He watched, breathless, as
appeared . . .

Paul lurched upright, grabbed to touch. Beneath his frantic fingers was cool satin, warm flesh. No delusion this, but corporeal; she had the substance, scent and sights of a living woman.

'I told you, Paul,' she said in a voice so faint he could scarcely catch the meaning of her words. 'Of sex so strong it can transcend the boundaries of time and place.'

'And death,' he said wonderingly, holding her hand, staring at her.

'Yes,' she said, raising her eyes to his. 'Of death, too. I didn't want to come back. I fought against it. But you brought me back. Your strength . . . Your passion . . .'

Then he was standing close to her. His arms went about the slithery satin and the pliant body within. She stood limply, arms at her sides, all slack surrender . . .

Also by Lawrence Sanders in Sphere Books:

TALES OF THE WOLF
CAPER
LOVE SONGS

Dark Summer

LAWRENCE SANDERS

SPHERE BOOKS LIMITED

SPHERE BOOKS LTD

Published by the Penguin Group
27 Wrights Lane, London W8 5TZ, England
Viking Penguin Inc., 40 West 23rd Street, New York, New York 10010, USA
Penguin Books Australia Ltd, Ringwood, Victoria, Australia
Penguin Books Canada Ltd, 2801 John Street, Markham, Ontario, Canada L3R 1B4
Penguin Books (NZ) Ltd, 182–190 Wairau Road, Auckland 10, New Zealand

Penguin Books Ltd, Registered Offices: Harmondsworth, Middlesex, England

First published in Great Britain by Sphere Books Ltd, 1988
Previously published in the United States of America by
Pocket Books, New York, as *Dark Summer* by Mark Upton

Copyright © 1979 by Lawrence Sanders
All rights reserved

Made and printed in Great Britain by
Richard Clay Ltd, Bungay, Suffolk

1

All day long people had been saying "It's trying to rain" or "It wants to rain." Finally, a little after three p.m., Paul Fayette saw it coming. He stood at the sealed windows of his 47th-floor office. He looked westward, across the stained tangle of Manhattan, across the mercury glint of the Hudson River.

A soiled cloudbank was moving east from New Jersey, billowing. As he watched, the smoke spread, blotting the sky. Beneath it, he saw pencil lines of rain. When the river was hidden, he turned away. There was a low thump of thunder, a few flashes of ocher light.

He sat at his desk, switched on the lamp. In this aseptic room, there was no smell of rain. But he could hear the lash on glass. He could hear the rising wind, a keening wail. He thought he felt the high building move. A faint sway.

Marie Verrazano came in with his correspondence.

"Looks like we're caught," he said cheerfully.

"I hope it clears the air," she said.

Something in her voice made him look up.

"I'm afraid of thunder," she confessed. "And lightning."

"They can't hurt you," he said. "Not inside this building."

"I know," she said. "But I'm still afraid."

She stood at his elbow as he read the letters. She whisked each away as he signed.

Clint Stahl came shambling into the office, a broken bird. He saw them working at the desk. He waved to them, slouched down on Fayette's leather couch. He put his feet up on the glass cocktail table. He lighted a cigarette with trembling fingers. He closed his eyes.

"Thank you, Mr. Fayette," the secretary said, gathering up the letters.

"Thank *you*, Marie," he said. "Nice job. You can leave whenever you like."

"I'll wait till it lets up," she said. "Have a good weekend, Mr. Fayette."

"You too," he said.

Stahl opened his eyes. He watched the girl stride to the door, slip through, close it softly behind her.

"You could get twenty years for what you're thinking," Fayette said.

"If that was true," Stahl said, "if you could get twenty years just for *thinking*, we'd all be in jail. Except you maybe."

"My God, I'm not that pure," Fayette laughed.

"Aren't you? You know why more men—and women, too, for that matter—don't cheat on their wives and husbands? Not because they don't want to. Or because they're afraid. It's the *logistics*. All that sneaking around. Out-of-the-way restaurants. Fleabag hotels. The *planning*. It's too much trouble."

"Logistics, hell. You're just lazy."

"That, too," Stahl said dreamily, closing his eyes again. "You've never been unfaithful to Laura, have you?"

"Of course not," Fayette said uncomfortably.

"Of course not," Stahl repeated. "Did I ever tell you what happened to me on that last Boston trip?"

"You have," Fayette said. "Several times."

"Twice," Stahl said, opening his eyes again. "Only twice. I was trying to make you jealous."

"Jealous, for God's sake?"

"Well . . . curious then. So you might be tempted to go out and try it yourself. Your trouble, m'lad, is that you and Laura are just too damned well-adjusted.

It's an offense to all us poor sinners. It reeketh in the
nostrils."

"How many martinis did you have for lunch?"

"Two. Both doubles. And why I bothered to come
back to the office, I'll never know. There was an eager
lady alone at the bar. I know she was smitten by my
manly charms."

"Asked you to pass the salted peanuts, did she?"

"I could have had her—" Stahl snapped his fingers.
"—like that."

"Why didn't you?"

"Logistics," Stahl sighed. "Those damned logistics.
Where would we go? And who might see us? With my
luck, I'd waltz her out of there and bump into Margaret's mother on the sidewalk. You and Laura going
to the club dance tonight?"

"Sure. Aren't you?"

"Of course. Friday night—club dance. Like death
and taxes. I think I'll get smashed and make a fool of
myself. Again. You better alert Laura. In case I come
pawing around."

"Paw away," Fayette said genially.

Stahl rose and pushed out his cigarette butt.

"Jesus," he said disgustedly. "Perfect trust. How
nauseating can you get? I think I'll spread the rumor
that the Fayettes have a secret vice."

"What makes you think we don't?"

"Ahh, you're too damned healthy," Stahl grumbled.
"And happy. If there's anything I hate, it's a happily
married couple."

"I know," Fayette said, tiring of this chivying. "Mis-
ery loves company." Then he saw Stahl's face. "Sorry,
Clint," he said. "Strike that."

"What the hell," Stahl shrugged. "Everyone knows
about Margaret and me. It's no secret. If it wasn't for
the kids . . . Well . . . see you tonight."

He waved a hand and wandered out.

Paul Fayette moved to the windows. It was like
looking into a fish tank. The city was submerged. The
world was drowning. He put a forefinger to the glass,

followed the track of raindrops jagging downward. He felt guilt and a kind of dread.

They were two games into the second set when fat drops began to spatter the clay court. They grabbed up sweaters, racket covers, extra balls, and dashed for the clubhouse terrace. They took a back table under the awning, laughing and drying their bare arms with handkerchiefs. They asked Carlos for gins-and-tonic, and a bowl of pretzels. Then they watched the rain pour across the courts, stream from the scalloped edge of the awning.

"Saved by the elements," Laura Fayette said. "You'd have creamed me; I couldn't do anything right."

"I was playing over my head," Margaret Stahl said. "Give the credit to Doc Terhune. He's got me on a new upper. Energy to burn."

"No fair," Laura smiled. "The next time we play, I'm going to insist on a saliva test."

They waited while their drinks were served. Margaret initialed the tab.

"These coasters," she murmured. *"So* tacky."

The sipped drinks, lighted cigarettes. They draped cashmere cardigans around their shoulders.

"I hope it lets up before train time," Laura said. "I hate to drive in the rain."

"He's sure to be late," Margaret said. "And Clint, too. That crazy car pool of his. Little Ed Webster is driving this week, and he's practically blind. I just hope it lets up before the dance. They were going to put the buffet out here."

"Chicken again?"

"What else? With that crappy Waldorf salad John makes. Laura . . ."

"What?"

Margaret Stahl shoved nervous fingers into the wig of tight blonde curls she was wearing.

"I've been thinking of leaving Clint," she said in a rush. "But thinking seriously this time, I mean. We said we'd stick it out for the sake of the kids, but maybe it's worse for them the way things are. Kids are so goddamned smart these days about what's going on. What do you think?"

"Well . . ." Laura said slowly, poking at the ice cubes in her drink, "what does Terhune say?"

"He never says. One way or another. He just listens. Clint's playing around again. I know he is."

"Margaret, you're not exactly innocent."

"Not for a year, I swear. Well, almost a year. Maybe we should attempt, you know, a trial separation? Get away from each other for a while. To sort things out."

"Have you talked to Clint about it?"

"No," Margaret said. "Not yet. Another drink?"

"Not for me. You go ahead."

Margaret Stahl turned to look for Carlos. He was inside, peering out one of the French doors. She held up a finger. He nodded and disappeared.

The watched the rain and didn't speak until he brought Margaret's drink.

"Thank you, Carlos," she said sweetly. "We're your only customers today, I see."

"My favorite customers, Mrs. Stahl," he smiled.

She looked after him as he retreated inside the clubhouse.

"He's ready," she said.

"Margaret," Laura said, "you're too much."

"Don't knock it if you haven't tried it," Margaret said. "You haven't, have you?"

"Don't be an idiot."

"Never had the desire? Not even the tiniest, tiniest urge?"

"Never."

"Bullshit," Margaret Stahl said. "It's not human. When you and Paul are in bed together, don't you ever think of being with another man? Occasionally? Now and then?"

"Oh sure," Laura said. "Richard Nixon."

Margaret laughed and took a deep swallow of her drink.

"You and Paul are something else," she said. "The nice, normal twosome that shows the rest of us how rotten we are."

"You talk like we're a couple of wax dummies."

"Marble statues is more like it."

"I think I will have another drink," Laura Fayette said.

Later, Laura finishing her second drink, Margaret her third, Margaret said, "We've got a new neighbor."

"Oh? Who's that?"

"A widow lady. Cheney. Mrs. Diane Cheney. She rented the old Barstow place?"

"My God! For herself? What does she want with that old barn?"

"Her father will be living with her. A retired military type. No children."

"How did you find all this out?"

"She told me," Margaret said. "Came down the hill to ask if she could use our phone. Hers isn't hooked up yet."

"What's she like?"

"Tallish. Slender. About thirty, I'd guess. Quite attractive in a dark, mysterious way."

"Great. A dark, mysterious widow lady. Just what Penlow Park needs."

"You'll get a chance to inspect her yourself," Margaret said. "I invited her to the dance tonight."

"Margaret, you didn't!"

"Why not? Because of Clint, you mean? Laura, I just don't care anymore. Besides, she's not his type."

"Famous last words," Laura Fayette said.

Three years previously, for Christmas, their daughter Christine had given them a small martini pitcher with the word "Ours" etched on the side, with two small glasses inscribed "Yours" and "Mine."

"Chris, how nice!" Laura had said brightly.

"Just what we needed," Paul had said bravely.

Later, in bed, they had discussed in hushed tones how they might contrive to drop and smash this cutesy gift. But now, three years later, they were using it without shame.

Laura had mixed the martinis, removed the ice, and placed the pitcher in the refrigerator. When she drove Paul back from the New Haven station, they went directly to the kitchen. Laura filled the "Yours" and "Mine" glasses while Paul sliced lemon peel. They took their drinks and the dividend in the pitcher into the family room. They sat in their customary chairs.

"Too much vermouth?" she asked.

"Just right," he said, slumping lower. "Any mail?"

"Bills and some junk. And a letter from Brian. He's changed his mind again. Guess what he wants to do this summer."

"Social work with the Navajos in Arizona?"

"No. Now he wants to bike through Northern Ireland."

"Great. He'll get his head shot off."

"What will you tell him, Paul?"

"Tell him to go ahead, of course. He's just waiting for me to forbid him to do one of those nutty things he's been suggesting. Then he can do it in triumph. But I agree to everything. It must be driving him crazy. Eventually he'll wind up doing something sensible—like getting a job as lifeguard in a girls' camp."

"You are so wise, great white father."

"Damned right. How was your day?"

"Lousy," she said cheerfully. "Our tennis game got rained out, and I had to listen to Margaret Stahl tell me how miserable she is."

He grunted.

"I got the same crap from Clint. They'll never learn that no one's interested in their troubles."

"I feel sorry for her," Laura said. "Both of them," she added hastily.

"I do, too," Paul said. "And I feel sorry for those people killed in that Iranian earthquake. And there's not a damned thing we can do about it. I suppose they'll split up. Eventually. Like the Blakes and the Cimentis."

"And Mary and Tony Smith," Laura said. "And the Renfrews. And Sally and Mark Parker."

"And the Bergers," he said. "My God, Laura, where did we go wrong?"

She laughed, and rose to fill his glass from the pitcher. Burnished light from the table lamp sheened her bare legs.

"You know the most erotic clothes a woman can wear?" he asked her.

"Babydoll pajamas and hip boots?"

"Tennis clothes," he told her. "Just what you're wearing now. The tight white T-shirt with your bra strap showing through. That short, pleated skirt. The naked legs and white sneakers. And those silly little fluff balls on the heels of your socks."

"Turns you on, does it?" she said.

"Oh," he said loftily, "I can take it or leave it alone."

"Liar," she said, flipping the short, pleated skirt at him.

She was a strong, handsome woman. Thickening in the waist now. The cap of curls an iron gray. Crow's-feet and laugh lines marking the complexion of heavy middle age. Arms were good: firm and muscled. Legs were magnificent: hard and sculpted. All of her warm and rosy. Blood coursed beneath the soft skin. Tendons pressed. Things rippled. A tingling there.

"Secretariat," he said approvingly.

"I remind you of a horse? Gee, thanks, boss."

"A thoroughbred," he said. "You remind me of a thoroughbred."

"Better," she said. "But not good enough. You'll pay for that. I think it's letting up, Paul. Maybe it'll stop before we leave."

"Clint said to warn you. He plans to get zonked, and he said he may come pawing."

"And what did you say?"

He paused for a second.

"I don't remember. Something stupid."

"My hero," she said. "I don't think he'll be a problem. Margaret is bringing a new woman."

"Oh? Who?"

"A new neighbor. Just moved into the Barstow place."

"Wait'll she gets her fuel bills next winter; she'll move right out again. That place is impossible to heat. What's she like—did Margaret say?"

"A widow lady. Living with her father. Margaret said she's attractive. Dark. Oh yes—and mysterious."

"Good," he said. "We could use a little mystery around here. We'd better get going. You want to shower first?"

"Okay."

"Need anyone to scrub your back?"

"Sure," she said. "Know anyone?"

He followed her up the staircase. Then, halfway up, he reached out to stop her. She smiled back at him over her shoulder. He leaned forward to kiss the tender skin behind her knees.

She whinnied like a horse. He laughed, and lightly slapped her tight rump.

He sat on the bed and watched her undress.

"After twenty-four years?" she mocked him.

"I never get enough," he told her. "Cross my heart and hope to die."

He accused her of tinting her pubic hair. She didn't, of course, but both agreed how remarkable it was that it had retained its original rich brown color with russet glints. The color of the hair on her head before it had grayed.

Her body was sturdy; she played tennis, golf, and every morning when the weather was fair, she jogged two miles up and down the hills of Penlow Park. She cosseted her body. Not, he knew, for her, but for him. The unwrinkled glow was for him.

She went into the bathroom. He remained seated on the bed, fully clothed, wondering why the martinis hadn't helped. He couldn't rid himself of his afternoon mood: the building's sway, city submerged, a haunting sense of opportunity lost and choice denied. He heard the shower begin to run. He undressed, then went downstairs naked and mixed another pitcher of drinks. He brought the full glasses upstairs, and when she stepped from the shower stall, fragrant and steaming, he held a full glass out to her.

"God bless you, sonny," she said. "You're a good little boy."

"Keep an eye on me tonight," he said. "If you think I've had enough, don't bother mentioning it."

"Not too much," she warned. "I have plans for later. When we get home."

"Laura, have I ever failed you in your hour of need?"

"Yes," she said. "April fifth, nineteen sixty-two. At precisely two-thirty in the morning."

"But I had the flu," he pleaded.

"That's what they all say, kiddo," she jeered, and goosed him gently when he stepped into the shower stall.

"What did you say?" she shouted above the sound of the running water.

"The name," he yelled again. "The widow lady."

She slid open the door.

"Cheney," she said. "Mrs. Diane Cheney. What's it to you?"

"I just want to be neighborly."

"Watch it, buster," she warned. "Or I'll fix your Welcome Wagon."

It was still drizzling; the buffet was laid out in the grill room. In the main dining room, tables and chairs had been moved against the walls. The floor had been waxed for dancing. Sammy Lobo and the Lamplighters were clumped on a small dais. The ancient musicians wore rusty dinner jackets and played show tunes from the 1930's and 1940's. They also played requests. "Smoke Gets in Your Eyes" was a great favorite. So was "Just the Way You Look Tonight."

Members of the Penlow Park Country Club loved those songs. They had danced to Benny Goodman and Glenn Miller. They recalled their youth with fondness and a sense of loss. Oh, their children were bigger, healthier, smarter—but what memories would they have? Poor, shriveled recollections of a charmless age. Where was today's "Dancing Cheek to Cheek"? The bar in the grill room was three-deep with mourners.

"Boring, boring, boring," Clint Stahl said. "Boresville, boresburg, and borestown. Listen to them. You'd think the world came to an end when Noel Coward died."

"Earlier," Paul Fayette said. "After *A Day at the Races,* it was all downhill. They're not bores, Clint. Just too familiar, that's all. We've lost the ability to surprise each other. Ingrown, we are. Almost incestuous."

"Watch your language," Stahl said. "There's a lot of fucking ladies around."

"Speaking of ladies," Fayette said, "Where are ours? How long does it take to powder a nose? I'm anxious to meet the mysterious widow."

"Mysterious?" Stahl said with a quirky smile. "Who told you that?"

"Laura. Said Margaret described Mrs. Cheney as, quote, mysterious, unquote."

Clint Stahl lighted a cigarette, his tremor more noticeable. He blew a plume of smoke upward and looked about from his lofty height: six feet four inches of lumpy tweed.

"Not so mysterious," he said. "But . . . well, different."

"I can hardly wait," Fayette said. "Ready for a refill?"

"Always," Stahl said. "I'm always ready."

Fayette caught the bartender's eye and held up two fingers. Ernie nodded, poured two dark Scotch-and-sodas, and handed them over the shoulders of the mob. Fayette gave one to Clint Stahl. The two men strolled into the main dining room. They found an empty table for four, and Clint dragged up another chair. Carlos was working their table. They told him the ladies would be along in a moment, but meanwhile he could bring two more Scotch highballs.

They sat sipping their drinks, listening to the Lamplighters play "Begin the Beguine," watching the dancers. Occasionally they smiled and waved to friends.

"Look at Bob Finch," Stahl said. "When's he going to spring for a new toupee? The moths have been into that one."

"Is that Babs Feldman talking to the Longviews?" Fayette said. "I never noticed her hair was red."

"It is now," Stahl said. "She's put on weight."

"In all the wrong places. There's that idiot Spencer. Is that a tango he's doing, a waltz, or what?"

"Maybe his underwear is creeping up. No bra for Helen Cantor tonight. Bless you, my dear."

"Any bets on who'll fall down first?" Fayette said.

"Me," Clint Stahl said. "Oh God, how can you stand it, Paul?"

"Stand what?"

"The general shittiness of things."

"Is that a Cole Porter tune?"

"Here come the ladies," Stahl said. "Laura looks good enough to eat."

"What makes you think I'm a vegetarian?" Paul Fayette murmured, standing up.

Introductions were made, chairs were shuffled, everyone was seated. Carlos came back with the highballs and took the ladies' orders. Cigarettes were lighted. They smiled determinedly.

"Well," Margaret Stahl said brightly, "here we are again."

She was only a few inches shorter than her husband. They were two of a kind: all lank twitchiness, all elbows and knees. Both stooped, both had the jerky gestures of marionettes with snapped strings. Margaret accentuated her skinniness with a knitted tube of a dress, a purple T-shirt to her ankles. Clint concealed his lack of heft with one of his tweed suits in earth colors: sand, mud, and swamp.

"As like as sister and brother," everyone said. And they were, with long, thin noses, sharp eyes, pointy chins. Their three children completed the basketball team: mixed twins and a boy, all tall, stretched, and ambling. A scornful, wrangling family, with contempt for the non-Stahl world.

"I understand you've taken the Barstow place, Mrs. Cheney," Paul Fayette said.

She turned slowly to look at him.

"Renting," she said. "Temporarily. I may buy."

"You'll love Penlow Paark," Clint Stahl said. "So exciting. Something going on every minute.'"

"Don't listen to him," Laaura Fayette laughed. "It's a very nice, quiet place. Friendly. Isn't it, Margaret?"

"What? Oh yes. Friendly as hell."

Clint asked Diane Cheney to dance. She politely declined, saying she'd rather have a drink first.

"Later," she promised Stahl.

So he asked Laura, and the two of them moved out onto the dance floor.

"If you'd like to dance," Mrs. Cheney said, looking back and forth, Margaret to Paul, "go right ahead. I won't mind."

"Not me," Fayette said. "I hate to exhibit my ineptitude in public."

Carlos brought the ladies' drinks. Then Bob Finch came along, smoothing down his ragged toupee, and asked Margaret Stahl to dance. They edged into the mob moving about slowly to "I Don't Want to Set the World on Fire.'"

"Alone at last," Fayette said to Diane Cheney, but she didn't smile.

"Do you know all these people?" she asked him.

"Almost all. Most of us are original settlers. Moved out from the city when Penlow Park was just opening up. It was farms then. I'm sorry your father couldn't come tonight."

"I think he's expecting a phone call," she said vaguely. "Your wife is very lovely."

"Thank you," he said. "I agree. She's mad for tennis. Do you play?"

"No."

"Golf?"

"No," Mrs. Cheney said. "I don't play any games. Does that disqualify me from joining the Penlow Park Country Club?"

"Not if you continue to drink like that," he laughed. "You're qualified. Carlos!"

He ordered another drink for her, and another brace of highballs for Stahl and himself.

"Your son and daughter are in college?" she asked.

"Yes. Brian at Princeton, and Christine at Radcliffe. Did Laura show you their pictures?"

She nodded. "Beautiful children. You must be very proud."

"Oh yes. You have no children?"

"No. None."

"Were you married long?"

"No," she said. "Not long. My husband was killed in a plane crash."

"Oh God," he said. "How awful."

"These things happen," she shrugged, and he looked at her in amazement.

He had the body of a fencer and the face of a friendly fox. He was physically slight, dapper, and wore a braided gold wedding band. His teeth gleamed, his own, but he smiled with restraint, slowly. He moved in a glide. He gestured rarely. He was not solemn but gave the impression of graveness. It amused him.

His eyes were his best feature: blue glass. Startling against dark skin. His fingers were unusually bony. He wore his flaxy hair long, puffed over his collar. He spoke so quietly that he was frequently misunderstood. No one but his wife had ever seen him anything but calm. He had few close male friends. And most of those respected him more than they liked him.

Women thought him a "perfect gentleman," not realizing the depth of his boredom.

"I'll dance now," Diane Cheney said, and he rose obediently.

Despite his disclaimer, he was a skilled and relaxed dancer, avoiding collisions on the crowded floor, leading his partner gently but firmly. Mrs. Cheney's hard thighs pressed, and he felt no bra strap beneath the thin stuff of her gown. Her scent was deep and fruity. The music stopped. The drummer rapped out a roll that signified a break. Fayette guided Mrs. Cheney back to their table.

"Thank you," he said. "You're a beautiful dancer."

She smiled faintly, and he wondered if she was naked beneath her dress.

Sequence seemed to vanish, and reason with it. They all ate and drank intemperately. They danced. There were comings and goings, laughter and drunken shouts, noise. Waterspouts of loud talk.

Around midnight, Paul Fayette and Clint Stahl hunched at adjoining urinals, then moved to adjoining sinks. They dried their hands, adjusted ties, combed their hair.

"We all fuck fantasies," Stahl said.

Fayette looked at that sardonic face in the mirror.

"What brought that on?" he asked.

"Just a philosophical observation."

"Clint, when you start thinking, you're dangerous."

"My trouble," Stahl said, "is that I'm a closet romantic."

"Your trouble is that you're a combination of D'Artagnan and Buster Keaton."

"Nevertheless," Clint Stahl said loftily, "I intend to screw the Widow Cheney."

"Bon voyage," Paul Fayette said.

Margaret Stahl and Mrs. Cheney . . .

"I don't know what to do, Diane. What do you think?"

Mrs. Cheney looked into her eyes. "It's your decision. But why? Because he's unfaithful?"

"That . . . and other things."

"What other things?"

"He says—in company—he says, 'My wife is a lady. I'd take her anyplace—once!' He's said that a dozen times. In company."

"And you?" Cheney asked. "Have you been unfaithful?"

"Not that I've enjoyed it," Margaret said. Shattered smile. "Just a way of getting back at him I suppose. Revenge. Something like that. Awful, isn't it?"

"Awful that you haven't enjoyed it, yes," the widow said, watching the dancers.

"Guilt," Margaret Stahl said moodily. "I feel guilty."

Diane Cheney laughed suddenly. She turned to Margaret, put a soft hand on her arm.

"Icing on the cake, love," she said.

Laura and Paul Fayette . . .

"What's your take?" he asked.

"Very quiet and thoughtful," she said. "But she doesn't miss much."

"No," he said, "she doesn't. Did you know that Helen Cantor collects boxes?"

"Boxes?"

"Little boxes. Antiques. Limoges china. Russian wood. Indian tin and brass. Jewel boxes. Snuff boxes. Things like that. Helen collects them."

"Helen told you?"

"No," he said, "Diane Cheney told me. Helen Cantor told her. She just met Helen tonight, and Helen told her. We've known Helen—what? Ten years? Twelve? And I never knew she collected boxes. Did you?"

"No, Paul. We've been to her home a dozen times. I never saw any boxes."

"Me neither. But she told Diane Cheney she collects boxes. The first time she met her. Odd."

"Isn't it. Will you deign to dance with me now?"

" 'Deign'? I don't believe I've ever heard that word spoken before."

"Sure you have," she said genially. "Hamlet, the Melancholy . . .'"

He laughed, but he remembered he had used the same pun months ago. She had that gift—or habit: playing back to him his wit, opinions, prejudices, observations. As if they were her own. To convince him she was not a dummy, he supposed. She needn't have bothered. He wanted no one but her.

Clint Stahl and Diane Cheney . . .

"I like your wife," she told him.

"Make me an offer," he said morosely. Then: "And now . . . on to finer things. Let's talk about us."

"Let's," she said.

"Do you ever come into the city?"

"Of course," she said. "Frequently.'"

"Logistics," he said, and when she stared at him, he showed his yellowed teeth and backed off. "Well . . . lunch," he said. "Could we?"

"I'd like that. Will you tell your wife?"

"No," he said. "Will you?"

"No," she said. "If you say not.'"

"Not," he said, grinning foolishly, afraid to stand lest his erection was poking out the earth-colored tweed.

Laura Fayette and Diane Cheney . . .

"Is your husband an artist, Laura?"

"Paul? Oh no. Nothing like that. He's in the New York office of a Boston bank. They factor various things. What made you think he's an artist?"

"The way he moves. His voice. His manner. He's a very graceful, loving man."

"Loving?"

"Isn't he? You. His children."

"Oh yes. Of course. If I hadn't had so much to

drink, I wouldn't tell you this, but a year after we were married, I was ready to split."

"Oh?"

"It just wasn't working. The physical thing I mean. He went into the bathroom to put on his pajamas. Funny?"

"Not very."

"No. It wasn't. He couldn't thaw. His upbringing, I suppose. Very cold, proper people. Church and all that. I knew he was trying, but it just didn't work. Oh God, why am I telling you all this? Then we went to—where was it—St. Croix, I think. A week in the sun. Hot. The beach. The ocean. A kind of bungalow away from the main hotel. He just melted. The coldness went out of him. What he had always wanted. Don't you think so, Diane?"

"Oh yes. I do. He surrendered. To himself. His nature."

"Exactly. How wise you are! And it's been marvelous ever since."

"So you were right from the start."

"What?"

"You must have seen that in him. When you married him. You must have seen the man he could become."

"Did I? Well . . . I suppose I did. The demon lover."

"Demon? Do you believe in demons?"

"Oh sure," Laura laughed. "Demons. Angels and devils. The good guys and the bad guys. I believe in all of them. Don't you?"

"Of course," Diane Cheney said.

Paul Fayette and Clint Stahl . . .

"Got her," Stahl said, stroking a nonexistent mustache.

"Bullshit," Paul Fayette said.

Sammy Lobo and the Lamplighters were playing "Don't Fence Me In," and the floor was mobbed.

The Fayettes and the Stahls sat lumpily at the table. Diane Cheney was off in the crowd, dancing. A success.

"Boop-boop-ee-doop," Margaret Stahl said, but no one responded.

A shriek. Laughter. A shout. The music stopped. The crowd congealed, pressing toward the center of the floor.

"What?" Paul Fayette said.

Clint Stahl stood, looking over bobbing heads.

"Someone's down," he reported. "First of the night. It wasn't me after all."

There were more cries. Someone yelled. "Doctor! Doctor! Doctor!"

Fayette said to the others, "Wait here." He pushed through the crush.

Stahl stood on a chair.

"It's Bob Finch," he said. "I think. His toupee is off."

Fayette came back.

"It's Bob Finch," he nodded. "May be cardiac arrest. Babs Feldman is giving him mouth-to-mouth."

"Let's hope she doesn't get emotionally involved," Stahl said. He nickered.

There were two doctors present. They worked on Bob Finch. An ambulance and police car came growling up. Bob Finch was removed.

Then Diane Cheney was back at their table, lighting a cigarette with steady hands.

"Who was he dancing with?" someone asked.

"With me," the widow said. "We were dancing, and suddenly he dropped."

"Maybe he fainted," someone said. "Or passed out."

"No," Mrs. Cheney said. "He's dead."

"Oh God," Laura said. "How awful."

"Yes," Mrs. Cheney said. She leaned close, whispering. "Will you and your husband drive me home?"

"Of course, dear. I understand."

"I should go with the Stahls," Diane Cheney said. "They brought me. But his car has a bumper sticker:

'Love thy neighbor, but don't get caught.' I'd rather go with you and Paul."

When they left, Sammy Lobo and the Lamplighters were playing "Moonlight Serenade."

She sat between them in the front seat of their station wagon. The windows were down; a shivery, rain-stained wind billowed in. It tousled her long hair. Tendrils whipped, stroked the cheeks of Laura and Paul Fayette.

"Did he say anything?" Laura asked in a low voice. "Bob Finch. Before he—before he dropped."

"He was telling me about a hobby he had. Well, perhaps not a hobby. A habit. A custom. He kept a record, a secret record, of everything in his life that had died. The date they died. Two dogs, a cat, a pet turtle when he was a child. Then, as he grew older, a boyhood friend. A schoolteacher. Then his father. Buddies in the army. Friends. Acquaintances. President Kennedy. A cousin. His wife's mother. Another dog. And so forth. He kept trace of them all, and wrote it down in a ledger. The date of their death. Even a dead bird he saw on the road."

"My God," Paul Fayette said. "Some hobby. Some habit."

"People do tell you things," Laura said.

"I suppose so," Diane Cheney said vaguely. "Sometimes it's easier to talk to strangers."

They were conscious of her scent, of her warmth between them. They went around a sharp curve, and all swayed, leaned together, and touched. When the car straightened, they were closer, pressing softly in the darkness. The Fayettes saw her pale features reflected in the black windshield. And beyond her, through her, the white road came unreeling.

They pulled into the gravelled driveway of the old Barstow house. Downstairs windows were lighted.

"My father will still be up," Diane Cheney said. "Please come in. There's brandy and coffee."

Paul leaned forward a bit to glance at Laura.

"Yes," she decided. "Thank you, Diane. I could use a coffee. You, Paul?"

"The brandy sounds good," he said. "But just for a moment."

Colonel Benjamin G. Coulter was a rubicund man, shortish, plumpish, wearing softly tailored doeskin slacks. a cashmere blazer with slate buttons. Paisley ascot at his throat. Tasseled moccasins glinting wickedly. All of him scrubbed and polished, gleaming with a ruddy light.

He offered a warm, ringed hand and got them seated, gentle fingers on Laura's elbow, then on Paul's shoulder. His smile was all manufactured teeth. He stood before a dully glowing fireplace and rubbed his palms.

"Well, now," he said. "This *is* nice. First guests, and all that. Celebration. Poison, anyone? Cognac, Scotch, martini—what?"

"Coffee, Colonel?" Laura asked. "If it's not too much trouble."

"Made and hot," he assured her. "Black?"

"Please."

"You, Mr. Fayette?"

"A brandy would be fine."

"Excellent. Ditto for Diane, and ditto for me."

He bustled, twinkling, scurrying in and out of the kitchen, hustling to a corner sideboard.

They sat in silence until they were served.

"Well, now," Colonel Coulter said, lifting his snifter. "To new friends."

He carried the conversation, asking them questions, making wry comments about the Barstow house, rising frequently to fill their glasses, to plump a pillow behind Laura's back, to put another small log on the dying fire.

"You're retired, Colonel?" Paul asked.

"From the military, yes. But I keep active. Not out to pasture yet. Hell no!"

"You're in business?"

"Import-export mostly. Do a lot of traveling. Europe, Africa, Asia. All over the place."

"Oh?" Paul said, interested. "What do you handle?"

"This and that," the Colonel said genially, waving a ringed hand. "Mostly heavy machinery. For roads, airports, land development, things."

"Earth movers?"

"Exactly!" the Colonel cried delightedly. " 'Our earth movers are earthshakers.' Company motto. Some advertising chap came up with it. Silly, I suppose, but quite right for all that."

"Are you British, Colonel?" Laura asked curiously.

"In a manner of speaking," he smiled. "But your cup is empty! More?"

"No thank you. But I would like a small brandy now, if I may."

"Of course, dear lady." He smiled, showing his porcelain teeth. "A pleasure indeed."

One dim corner lamp and the fragile fire provided illumination. They sat, two by two, on couches end on to the hearth and facing. So they were all half in flickering light, half in gloom. The room tasted of wood smoke, a faintly bitter scent of scorch and ash.

Laura Fayette, sitting alongside the Widow Cheney, saw only her sharp profile with a thin highlight of red along brow, bridge of nose, sculpted lips, chin, long throat, and one bare, burnished shoulder. Paul Fayette, sitting opposite, saw the pointy thrust of her breasts, accented by black shadow. She was leaning forward, legs crossed, staring into the blue flame. One evening slipper dangled from thin, naked toes.

"Colonel," Diane Cheney said slowly, "a man died at the dance tonight. Heart attack, I suppose."

"Damned shame," Coulter said promptly. "Put a damper on things, I suppose. A close friend?" he asked Paul.

"Not close, no, sir. But I knew him."

"Just like that, eh?" Coulter sighed. "So it goes. In life we are in death. The Good Book. Lots of jolly stuff in *that,* I can tell you. You're in banking, Paul? May I call you Paul?"

"Of course. Not exactly banking," he said, wondering how the Colonel knew. "But part of it. The factoring division of Fourth National of Boston."

"Know it well," Colonel Coulter nodded. "Old Bernie Stiffens. Soldiered with him years ago. Give him my best, will you?"

"That might be a little difficult," Paul laughed. "He's Chairman of the Board, up in Boston, and I'm just a peon slaving in a division office in Manhattan. I wouldn't say we're exactly buddy-buddy."

"Just between you, me, and the lamp post," Colonel Coulter said, "he's a bit of nice-nelly. True blue and all that. Absolutely straight up. No doubt about it. But not one for a fight or a frolic. Well, I shouldn't be putting down the poor man. He's not long for this world."

"What?" Paul said, bewildered.

"You haven't heard?" the Colonel said. "Not long to go. Here——" He tapped his chest. "Not a chance. Too bad. In some ways he's quite a man. In some ways. Well . . . who's ready for a dividend?"

"Oh no, Colonel, thank you," Laura said hastily, rising. "We've overstayed already. Thank you so much for your kindness."

"My pleasure, dear lady, My *pleasure!*" Coulter bowed low over Laura's hand, kissed the fingertips lightly.

"We will be seeing more of you, I hope. I'm here there, everywhere. Scooting all over the place, as I said. I keep an apartment-office on Madison Avenue, but Penlow Park will be my command post, for a while at any rate. I do hope we see much more of you and Paul."

"I'm sure you shall," Laura said. "Penlow Park isn't all that big. Perhaps you'll come over for dinner some night?"

"Delighted," he assured her. "Absolutely delighted. Just check with Diane. She'll know when I'm due in."

Meanwhile Mrs. Cheney and Paul Fayette were saun-tering toward the door.

"You're all right?" he asked in a low voice.

"Of course," she said, surprised at the question. "Thank you for driving me home. Will I see you again?"

"I hope so." he said. "Laura will arrange something. If you're serious about joining the club, I might be able to help you. I'm on the Board."

"You're very kind. The Colonel, too? He'd like that. He's such a joiner. He likes people. Always making new friends."

"I can understand why," Paul smiled. "It hasn't been much of a welcome for you, but welcome to Penlow Park anyway."

He pulled the outer door open and had to step back. When he turned to look for Laura, he found himself standing quite close to Diane Cheney. He looked into her eyes, startled.

"I hope I see you again," she said. "I like you."

"Thank you," he said, wondering if the cognac had gotten to her. "We like you, too."

"I'll see you again?" she insisted.

"You won't be able to avoid it," he laughed, de-termined to keep it light.

"Laura! Coming?"

They waited in silence for Laura and the Colonel. Paul looked around the musty hallway. On a small, marble-topped table, he saw a brown bowler, the stiff brim curved rakishly.

"I haven't seen one of those in years," he told Mrs. Cheney.

"The Colonel likes to dress up." she said.

In the car, driving home, Paul Fayette turned to his wife in wonderment.

"Jesus Christ," he said, "what was *that?*"

He sat on the edge of the bed, watching his wife undress, darkly stirred.

"What do you think?" he asked her.

"Well . . ." Laura said slowly, "they're certainly different."

"You think she's mysterious, like Margaret said?"

"More odd than mysterious."

"Odd is right." He stood, began to unbutton his shirt, "Colonel Blimp and the Dragon Lady."

Laura laughed. "He wasn't exactly gossipy about his business, was he?"

"Oh, you caught that, did you? Maybe he's running guns or smuggling opium. Maybe he's a white-slaver."

"That imagination of yours, buster! He's probably just what he implied: a dull businessman. She's the one who interests me. She's weird."

"Weird?"

"Takes things so casually. Bob Finch dying. Her husband's suicide."

He stopped, stared at her.

"Suicide? Did she tell you that?"

"Yes, she did. Why?"

"She told me he was killed in a plane crash."

They were silent a moment, moving about the bedroom, hanging away their clothes.

"It could be both," Paul Fayette mused. "Suicide *and* a plane crash. It's possible."

"Do you believe that?" his wife demanded, climbing naked into bed.

"No, not really. Sleepy?"

"Never *that* sleepy, kiddo," she said. "Light or no light?"

"No light," he said. "For starters."

He switched off the lamp, slid next to her under the sheet and single blanket.

"Your hands are cold," he complained.

"They won't be for long. Let me toast them on your ass. You think she's beautiful, Paul?"

"Not in a conventional way. Face too thin. Too much chin. But I like her eyes. Her hair. She's attractive enough. 'Interesting' is the word."

"Marvelous body. Did you notice?"

"I noticed," he said.

"I noticed you noticed," she said. "Brute! She'd like to see us again."

"So she told me. Several times. Wants to join the club. She and daddy."

"What do you think?"

"Why not? They'll give us something new to talk about, and God knows we need it. Clint is convinced she's going to roll over for him."

"Clint dreams *every* woman is going to roll over for him. Margaret's wild about her. Says she's so understanding. Margaret's word: 'understanding.' "

"Almost too understanding."

"What does that mean?"

"Damned if I know. Except she found out a hell of a lot about us in a short time. But you haven't said whether or not you like her."

"Oh, I like her well enough. That bod—really fabulous. I don't blame you for staring."

"I wasn't staring."

"Well, noticing then. I had a carcass like that once, didn't I, Paul?"

"You did. Until it improved."

"Oh, lover, you know all the right things to say. Well . . . enough of this pillow talk. Let's get down to business."

"I think I'll call Boston and see if they know anything about Colonel Benjamin G. Coulter."

"Shut up," she said.

"All right," he said.

She moved closer, took him into her strong arms. She pressed tightly at first, shivering a little, then relaxed as she warmed. She kicked the sheet and blanket lower until only their legs were lightly covered.

She kissed his lips, the corners of his mouth, his chin, temples, closed eyes. He began to make a noise, a deep, low hum. She sucked gently at the point of his chin, bit his ear lobes, laved her tongue along his smooth throat, nibbled at juncture of neck and shoulder.

She moved him onto his back, her hands feeling

him out: touching, prying, opening. He helped her roll atop him. They clasped fingers, and she held him pinioned, hands forced flat at shoulder level. Open mouths mingled. She squirmed closer to him. The skin of her belly brushed back and forth. Then her weight punished.

She thrust at him. He spread his legs as wide as he could, until he felt the strain, then lifted his knees. He hooked ankles and feet behind her knees, panting with the effort to envelop her, swallow her. He wrenched his hands free, gripped her buttocks, pulled her more tightly down between his thighs.

She pounded him. Their movements became more frantic, sweated. Her mouth ravaged his breast, her teeth at his nipples, and he moaned with delight. Her fingers pried between them. Pinching. Tugging. Rubbing.

She lifted slowly to a sitting position. Her solid weight was hot atop him. She pushed his legs together and spread hers wide. She guided him, gripped him with wet muscle, slammed down to meet his sobbing thrusts. She rode him like a demented jockey, hunched, rocking, and intent.

Until they cried out. Something thick and exultant. And slowly melted to a warm languor, vaguely stirring, murmuring, tasting each other's swollen mouths. Consciousness came creeping. They both had a fleeting vision that it was the sudden death that night that had driven them to such a desperate and mindless paroxysm. But it was a fleeting thought, conceived and aborted.

They lay a long time, she still astride, uncovered on the cooling bed. Neither wished to move. They were entwined, dreaming of Mrs. Cheney. He saw a naked supplicant, and she a naked boss. So they were both content.

2

Laura Fayette, waking first, blinked, stared at early June sunlight hazing through the bedroom window, glanced at her sleeping husband, slipped naked from the bed, stood, stretched, heard her spine creak, padded to the bathroom, closed the door quietly, peed, brushed her teeth, washed, tugged a comb through her short, gray hair, went back into the bedroom, pulled on cotton panties, a white T-shirt, jogging shorts, sneakers, went downstairs to the kitchen, took in *The New York Times* from the back stoop, put the coffee on, drank a small glass of grapefruit juice, heard her husband moving around overhead, sat down with a cup of black coffee, flipped idly through the paper, heard Paul coming down the stairs, poured him a cup of coffee, set the paper neatly folded alongside his place, and looked up when he came into the room.

"Good morning, love," she said brightly. "Did you sleep well?"

Laura Fayette turned off the percolator, found her car keys, eased the station wagon from the garage, waited in the driveway until her husband came out carrying his attaché case, drove him to the New Haven station, waved to friends, kissed her husband goodbye, sat in the car until the 8:46 arrived and departed, started the car, drove home, pulled into the garage, lowered the door, went into the house from the garage entrance, swallowed a Vitamin E capsule, put a terry cloth sweatband around her forehead,

locked up, went outside, and began jogging down the
long circle that led, eventually, to the First Presbyterian Church of Penlow Park.

The men were gone to the city. The children were
in school. It was too early for the women to be out
shopping. So the curved roads of Penlow Park were
almost deserted. The new sun was warm behind a
morning fog. New foliage hung unmoving in still,
cool air. New Grass, dew-glinted, stretched neat and
manicured before each ranch, split-level, Tudor, tra-
ditional, contemporary, modern, A-frame, and Medi-
terranean Villa.

A few tots were out, toddling around on lawns,
pedaling their tricycles on driveways, chasing butter-
flies. A birdcall came briefly from somewhere. Helen
Cantor, sweeping her porch, waved as she jogged by,
and the Spencers' brown-and-white beagle came loping out and ran alongside her for a few yards, ears
flopping, before he stopped and turned back. She
passed two other early morning joggers: the Reverend
Timothy T. Aiken puffing solemnly, red-faced and
erect, and old Mr. Hopkins jerking along in his awkward, tireless stride, elbows out, knees lifted high.

Laura Fayette could do a ten-minute mile, but she
rarely ran at that speed. She just jogged steadily down
to the First Presbyterian, up to the old cemetery, and
back by a different route. Most of her track was up or
down, and she saved her strength for the steep climb
to Cemetery Hill. She ran freely, loose-limbed, her
brown thighs flashing, sneakers slapping down on as-
phalt, gravel, or packed earth. She breathed deeply
through her nose. She tried to think of nothing but
catching and holding her mesmeric pace, a rhythm
that filled everything, blotting out sights, smells,
sounds.

"It's like you're falling forward," she had tried to
explain to Paul. "And you have to take another step
to keep from flopping on your face."

He didn't understand.

She circled the church and parking lot and started

up Cemetery Hill, feeling the strain in her calves. She was sweated now, wet under her arms and between her thighs, her scalp sticky, rivulets along her jawline and neck. She topped the crest, not glancing at the tombstones, and started down. She leaned back slightly, lengthened her stride, let the slope carry her down. When she hit the flat, she saw, a hundred feet ahead of her, another woman jogging easily with a floating step, elbows held in close, shoulders back, head up. Fayette saw long, black hair braided into a single plait, tied with a small, yellow silk scarf.

She ran faster, gained, and recognized Diane Cheney, wearing a dark blue jogging suit with yellow stripes on jacket sleeves and pants. She drew alongside. The two women smiled at each other, but wasted no breath on greetings. They ran side by side, Mrs. Cheney subtly altering her stride until they were running in tandem, two right knees rising simultaneously, two right feet slapping down as one. They were close; when Laura made her turns through the clean, quiet streets of Penlow Park, the widow made the turns with her. The sound of their heavy breathing. The spat of running feet on paved road. The birdcall that came briefly from somewhere.

They pounded down Chancery Lane, slowed, stopped on the Fayettes' blacktop driveway. They looked at each other and laughed. They walked about in circles, hands on hips, on the driveway and lawn. They took enormous gulps of air.

"Paul said. I looked. Like a horse," Laura Fayette puffed. "I feel. Like one. Especially. Doing this. Cooling off. I didn't. Know you. Jogged."

"Haven't," Diane Cheney gasped. "For years. But this. Place. So perfect. For it."

"Come in," Laura said. "For coffee. A muffin. Whatever."

They sat in the cheery kitchen. They drank black coffee and nibbled on wedges of pecan coffee cake Laura took from the freezer and warmed in the electric baker. They talked about the pleasures of running. Diane Cheney said that once, during a college vacation, she had lived for a month in a small Nebraska town. She had run the roads at night. She wore a lightweight lamp about her head, like a miners' lamp, battery-powered. She would run at midnight, sometimes even later, and the puddle of pale, orange light would jerk along at her feet, leading the way on the dark, country lanes.

"Weren't you frightened?" Laura asked. "Running at that hour?"

"Frightened?" Mrs. Cheney said, astonished. "No. I'm never frightened."

"Then you're braver than I am!"

The widow smiled vaguely. "That's what it's all about, isn't it? Risk?"

They sipped their coffee in silence a few moments. The morning sun, flooding the kitchen window behind Diane Cheney, cast a nimbus about her head, shadowed her features. For a moment her closely drawn hair, shoulders, and upper arms seemed to Laura to be aflame, flickering with a reddish glow.

And surrounded by this radiance, the darkened face was grave, remote, magisterially Spanish: long nose, serene mouth, eyes that gleamed inordinately large and fathomless. A disturbing image; Laura stirred uncomfortably.

"Your jogging suit," she said suddenly. "It's very professional looking, Diane."

"But too warm for summer." Mrs. Cheney leaned forward, placed a hand lightly on the other woman's naked thigh. "Shorts are much more practical. I must get a few pair. Like yours. Where did you find them?"

"At Saks," Laura said. She rose abruptly to bring the percolator to the table and refill their cups. "At the Four Corners Shopping Center. I'm going over this afternoon with Margaret Stahl. We thought we'd have lunch there. Would you like to come along? Love to have you."

"Thank you, but I'm going into the city at noon," Mrs. Cheney said. "Business. I hope you'll ask me again."

"Of course."

They talked about the Fayettes' children, about Brian's wild ambitions and Christine's passionate, if brief, romances. Diane Cheney listened intently, faintly smiling, nodding occasionally.

"I'd like to meet them," she said. "They sound so curious and eager."

"You're exactly right," Laura said. "They *are* curious and eager. I just hope they don't get hurt."

"I promise you they'll survive."

"I suppose so. But I have a terrible desire to grab them and shake some sense into them."

"*Your* sense," Mrs. Cheney said. "It might not be right for them. We all do what we must do."

"Even children?"

"Even children. I believe that. When I was a child, the Colonel raised dogs. For a time. Welsh springers for show. In a litter of four, say, each pup would have a very different and very individual personality. People are the same. What's right for you and Paul might not be right for Christine and Brian."

"I know in my mind that you're right," Laura said. "But I want to tell them everything I know, everything I've learned. So they can benefit from my experience."

Mrs. Cheney put her fingers lightly on the other woman's bare knee. She looked gravely into Laura's eyes.

"They must make their own mistakes," she said in a low voice. She paused. . . . "As you make yours."

Each table lamp had a little pink shade with short, beaded fringe.

"Reminds me of a Kewpie doll's skirt," Clint Stahl said, fingering the strands of beads. "How old is this place?"

"Very old," the Widow Cheney said. "But the Colonel likes it here. They know him; he gets excellent service."

" 'The Colonel,' " Stahl repeated. "Don't you ever call him daddy, or daddums, or pop?"

"No," Mrs. Cheney said, "I never do."

Stahl looked around the cavernous dining room. He was the only man lunching. Most of the other tables were occupied by elderly ladies with hair, or wigs, that ranged from pure white through all shades of blue to lavender.

"Beautiful," Stahl said. "Cream sherry and watercress sandwiches. They don't know what they're missing; my trout was great. How was your Steak Tartare?"

"Good," she said. "Very fresh. Very spicy. They know how I like it. The Colonel's apartment is on the eleventh floor."

"I know," he said. "You told me."

"More office than apartment," she went on. "He went downtown this afternoon. His secretary is with him."

"I'd like another brandy," Stahl said, throat suddenly dry and aching. "Would you mind?"

"Why don't we have it upstairs?" Mrs. Cheney said. "The Colonel is well-supplied."

He went stumbling after her. She initialed the check and murmured something to the mutton-chopped maître d' that made him laugh.

The superannuated operator of the birdcage elevator was wearing a pillbox cap.

"Haven't seen Lillie Langtry around lately, have you?" Clint Stahl asked him.

The old man wasn't at all fazed.

"She stayed here, you know, sir," he quavered. "Lillian Russell too, it's said. But that was before my time."

"Go on," Stahl said. "I'll bet you knew Jenny Lind."

"Don't listen to him, Ben," Mrs. Cheney said. "He's

just jealous because all the beautiful women are gone."

"Not while you're alive, Mrs. Cheney," the antique said, and she bent to kiss his veined cheek.

The apartment-office was a suite with high ceilings, damask walls, oak beams, mahogany furniture, and an enormous fireplace with a carved marble mantel. Cherubs and nymphs.

"Be it ever so humble," Stahl said, laughing nervously. He looked around and flinched, a little, when she double-locked the door.

"The Colonel likes it," Mrs. Cheney said. "And so do I."

"Oh, I like it, I like it," he said hastily. "It's just—" He had a sudden fit of giggling. "—I expect Evelyn Nesbit and Stanford White to come strolling out of the bedroom."

"I like you," she said. "You're funny."

"Yes," he said, sobering. "A very funny guy. Could I have that brandy now, please."

She was wearing something loose-fitting in black silk crepe. When she moved, it touched breast, hip, haunch. The mass of black hair swung wildly free. But all Clint Stahl could see were her naked feet in sandals that were straps. Her toes were long, slender, unblemished. Could they grasp? The nails were painted vermillion.

He sat in a leather wing chair facing the empty fireplace. He accepted a balloon of brandy from her, thinking how like her toes her fingers were. She sat in a matching chair, set at an angle to his. He sipped his brandy delicately, feeling lord of the manor.

"About toes," he said. "Bare toes. Women aren't so much like that, are they? As much as men?"

She knew at once what he meant.

"You mean the fantasies?" she said. "No, not as much. Sexual dreams, of course, but not as quirky. Generally, men are the flashers, the fetishists. Not women. We're more straightforward in our desires."

"I'm glad you didn't say 'normal,' " he said.

"Normal?" she asked. "What's that? I understand, Clint, I really do. I'm an only child, you know, and the Colonel wanted a son. But I remember, years and years ago, overhearing him say to someone, 'I got my boy after all.' So I do understand."

"Is your mother living, Diane?"

"In a manner of speaking," she said. "Hospitalized for the past twenty years. Mental. In England."

"Ah," he said. "Terrible. See her often?"

"The Colonel and I visit once or twice a year. But she doesn't recognize us. Or won't. Did you mind my phoning you?"

"Of course not. Loved it."

He drained his glass, and before he knew it, it held more.

"Thank you," he said. "Last one."

"If you say so," she said. "But before you go back to the office, don't you have something to ask me?"

"Ask you?" he said.

"Tell me first, then ask me."

"As a matter of fact I do," he said hoarsely, setting his drink aside and flopping out of the chair onto his knees.

Factoring can be a beautiful business. It can make zillions with nothing more sweat-stained than the papers it deals with. It can also, easily, result in frauds, bankruptcies, suicide. It's a game for young men with strong nerves and the ability to give a grinning No.

Essentially, a factor buys (or lends on) accounts receivable. A merchant applied to a factor. The merchant has made a sale, but for a variety of reasons he cannot wait for payment. If the sale was not for immediate cash, the wait could be a week, a month, ninety days, or forever. So the merchant "sells" the sale to a factor, at a cost of, say, ten percent. The factor, after investigating the trustworthiness of the debtor buyer, then pays the creditor merchant ninety percent of the sale immediately and waits for payment from the buyer. The factor's profits can be enormous. But one heavy bankruptcy, between advance to the seller and collection from the buyer, can wipe him out.

The New York factoring division of Fourth National of Boston was divided into sections, by business. Clint Stahl, for example, supervised loans in the textile and garment industries. Len Babson handled factory machinery. Morris Ellen was supervisor of retail establishments, and Henry Winant was responsible for contractors and builders. And so forth. Top man was Paul Fayette. His title was Chief Supervisor. In addition, he served as Office Manager, overseeing Accounting, Personnel, and Research.

Clint Stahl came unfolding in Fayette's paneled office, his sardonic features wavering in a shitty grin. He shambled across the plummy carpeting, flopped down on the leather couch.

"You wanted to see me, boss?" he drawled.

Fayette made a great show of looking at his watch. "About three forty-five," he said, "and a new world's record. Mind telling me where you've been?"

"Heavy lunch with Diamond Textiles," Stahl said.

"Want me to call them?" Fayette asked.

"No," Stahl said quickly. "Don't do that."

Paul Fayette sighed. He got out of his swivel chair. He came over and sat at one end of the leather couch, pushing Stahl's feet out of the way. He gave Stahl a cigarette and took one himself. Fayette lighted them both with his gold Dunhill. Stahl's cigarette bobbed in his trembling fingers.

"I may possibly have mentioned this before," Fayette said casually, "but when I was in the Marine Corps, our translation of *Semper Fidelis* was 'Hooray for me, fuck you.' I live my life by that noble creed. What I'm trying to tell you, Clint, is that we're good friends. I like that. But never get the notion that I wouldn't throw you to the wolves to protect my own sweet ass. You understand that?"

"I understand that," Stahl nodded, frowning. "Always have."

"All right," Fayette said. "Maybe we shouldn't

have become so close. Maybe that was my mistake. But it's happened, so fuck it. All I'm trying to get through your pussy-whipped brain is that, if push comes to shove and my survival is threatened, you're down the drain."

"I told you, I understand that."

"Good," Fayette said. He rose, went back behind his desk, sat down in his swivel chair. He picked up a folded length of computer printout. "Now what we've got here are the estimated loss numbers for the second quarter."

"Oh, that," Stahl said.

"Yes, that," Fayette said. "Any comments, excuses, alibis, explanations, or scams?"

Stahl hunched forward on the couch. He stubbed out his half-smoked cigarette in an ugly ceramic ashtray Christine Fayette had made in Scout camp.

"Paul, it's been a lousy season on Seventh Avenue. You know that. They're jumping out the windows."

"Bullshit," Fayette said cruelly. "It's always a lousy season on Seventh Avenue. Not only are your losses almost double the next highest section's—Al Wimpler's in publishing—but they're more than double your losses for the same quarter last year. How about it?"

"A lousy season," Stahl repeated. "Bankruptcies. Jesus Christ, every one of those delinquent accounts was checked out. Research gave the okay."

"Research," Fayette said disgustedly. "If we ran this shop by computer, we'd all be pushing Good Humor wagons, and you know it. Your job is to be aware of what's going on, and to be very, very skeptical of Research's okays. Since when have you let them run your section?"

"I've had problems," Stahl muttered.

"Oh boy, have you had problems. Have you *got* problems. There's no way in the world I can cover you on this, Clint. The report goes to Boston as is. They may want your ass. You know that, don't you?"

Stahl nodded miserably.

"Well, for God's sake, man, give me some ammunition! Are you ill? Do you want a leave of absence? Are you overworked? Need more staff? Give me *something!*"

Stahl shook his head. He leaned back, shoving his disordered length into a corner of the couch. He began gnawing furiously at the hard skin around one thumbnail, spitting little bits of matter onto the rug.

"Maybe I need a shrink," he said. "Maybe I should go to Margaret's Doc Terhune. Maybe he'll give me a discount. You know——" Brittle laugh. "——family rate. Paul, for God's sake, I'm falling apart!"

Fayette stared at him. "You zonked?"

"No."

"How much did you drink at lunch?"

"Not enough." Stahl said. "And I'm not going to tell you where I was."

"Good," Fayette said. "Because I couldn't care less. All I care about is that you're not carrying the load, and when Boston sees these numbers, you may be walking the streets. I want you to absolutely understand that."

"I understand it absolutely," Stahl said in a low voice. "I don't give a damn."

"Oh Jesus," Paul Fayette sighed. "Don't give me any more of that What-have-I-got-to-live-for? crappola. I can't take that."

"Oh no," Stahl said, looking up. "I've got something to live for."

"Glad to hear it. So?"

"So it's got nothing to do with Fourth National. The job's incidental. Unimportant. This has got to do with me."

Paul Fayette tossed up his hands in a comical gesture of bewilderment.

"Whee!" he said. "Nothing to do with your job, your livelihood, liverwurst on the table for the wife and kiddies. But it has to do with *you*. That's swell."

Suddenly, without warning, Clint Stahl was bent far forward. Elbows on his knees. Palms to his face. He was weeping. Shoulders shaking. Breath coming in heaving sobs.

"I feel so," he choked. "So soiled."

Fayette stared at him in astonishment, unable to comprehend this melodramatic moment. He was so inured to Stahl's manic moods, he thought this another of his dreadful impersonations.

"Who's that supposed to be?" he faltered. "Joan Crawford in *Mildred Pierce?*"

"So fucking soiled," Clint Stahl wailed, and then Fayette knew he was really hurting. He rose, went over to the outside door and locked it. He returned to his desk, took a half-filled bottle of Cutty Sark from the bottom drawer. He filled the water glass next to his desk thermos, then brought the whisky over to Stahl. He pried loose one of the trembling man's wet hands and pressed it around the glass.

"Drink," he ordered.

Shaking, spilling the Scotch, Stahl managed to gulp down half of it. Some ran down his chin. Dripped onto his tie and shirt. Stained his trousers.

"I can't tell you, Paul," he spluttered. *"Can't."*

"I don't want to know," Fayette said.

Laura had closed the toilet seat cover and put a towel across. She leaned back, naked, her tanned legs stretched out. On the floor, kneeling between her legs, her husband was spraying a layer of shaving cream over her calves, knees, thighs. He was wearing white bikini briefs.

"I don't know what it was all about," he said. "Something broke him up. Something that happened at lunch. He was gone almost four hours."

"What happened?" Laura asked. "After you gave him the drink?"

"Embarrassment. We couldn't look at each other. He mumbled something about shaping up. Oh God, it was terrible. He just came apart. While I watched."

"The poor man," she mourned. "How awful for him. And for you."

"Screw me," Paul said. "I told him I couldn't cover for him. He just didn't seem to care. Enough soap?"

"On my knees," she said. "I happen to have very hairy knees."

"All the women in the world," he grumbled, "and I've got to marry one with hairy knees. That should do it. I'll do the fronts first, and then you'll have to stand, and I'll do the backs."

"The fun part," she said.

"It's all fun," he said. "I love all of it."

Still on his knees, he began to shave her legs. He started at crease of groin, drawing the safety razor down slowly and carefully. He rinsed it in warm water running in the bathroom sink. As he shaved with one hand, he drew the skin taut with fingers of the other, then stroked the shaved area softly, searching for stubble he might have missed.

"About the dinner," he said. "No way to call it off?"

"Honey, I told you, it was just a spur-of-the-moment thing. She was jogging when I was and came back with me for a cup of coffee, and we talked. She had to go into the city on business—she didn't say what—and I suggested she and the Colonel come by for a pickup dinner about eightish. Nothing fancy. She jumped at it. We did say we'd have them over, Paul. I warned her: just knockwurst, boiled new potatoes, and sauerkraut. She said they'd love it. Are you really angry?"

"Ah, not really," he said, shaving away. "What's this here? Pimple? Mosquito bite?"

"A bite, I think."

"Itch?"

"A little. Kiss it."

"All right," he said, and did.

"So the dinner's okay?" she asked anxiously.

"Sure," he said. "As long as I don't have to dress up. I refuse to put on a tie for knockwurst."

"No, no, love," she said hurriedly. "Diane and I agreed: no dress-up. Very, very informal."

"Which means the Colonel will wear a cotton ascot. Am I scraping too hard?"

"Just right. As usual. Much better than I could do myself."

"You say."

He shaved the insides of her thighs as she spread her legs wider.

"One of these days I'll shave the whole cooze," he said.

"Promises, promises."

"Or start a brush fire. What did you and Diane talk about?"

"This and that," she said. "Funny thing, Paul, whenever I talk to her, eventually it gets to deep things. I mean, we can start gabbing about the weather and shopping and so forth, and before I know it, we're spilling our guts."

"Both of you?" he asked shrewdly. "Or just you?"

She considered a moment.

"Both of us," she decided. "But mainly me," she admitted. "It's very unusual. I mean how the talk gets around to deep things."

"Nothing meaningless," he said. "Things of consequence. Talk that might embarrass us if we had it with, say, the Stahls or Cantors or Spencers."

"Right," she nodded. "You do understand. Deep things."

He shaved her legs slowly, with care, humming as he worked. He rinsed the razor frequently, and thinned the lather with his fingertips, and felt for places missed. The shaved skin gleamed wet and slick. It dried to a suede finish. He did shins, the sides of her calves, ankles. When all the lather was shaved away, he ran his palms lightly over her legs, groin to feet.

"A-OK," he said. "Let's do the back."

She stood, turned, stepped up on the toilet cover. She leaned forward, propping her hands against the wall. The long muscles of her thighs and the round muscles of her calves tightened her skin, thrusting.

He also stood, and sprayed lather slowly, shaking the shaving cream can occasionally.

"Ass, too?" he said.

"Let's go for broke," she said, so he sprayed her ass.

"But not too high," he said. "Above the crack, that fuzz of golden hair—I wouldn't want to touch that."

"Then don't," she said.

"I know what you mean," he said. "About the deep talk. Listen, tonight you take the Blimp and I'll take the Dragon. Let's see what we can get out of them."

"About what?"

"Everything. Where they're from. Their background. What his business really is. How her husband died. What the hell they're doing in Penlow Park. Let's really be curious and dig."

"Not very polite, Paul."

"Why the hell not? Just neighborly interest. We answer any questions they have, don't we? So why not them? They're so fucking mysterious."

"Ah-ha!" she said. "So Margaret *was* right."

"Oh hell, she's not a dark, mysterious widow lady. Just close-mouthed, that's all."

He shaved the tender leather behind her knees, going ever so slowly and ever so cunningly, his razor following curve, fold, and crease of skin. He was aware of his hardening.

"I may come," he said.

"Don't you dare," she said.

He shaved away the fine, blonde hairs of her thighs with short, light strokes. His tender fingers pried her legs apart gently.

"A little more," he murmured.

Silently, she spread her legs a bit wider. His clever blade began to scrape softly at skin so limpid it was almost liquid.

"Lanugo," he said, but she made no answer.

He shaved her buttocks, spreading the cheeks apart with thumb and forefinger. He worked with solemn intentness, leaning close, peering. He touched the beige rosebud with the tip of his little finger. She shivered.

"Oh, lover," she said.

"Almost finished," he said.

"Yes," she said.

The lather was shaved away. He rinsed the razor. He soaked a cloth in hottish water and wiped her legs with long, slow strokes. Then he stood back, admired the pellucid gleam.

"Perfect," he said.

He helped her down from her perch. She sat on the toilet cover again. She raised her knees, put her heels on the seat, spread wide her thighs.

"Aren't you going to finish the job?" she asked.

"My pleasure," he said.

"No," Colonel Benjamin G. Coulter said. "No, no, dear lady. You'll never convince me *that* sauerkraut came from a can."

"It did," Laura Fayette smiled. "But I may have gussied it up a bit."

"Of course you did." Coulter said, leaning forward to pat her bare knee. "I should think you added caraway seeds and steamed it in white wine."

"Something like that," Laura said vaguely. She gave up trying to see her husband and the Widow Cheney through the screen wall of the patio. They were strolling about the backyard, two white blurs. She turned back to Coulter. "Are you a gourmet cook, Colonel?"

"A dabbler," he said. "This and that. In my travels I've picked up a few unusual recipes. When you come to us for dinner, I'll try something exotic. Do you like snake meat?"

"No," she said hastily, but he didn't laugh.

"Too bad," he said. "Marvelous creature, the snake. You can do so much with it. The meat's not unlike your knockwurst, as a matter of fact, but a bit more delicate."

"More snaky," she said.

"Precisely," he said. "More snaky."

The dinner had been a success. Mrs. Cheney and the Colonel had arrived with a case of chilled Alsatian beer, bewildering the Fayettes with this generous gift. Everyone had eaten enough to please the hostess. Then they had adjourned to the screened patio for coffee and brandy.

Coffee finished, Mrs. Cheney and Paul Fayette took their brandies out of doors, to wander about the small backyard and inspect the smaller garden by the light of a scabrous moon.

"Full in two days," the Colonel reported to Laura. "You are not, by any chance, a full-mooner, are you?"

"I'm not sure I know exactly what a full-mooner is."

"An individual excessively affected by a fat moon. The world's police are aware of them. Crime rates go up, otherwise normal people dash naked down the street, and the loonies of this earth have their walpurgisnacht. As well they should, since the name itself comes from the moon. Loony. Lunar."

"I don't *think* I'm a full-mooner," Laura said. "At least I don't dash naked down the street."

"Pity," the Colonel said dryly, and this time they both laughed.

"A close night," Paul Fayette said. "I'm afraid we may be in for a hot summer."

"I hope so," Mrs. Cheney said. "I love heat. The hotter, the better. I can't stand the cold."

"Then I'm surprised you settled in Penlow Park," Paul said. "Why not Florida, or the West Indies, or French Riviera? Or Africa, for that matter."

"It's really for the Colonel's sake," she said. "He has business here."

"In Penlow Park?" Fayette laughed. "Impossible!"

"I wouldn't be a bit surprised," she said seriously. "He has so many things going. I just can't keep up with him."

"Remarkable energy for a man of his age."

"How old do you think he is, Paul?"

"Oh about sixty?" he guessed. "Sixty-five tops?"

She laughed merrily. "You're not even close."

They strolled a moment in silence, she tinking her brandy glass lightly against her teeth.

"Where did you live before you moved here?" he asked her.

"Oh, here, there, everywhere. The last place was Cedar Rapids, Iowa. For a short time. And before that in Liverpool, England."

"My God," he said, "you do get around. You must enjoy traveling."

"Not particularly," she said. "But, you know—business."

"Never had the urge to settle down? Permanently?"

"Oh, every now and then I think I'd like to put down roots. But I know I'd probably be bored to tears in a year. Or less."

"What?" he said, surprised. "Then you don't intend to stay in Penlow Park?"

"Only as long as it takes," she said.

"You mean your father's business?"

"Yes," she said. "And mine, too, of course."

"I'm afraid I can't get interested in golf," Benjamin Coulter was telling Laura, filling their glasses from the brandy decanter. "One can bowl a perfect game. And a baseball pitcher can toss a no-hitter. Even a tennis player can take a match in love games. But perfect golf? That would mean nine holes-in-one. Quite impossible, I should imagine."

"Colonel, you're a perfectionist," Laura said.

"Always have been," he agreed. "As the old song goes, all or nothing at all."

"You have no hobbies?"

"As a matter of fact I do, dear lady. I'm something of an amateur magician. A rank amateur, I might add."

"A magician?" she said, brightening. "But that's wonderful! I love magic."

"Do you?" he said, peering at her. "Delighted to hear it. Take a look at this . . ."

He unbuttoned his suede hacking jacket. He fished in a pocket of his tattersall waistcoat. He brought out a silver dollar. He held it up for Laura to see in the watery light coming from the family room window.

"Take it," Coulter said, holding it out to her.

Obediently, she held out her hand. She saw him place the silver dollar in her palm. She felt the pressure of the coin. But when she brought her hand close to look, there was nothing there. Nor was the dollar in his fingers. He spread them wide to show her.

"How did you do that?" she said wonderingly.

He laughed. "Illusion, dear lady. What makes the world go 'round. It's all illusion."

"Where's the silver dollar now?"

"Under your seat cushion."

"It's not!" she cried.

"Look."

So she did, and there it was.

"But that's marvelous," she said. "How did you *do* it?"

"I told you, Laura. Illusion. The hand is quicker than the eye. Now you see it, now you don't. Shall I show you another?"

"Oh yes," she said eagerly. "Please do."

Mrs. Cheney leaned forward to light her cigarette. She held Paul's hand to steady his lighter. She continued to hold it while he lighted his own cigarette. Then they stood side by side in the warm darkness. He glanced back to the patio. Laura and the Colonel were sitting close, heads together.

"I thought you'd smoke a pipe," Mrs. Cheney said. "I saw the rack on your sideboard."

"What?" he said. "Oh. A pipe. No, I'm not enthusiastic about pipes."

"You have a lot of them," she observed.

A thin laugh. 'When I was getting started in business, after college, I felt very young. I thought I *looked* young. I wanted to look like a mature executive. It was the blond hair that bothered me, I suppose. So I tried to grow a mustache. But that came in blond, too, and wasn't much help. So I took up a pipe. Thought it helped my image."

"Did it?" she asked.

He shrugged. "Maybe it did. Who knows? Then one day I woke up and realized I really didn't enjoy smoking a pipe. Now I hardly touch them."

"Things like that happen," she said. "We do things from habit. Without questioning. Then one day we realize how empty the habit is. There's no real pleasure in it anymore, if there ever was. Then, if we're strong, we just kick it."

"And if we're not strong?"

"Oh, habits can chain you," she said. "Even relationships can become habits. I know a lot of marriages that are habits, nothing more. People keep going because it takes too much emotional energy to change, too much resolve. It's easier just to go along. Velvet-covered chains."

"You're not chained," he said. Then: "Are you?"

"Oh yes," she said. "But I'm aware of it, and have no desire to change."

"Chained to what?" he asked. "To whom?"

"Oh . . ." she said thoughtfully, "to the Colonel, for instance. I'm chained to the Colonel. Voluntarily, of course."

"You never go it alone?"

"Never," she said. "We've had our disagreements, but he always gets his way. In the end."

"A very persuasive man," Paul Fayette said. "I've noticed that."

"You have no idea how persuasive he can be," she said. "A master."

"And you have no desire to go your own way?"

"Where would I go?" she asked. "I tried it once. It didn't last long."

He was silent a moment, then: "I don't mean to pry, and don't answer if you feel I am, but we're not talking about financial dependency, are we? Is that why you're chained to him?"

She moved her head back and laughed. He could see the sheen of her polished throat in the pale moonlight.

"Money?" she said. "Oh no, nothing like that. My husband left me well-provided for."

"Not money," he said, "then *what?*"

"Let's just say I'm a dutiful daughter," she said, taking his arm. "Can we go back now? I'd like a little more brandy."

"Of course," he said, hoping Laura was having more luck than he.

They sauntered back to the patio. She held his arm against her soft breast. Just before they came to the weak wedge of light, she leaned to him and whispered in his ear. He stopped, shocked, not believing what he had heard. His mouth stretched, eyes widened. She disengaged her arm and swept ahead. He stumbled after, still incredulous, trying to convince himself he had misheard her.

"Paul!" Laura shouted. "The Colonel has been showing me the most wonderful magic tricks. Show him one, Colonel. Please do!"

"Just sleight of hand, you know," Coulter said deprecatingly. "A bit of legerdemain; nothing more."

"But I don't know how you *do* it," Laura cried. Almost feverishly, Paul thought. "Do that one with the coin. Do it slowly, just like you showed me."

"You mean this one?" the Colonel said.

He pulled shirt and jacket cuffs high on his wrist. He showed Paul his bare hand, turning it this way and that. The fingers were surprisingly long and slender for such a plumpish man. Joints were unwrinkled; nails gleamed.

"Hold my cuffs if you like," he offered.

Paul grasped both his hands about the Colonel's wrist.

"Now keep a tight hold," Coulter said, "but let me move my hand."

Still gripping the man's cuffs and wrist, Paul allowed the Colonel to lift his hand slowly. His fingers touched behind Paul's ear, came away holding a silver dollar in their tips.

"My God," Paul said.

"I *told* you," Laura said. "Have you ever seen anything like that?"

"I didn't even see *that*," Paul said. "How did you do it, sir?"

"Tricks of the trade," Colonel Coulter smiled. "Against the rules to reveal magicians' secrets."

"Do another," Paul said. "Please, I want to see if I can figure out how it's done."

"Let's go inside," Coulter said. "Diane and I will give you a demonstration of mental telepathy."

"Oh Colonel, not again," Mrs. Cheney protested. "I think you've done enough for one evening."

"No, no . . . please," Laura begged. "We'd love to see it, wouldn't we, Paul?"

"Of course," he said. "If it's as good as that coin trick, you'll make a believer of me."

"We intend to," Colonel Coulter said, smiling coldly. "Don't we, Diane?"

They moved into the living room, comfortably crowded with easy furniture, good watercolors, and the accumulated mementoes and bric-a-brac of twenty-four years of married life.

"Now let's turn on a few more lights," Colonel Coulter said briskly, taking charge. "Mustn't have any gloom or dark shadows. No hocus-pocus here. Everything open and aboveboard. Now Laura, you and Paul sit in your favorite chairs, and get comfortable. All settled? Good. Now Diane, you stand over there facing the wall, that's a dear. A bit closer. Fine. Now you'll notice Diane is facing an absoutely blank wall. No mirrors, no glass in which she might see a reflection. Agreed?"

"Agreed," Paul nodded.

"Now I shall move about the room behind Diane, taking care that there is no possible way she can catch me in her peripheral vision. I will point at various objects and ask her to identify them. I will not pick them up because the sound might give her a clue; I shall merely point. Are you ready, O divine seer?"

"I am ready, O swami," Diane Cheney said.

Laura and Paul laughed.

Colonel Coulter stepped close to the antiqued oak cocktail table. His long forefinger stabbed at a pewter cigarette box.

"What am I pointing at?" he demanded.

Mrs. Cheney paused only a blink, then said, "A pewter cigarette box."

Laura gave a little gasp of surprise, then clapped her palms together.

"And what is this?" the Colonel asked, pointing.

"A china cigarette lighter."

"And what have we here?"

"A glass ashtray."

"And now what am I pointing at?"

"A book. It has a red cover."

The Colonel turned to the Fayettes, and made a small, mocking bow.

"And that concludes our little demonstration, lady and gentleman," he said. "Proving conclusively that Diane, through her highly developed psychic powers, is able to read my innermost thoughts."

"Bravo!" Laura cried, applauding enthusiastically. "That was wonderful! Wasn't it, Paul?"

"Very well done," he said, smiling. "Very professional."

Coulter caught him up at once. "Professional?" he repeated. "Do I detect a note of doubt here? Can it be you question my daughter's supernatural authority?"

"Well, as a matter of fact, sir," Paul said, a bit uncomfortably, "I have seen something similar done before. In nightclubs and the theatre. The two of you have a code; isn't that it? Diane identifies the object by the way you ask your question. For instance, the word 'What' might signify a book. 'And now' would

indicate an ashtray. And so forth. But I must say you
do it very well."

"Diane, did you hear that?" the Colonel called.
"This unbeliever actually thinks we're using a code!"

She had turned from the wall and was facing them,
smiling faintly. In a tailored, white garbardine pantsuit, she looked seven feet tall. The silky hair floated
about her shoulders, a dark cloud. She wore no sweater
or blouse. About her neck hung a fine silver chain.
Suspended from it was a single shark's tooth, polished and gleaming against tanned skin.

"A code!" she repeated. "Very insulting, Colonel,
wouldn't you say!"

"Isn't it?" he agreed. "Paul, to prove to you how
unjust your suspicions are, we will give another demonstration at absolutely no additional cost. This time
I will use the same inquiry for each of the objects selected. Code indeed! O divine seer, will you face the
wall again?"

Mrs. Cheney turned and pressed close to the blank
wall. Colonel Coulter moved easily around the room,
pointing, calling out to this daughter . . .

"This?" he asked.

"Petit point footstool," she said promptly.

"This?"

"Brass candlestick."

"This?"

"A crystal decanter."

"This?"

"A magazine—no, a stack of magazines."

"This?"

"A little wicker frog."

"Thank you, my dear." The Colonel turned to Paul.
He was not smiling. "Well? Still think we're using a
code?"

"They couldn't be, Paul," Laura said nervously. Her
features were wrenched with distress.

"Wait a minute, wait a minute," Paul said angrily.
"Let me figure this out. All right, you weren't using a

code. There must be another trick to it. Let me think."

They let him think. He leaned forward, head in hands. The Colonel strolled about casually, lighting cigarettes for the ladies and himself. He smoked a brown cigarillo in a short, ornate meerschaum holder carved in the shape of a dragon. The little cigar fitted into the dragon's mouth.

"Got it!" Paul shouted suddenly. He straightened up, grinning. "We were in this room for an hour, for drinks, before we went in to dinner. There were a few moments when both Laura and I were out of the room. The two of you had an opportunity to agree on certain objects. No, it wasn't a code. But you agreed on the *sequence!* Right? You selected a half-dozen objects the Colonel would point to, and the sequence in which they'd be selected. Am I right? Wasn't that how it was done?"

The Colonel looked at them both, back and forth. Then he shook his head sorrowfully. He learned forward to stub out his cigarillo in the glass ashtray.

"O ye of little faith," he said softly. "Is there no way we can convince you that Diane is possessed of superhuman powers and can read the mind of anyone she chooses? No way at all?"

"Sure there is," Paul said, still grinning. "You want to make us believe Diane is a psychic? Okay, let's do the trick again. Diane, you face the wall, but this time *I* will point out the objects. You read my mind and tell us what I'm pointing at. Should be easy as pie for any self-respecting medium."

There was silence for a moment. The Colonel looked at Mrs. Cheney. She had turned to face them again. She was staring at Paul. He could not fathom her smile. Almost sad. Almost regretful.

"Well, my dear," the Colonel said, "what do you say? Willing to play Paul's little game?"

She nodded.

"Are you spiritually in tune with him?" Coulter asked with mock solemnity. "Do you feel the incorporeal emanations pouring from that beautiful soul?"

"I feel them, Pandit Coulter," she said in a low voice. "They are very strong."

"Good, good, good," the Colonel said, rubbing his palms together and smiling. "Then—on with the show!"

Once again Mrs. Cheney faced the wall. Paul inspected her to make certain she was not using a small mirror or reflective jewelry. Then he moved across the room, directly behind her.

"All set, Diane?" he called.

"I'm ready, Paul," she said.

He looked about, selected a small silver filigree pillbox on the mantelpiece. He brought the tip of his forefinger close.

"Diane," he said loudly, "What am I pointing at?"

She was silent for a few seconds. Then . . .

"Concentrate on it," she said.

"I am," he said.

"Harder."

He stared intently at the pillbox, bringing his pointing finger closer.

"What is it!" he asked again.

"The silver pillbox on the mantelpiece," she said clearly.

Paul let his finger, hand, arm fall slowly. He stared at Laura. She stared at him. Their faces were blank. Colonel Coulter was sitting immoble in an armchair, knees crossed, gleaming moccasin bobbing. He had clasped his hands. He was pressing forefingers against his lips, regarding Paul gravely.

Paul pointed at the Colonel.

"What is this, Diane?"

"You are pointing at my father."

"And this?"

"The leather club chair."

"This?"

"The glass ashtray again."

"And this?"

"You are pointing at yourself, your heart."

"All right," Paul said faintly. "Thank you, Diane. Come sit down."

She moved gracefully to the couch to sit alongside Laura. She lighted a cigarette slowly, blew out a long plume of smoke. She looked at Paul quizzically.

"Well?" she said.

"Perfect," he said, trying to smile. "I give up; I don't know how you're doing it. It's one hell of a trick."

"*Trick?*" Colonel Coulter said explosively. "Ye gods and little fishes, man, can't you recognize the real thing when you see it?"

"Diane," Laura faltered, "are you really psychic?"

"Of course she is," the Colonel said immediately. "Wonderful gift. But not as rare as you might think. Dabble in it myself, as a matter of fact."

"*Dabble!*" Mrs. Cheney laughed. Then, to the others, "The Colonel taught me all I know."

"And a most apt and willing student you are, love," Coulter said fondly. "My best. Absolutely my best. We must have you people in for a seance. No blowing trumpets of floating tables. None of that trash. Just the past revealed."

"And the future," the Widow Cheney said. "Don't forget the future, Colonel."

"Ah yes." He smiled without mirth. "The great and glorious tomorrow." Here he consulted a lumpy timepiece he hauled from a waistcoat pocket on a gold chain. "But it's getting on to the witching hour, and there's a heavy schedule awaiting us. We really must run."

Mrs. Cheney and Colonel Coulter expressed thanks for the dinner. Laura and Paul said how much they had enjoyed the evening, especially the unexpected entertainment. The widow kissed both Fayettes on the cheek. Coulter kissed Laura and shook Paul's hand. The Colonel was strong on touching, patting, stroking. . . .

Diane Cheney exited first. Coulter turned at the door to wink at Paul, and laugh.

"There *is* a trick to it, you know," he said, and then he was gone.

Laura and Paul stood in the open doorway, watching as their guests climbed into the Colonel's car. It was a black Cadillac limousine.

"Damned thing looks like a hearse," Coulter had grumbled to Paul earlier in the evening. "Must turn it in for something sprightlier."

"A sports car?" Paul suggested.

"Oh lord, no. Same model, but a different color. Blood-red perhaps."

The long car backed slowly out of the Fayettes' driveway. They continued to stand at the doorway until the Colonel got turned around on Chancery Lane. He waved from his open window. They waved back. They watched until the black car was lost in night shadows. Then they came slowly inside. Paul turned off the outside light. He double-locked the door, put on the chain. Then he turned. Laura was standing close to him.

Paul Fayette looked at his wife, troubled. "Who *are* these people?" he said. Then, seeing her face, he asked anxiously, "Butch, what's wrong?"

"Something," she said desperately. *"Something."*

At night, even to God's jaundiced eye, Penlow Park seemed a fair and pleasant place. In thin moonlight the June foliage gleamed blackly, a shroud of glints. Here and there a roof poked through, the Lucite cross atop the First Presbyterian Church, the tower of the firehouse, the courthouse steeple. Curving roads made a dully shining seaweed, and swimming pools showed in their centers the moon's dim glow.

Up and down hill it went, with many sly corners and cunning culs-de-sac. The houses were not of a single style—but who cared for that? Gardens there were, and trig lawns. A baseball field. Riding paths. The high school bleachers. All shone silently in that washed moonlight. A few late lights burned. A solitary stroller. Dog bark and cicada song. But mostly the soft quiet of satisfied homes, the peace of monied ease.

Little crime and violence in Penlow Park. A nice place. Relaxed and informal. A place where eccentrics were happily tolerated, and youth found it difficult to revolt. The enameled air itself might have been purchased and delivered in pale blue Tiffany boxes. The suburb was young enough to hope, and old enough to laugh. Even at itself. The small shopping section had three stores with names beginning "Ye—" but there was also a head shop and a store that specialized in blackstrap molasses, wheat germ, and kelp. The proprietor's beard was almost as bushy as the mayor's.

No backwater was Penlow Park. It knew the world and was determinedly part of it. Committees for this and that, generous contributions to unpopular causes, adoption of a Nigerian village, and charity auctions, charity bake sales, charity dances, charity banquets, and charity subscriptions without end. Good giving people in Penlow Park. No one starved, and the deserving poor were heaped with more castoff clothing than they could ever wear. The volunteer fire department had a brand-new $150,000 pumper, and the high school cheerleaders had been clad in silver plastic miniskirts by an anonymous donor.

"Penlow Park: A Good Place to Live—and Grow!" claimed the Junior Chamber of Commerce billboard. It was true.

Toward this charming suburban oasis, in the early morning hours following the Fayettes' dinner for Mrs. Diane Cheney and Colonel Benjamin G. Coulter—the night still pitch, the air as still—a scrofulous alley cat came loping down from the north, steadily through the darkness.

It was an ugly beast, chawed and skewbald, hair missing in patches, one bloody ear hanging limp, a tooth jagging up through torn lips. Ribs pressed; pelvic bones jutted. This cat, perhaps ten years old, trotted purposefully, as if with a remembered destination. It threaded its way through the trees of Penlow

Park, around buildings, across lawns, between the pickets of white fences. At times it moved along the shoulders of roads, then cut through sprouting gardens and wooded lots. Mouth open, thin chest heaving, it stopped to crouch only at unexpected dog bark or the grind of a passing car. Then it rose again to continue its determined journey.

It came finally, limping slightly, to Chancery Lane. It paused to look about, an idle tourist getting its bearings. The remainder of its search was made at a slow, ambling walk, hips swinging. It padded up to the home of Laura and Paul Fayette. It sniffed the front steps, then arched its back and yawned, showing broken teeth to the failing moon.

Then, slowly, one paw placed delicately before the other, it moved around to the back of the house. It mounted the three steps to the back stoop. It sniffed again at the door. Yawned again. Stretched again. Then suddenly fell over on its side, on the stoop, legs extended. The beaten head went down. The cat was still, staring at the door of the Fayette home with green, unwinking eyes.

3

The 8:46 was late—not the first time, not the last. Paul Fayette waited grumpily on the station platform, trying to read his vertically folded *Times,* raising his head occasionally to peer down the naked tracks. A light touch on his sleeve; he turned.

A Negro, high, whip-thin, wearing black livery. Possibly the handsomest colored man Paul had ever seen. Not handsome as an imitative white, with delicate features, straight nose, thin lips. But handsome as a negroid, a Benin mask: bold brow, fluted nose, sculpted lips.

"Mr. Fayette, sir?" he asked softly. West Indian accent.

Paul nodded, startled.

"Sir, Colonel Coulter is waiting outside in his car. He respectfully requests the pleasure of Mr. Fayette's company. We're driving into the city, sir. Into Manhattan. Would Mr. Fayette care to join us, sir?"

"Mr. Fayette would," Paul grinned. "With gratitude. Lead the way."

"Went by your place too late," Colonel Coulter explained. "Laura was just setting out on her morning jog, and said you might still be here. So we stopped by on the off-chance."

"Glad you did. God knows when that train will be along—or they might cancel it entirely. How have you been, Colonel?"

"Tip-top, sir! No complaints whatsoever."

"And Diane?"

"Smashing. No other word for it. That girl grows lovelier by the day, if I have to say so m'self."

"I'll say it, if you won't."

"Nice to hear we're of a mind," Coulter smiled, putting a hand on Paul's knee. He leaned forward, pressed a button that lowered the glass partition separating the passengers in the back from the chauffeur up front. "Jacque," he called, "just to make it official, I'd like you to meet a good friend of mine, Paul Fayette. Paul, this beautiful beast is Jacque, and I don't know what Diane and I would do without him."

The chauffeur turned briefly from the limousine wheel to show a flash of white teeth.

"Mr. Fayette, sir," he called. "A pleasure to make your acquaintance."

"Nice to know you, Jacque," Paul said. "How are you going—Saw Mill River?"

"Right, sir. Then into Manhattan and down Fifth. Deliver you to your door, sir."

"Beautiful," Fayette said, having no doubt whatsoever that the Colonel, and Jacque, knew exactly where he worked.

"A bit of air conditioning would be in order, I think," the Colonel told his chauffeur. "Better put it on exhaust."

The glass partition slid up noiselessly. Coulter leaned back against the leather upholstery, took a pigskin cigar case from his inside jacket pocket.

"First of the day," he said. "Join me?"

"I'd better pass," Fayette said. "I'm not much of a cigar smoker."

"Try one," Coulter urged. "Genuine Havana. Absolutely. I get them a never-mind way. Mild, morning cigar. You'll like it."

In a moment they were both puffing contentedly, lolling back in the sealed club room, cooled, grandly watching the world flash by.

"Better than the 8:46." Paul murmured.

"Isn't it?" the Colonel said equably. "Happy to have

this chance for a bit of a chat with you. First of all, Diane and I would like it if Laura and you could drop by for dinner on Saturday, if you can make it."

"Thank you," Fayette said. "Sounds fine to me, but I don't know if Laura has anything planned. Suppose I call her when I get to the office, and have her call Diane—one way or another."

"Good-o," the Colonel said, "The second thing is—"

But just then a phone rang. Fayette wasn't surprised; he had seen the long whip antenna mounted on the rear of the limousine's roof. He saw Jacque pick up a white handset and speak briefly. In a moment, an intercom clicked on . . .

"Colonel," the chauffeur said softly, "it's Beirut. Will you take it, sir?" He glanced in the rearview mirror.

Coulter nodded, opened a small flip-down door in the back of the front seat. His handset was red.

"Excuse me," he said to Paul. "Won't take a moment." He pressed a button. "Colonel Benjamin G. Coulter here. Yes . . . I see . . . All right, we'll wait."

He replaced the phone in the recess, slammed the little door. He flung himself back against the seat again.

"Damned doctors," he said wrathfully. "Always interfering."

Fayette was silent. The Colonel sat turned away a bit, glowering. Finally he turned back to Paul, all geniality.

"I better go over," he said. "But it'll be a turn-around trip. Be back in plenty of time for our Saturday dinner, if you can make it."

"Of course," Paul said.

"The other thing I wanted to mention is our joining the country club. Diane and me. How might that be managed?"

"No problem," Fayette told him. "You need a sponsor. I'll be happy to put you up. And two seconding sponsors. I'll get Clint Stahl and someone else. Then it's just a matter of filling out forms; banking references,

and so forth. Meanwhile, I'll get you temporary cards
until the Board meets in July. How does that sound?"

"Excellent," the Colonel said, restored to good humor. "Give you a stack of references, if you like.
Clubs all over the world, you know."

"I'm sure there'll be no problem," Paul said. "The
application form is brief: age, birthplace, personal his-
tory—that kind of thing. What branch of Army were
you with, Colonel?"

Coulter looked at his cigar. It had burned down to
two inches in length, with a fat, white ash. He set it
carefully aside in a glass tray inserted in the armrest.
Then he leaned forward to press another button. It
released the lid of a small, lighted bar inset into the
rear of the front seat.

"Refreshments!" he cried gaily. "Cleanse the nasal
passages and the stuffed bosom of that perilous stuff
which weighs upon the heart. Shakespeare. Almost
anything you might want here, Paul m'lad. Name your
poison."

Fayette gazed with admiration at the neat set of
small crystal decanters and glasses, the aluminum thermos of icecubes, the silver knife and stirring spoon,
And, on a wee cutting board, one fresh lemon and
one fresh lime.

"A little early in the morning for me, Colonel," he
said. "But you go right ahead."

"Nonsense," Coulter said sharply. "Never too early.
What would you say to a spicy Bloody Mary, icy as a
witch's tit, with a squeeze of lime?"

"You're right," Paul said. "It's never too early."

The Colonel laughed, and set to work. Fayette
crossed his legs, savored the last sweet drags of his
morning cigar, enjoyed the chilled, filtered air, looked
indolently out the window, scorned the drivers and
passengers in the small, dusty cars they passed so ef-
fortlessly. He even saw roadside workers and, in the
distance, men wheeling barrows and carrying loads.

"The fools," he said idly.

"What?" the Colonel asked, pressing a tall, frosted glass into his hand.

Paul sniffed the tangy scent of the drink, smelled the smoke of his good cigar, the cool perfume of new car and leather upholstery.

"I was just thinking," he said, "that heaven must be like this."

"More like hell," the Colonel said, smiling thinly. "No fun in heaven, I do assure you. Well—" he lifted his glass. *"Haw bon ching d'how yin sak."*

They both sipped their drinks.

"What was that?" Fayette asked. "Your toast?"

"Means 'May all your troubles be little ones.' Or something like that."

"In what language, Colonel?"

Coulter thought a moment, frowning.

"Damned if I know," he said finally. "Can't remember. Or I may have made the whole thing up. I'm capable of that."

"I'm sure you are," Fayette said, sipping his drink and wanting his fantastical ride to go on forever. "About your army service . . . I was asking what branch it was."

"Ah." the colonel said, "So you were. Care to guess?"

"Tank corps?"

Coulter smiled. "Not even close. No shot and shell for me and my lads. Oh, a few forward posts got bombed every now and then, but nothing serious. I was with Graves Registration. Surprised? Identification of the dead, transportation, burial—that sort of thing. Not very romantic or glamorous, I'm afraid."

"But necessary," Fayette said slowly, deciding the Colonel had put too much lime into the Bloody Mary; it had a bitter, puckering taste.

"Necessary?" the Colonel said. "I should think so! Absolutely essential. Pick them up—somet'mes in pieces, you understand—put a name to them, tuck them away. Had to be done, you know. Reams of paperwork."

"I can imagine," Paul said faintly. "Not the happiest job in the world."

"Oh . . . I don't know," Coulter said thoughtfully. "It had its compensations."

The remainder of the ride was made in silence. As they were coming down Fifth Avenue in Manhattan, the Colonel asked, "What did you decide about that stray cat of yours?"

"Word does get around," Paul smiled. "That's Penlow Park for you. Well, first we were going to call the S.P.C.A. But then Laura put out a dish of milk and a can of tuna for him. I thought the damned thing was diseased and dying. But he's looking better now. We've bought some cat food for him. Put it out on the back stoop. Sometimes he eats, sometimes he doesn't. He disappears for days, then comes back. An outside cat. A rover. So ugly, he's attractive."

"Marvelous creatures, cats," Colonel Coulter said. "So independent. Have you named him yet?"

"No, not yet," Fayette said. "We've considered everything from Henry James to Millard Fillmore, but can't decide."

"Why don't you call him 'Ben'?" Coulter said suddenly, completely serious. "After me. Good, straight, stand-up name: Ben. And you say he's a rover. I'd be proud to have him named after me."

"All right, sir," Paul Fayette laughed. " 'Ben' sounds like a good name to me, if you have no objection. But he's hardly civilized. Hasn't even tried to get into the house."

"Still," the Colonel said, "he might."

Margaret Stahl, sweaty and peevish, came trudging from the tennis court. She searched about and finally found Mrs. Cheney sitting at an umbrella table alongside the swimming pool. She was watching a gang of tots thrashing about in the shallow end.

The widow was wearing a strapped sun dress of white pique. A wide-brimmed straw hat cast her face in blued shadow down to her mouth. Her lips gleamed.

"You look so calm, cool, and collected," Margaret said. "Dammit, don't you ever sweat?"

"Not in public," Mrs. Cheney said lazily, showing her teeth. "How did the lesson go?"

Margaret muttered something. She slumped into a wrought iron chair, thrust her thin, bared legs under the table. She put her head back, squinted up at a pellucid June sky.

"Why do I do it?" she demanded of God. "Spend Clint's money on tennis lessons? I don't even *like* the damned game. And golf lessons. And therapy. And clothes I don't need."

"Doesn't he complain?" Mrs. Cheney asked.

"No," Margaret said shortly. "That's what's so maddening."

Mrs. Cheney regarded her gravely. The widow was wearing black eyeliner. It gave her a vaguely Egyptian appearance. A face on a temple frieze: coal-dark hair, brilliantly carmined mouth (subtly outlined in a deeper shade), a chalky complexion.

"Margaret," she said softly, "it's such a silly way to get your husband's attention: spending him into bankruptcy."

"I want him to be aware of my existence," the other woman said stiffly.

"No sex life? You two, I mean? At all?"

"Zilch. I forget how long it's been. No, I don't. Almost five months. And the last time he was so drunk, he couldn't do anything."

"He must be a very unhappy man."

"What has he got to be unhappy about? A good job I keep a nice house for him. I'm a reasonably good cook. And he's unhappy? Screw him. I want some happiness, too."

Mrs. Cheney was silent.

"A little love, companionship, understanding," Margaret went on furiously. "All that shit. And what do I get? A stick in the eye."

"Have you tried?"

"Tried? You mean with Clint?"

"I meant with other men."

"A few one-night stands," Margaret Stahl said morosely. "With local talent. Not very satisfying. There's got to be something better."

"Perhaps there is," Mrs. Cheney said.

Margaret looked at her.

"I'll take anything," she said. A barked laugh. "Oh God, I smell like a goat. Let me grab a shower. Then we'll have a drink or two and some lunch. You wait here for me."

"I'll come along," Mrs. Cheney said.

"All right. If you want to."

In the deserted locker room, Mrs. Stahl stripped off her soaked tennis dress, bra, panties. She stood naked in short socks and white sneakers. She pulled off her wig of tight blonde curls. Her natural hair was short, brownish, sweated to her skull.

"You're a long one," Mrs. Cheney said, staring at her.

"Look at these bones, will you?" Margaret said, peering down at herself. "I look like something out of Auschwitz or Buchenwald. And that fish-white belly!"

"Don't keep putting yourself down," Mrs. Cheney advised. "You've got a good body. Very elegant."

"If no tits, no hips, and no ass is elegant, then I'm elegant. Clint says I'm built like a ballpoint pen."

"I like your body," Mrs. Cheney said.

"I'll get that shower now," Margaret said.

"I'll come along."

"It's steamy."

"I don't mind."

"All right then."

The widow leaned against the jamb of the shower room door, ankles crossed. She lighted a cigarette.

"Leave the curtain open," she said. "So we can talk."

She watched Margaret Stahl stand directly under the hard spray. The stream plastered her hair, ran over her closed eyes, her small, hard breasts. It poured over her ribs, across her groin, made rivulets down her long legs. She began to soap herself busily.

"What did you mean?" she yelled. "I said there's got to be something better, and you said perhaps there is."

Mrs. Cheney shrugged.

"Whatever you want," she said. "What *do* you want?"

"A little fucking love," Margaret Stahl said. "Is that so much to ask?"

"No," the widow said, "not so much. Do you dream of sex? Fantasies?"

"Of course. All the time. Don't you?"

Mrs. Cheney didn't answer. She looked around for an ashtray.

"Throw it on the floor," Margaret called, rinsing the suds away. "Someone will clean it up."

She turned off the shower, came padding out. She led the way, dripping, back to the locker. She began to scrub her short hair dry with a pink towel.

The widow took the towel from her hands and dried her back slowly. Margaret turned. Mrs. Cheney continued to wipe her breasts, ribs, belly, below. The two women were close, staring into each other's eyes.

"I'm dying for a cold drink," Margaret Stahl said. "Aren't you?"

The gloomy living room of the old Barstow place was lumped with overstuffed chairs and couches, rickety endtables, puffy hassocks, chipped china figurines, wooden lamps with fringed satin shades and, over the fireplace, a large steel engraving of Theodore Roosevelt in the uniform of a Rough Rider.

"Damned place looks like a theatrical warehouse." Colonel Coulter said. "But I like it; suits my purpose. Now here's what we've been waiting for!"

Jacque, wearing a white mess jacket, came in smiling from the dining room. He was carrying a silver tray with four tall glasses filled with a bubbly pink liquid, each garnished with slices of lemon and orange and a stalk of fresh pineapple.

"You'll like this," Coulter assured them. "You've heard of a Singapore Sling? This is called a Hong Kong Crush. Rum, brandy, sugar, bitters, nutmeg, and this and that."

"Creme de Menthe, sir," Jacque murmured. "White."

"Ah yes. Creme de Menthe. But no opium this time, Jacque—right?"

Servant and master laughed. When they all had their drinks, Jacque gone, the Colonel said, "That business about opium—don't let that give you the jim-jams. Silly joke. Well . . . here's to our hearts' desires."

They sipped.

"Delicious," Laura said. "What a flavor! Even without opium, I can see how it could become habit-forming."

"Why did you mention it, Colonel?" the widow rebuked him. "Now the Fayettes will be wondering all evening if they're being drugged."

"Not me," Paul protested. "I always put opium in my drinks. Keeps the ice from melting."

"What happened, you see," the Colonel explained, "was that we found Jacque in Port-au-Prince. He was a busboy at our hotel, and steering tourists to a fake voodoo ceremony. All staged, of course. Cost ten dollars a head, including a drink they claimed contained opium. Absolute fraud, y'know. No opium in it. I know. Though they do have some interesting native drugs down there. Hallucinogens."

"Did you ever go to a real voodoo ceremony, Colonel?" Laura asked breathlessly.

"I'd say yes, dear lady," Coulter smiled. "Wouldn't you agree, Diane?" he asked, turning suddenly to his daughter. "Wasn't that genuine?"

"I believe it was," she said. She looked down at the snake bracelet on her bare arm, twisted it so the sapphire eyes glittered out. "I was quite impressed."

"You were indeed," the Colonel laughed. "For two whole days! But that business with the headless chicken was just a mechanical trick, of course. I could have done that."

Paul looked up from his drink. "Speaking of tricks, I'd still like to know how Diane did that mind reading stunt over at our place. I haven't figured that out yet, but you said it's a trick."

"Well, it is and it isn't." Coulter said slowly. "Not mechanical though. Oh no."

"Do another magic trick, Colonel," Laura urged. "Please do."

"Dinner will be ready in a few minutes, but perhaps we have time for a little one. Laura, think of a number between one and ten."

"All right."

"Got it?"

"Yes."

"What is it?"

"Six."

"Six," the Colonel repeated thoughtfully. "Very good. Now would you walk over to that vase on the mantelpiece, lift it, and read the slip of paper underneath?"

Laura rose obediently, went to the vase, retrieved the note, and read it aloud: "The number you have chosen is six." She gasped, turned to Coulter. "How do you do it?" she demanded. "How do you *do* it?"

"Oh, I know how that one's done," Paul said, grinning at the Colonel. "You prepared ten notes, one for each number. They're concealed all around the room. Then, when Laura told you which number she selected, you merely directed her to the note with number six on it."

"Is that how it was done?" the Colonel said with an ironic smile. "Take a look around the room, Paul. Pick up everything: bric-a-brac, lamps, telephones. Behind pictures, under cushions. Everything, everywhere. See if you can find another note."

Paul went about busily, lifting, peeking, pushing, searching. He didn't find a thing. "Colonel," he said slowly, shaking his head, "you never cease to amaze me."

"Delighted to hear it, m'lad," Coulter cried, clapping him on the shoulder. "Now let's see what tricks Jacque has prepared for us."

They filed into the high-ceilinged dining room. The Colonel got them seated, and opened a bottle of white and a bottle of red wine, both Spanish, both chilled. Then a beaming Jacque carried in an enormous black iron pot and placed it on a trivet in the center of the table. He began to serve them, working rapidly and dexterously with spoon and fork.

It was, Coulter explained, "a kind of paella," with shrimp, mussels, chicken, lobster, clams, vegetables, hot sausage, and saffron rice.

"And something else," Laura Fayette said, tasting. "A flavor I can't identify."

"Probably imported saffron," her husband said, after his first nibble of rice. "A different flavor from the powdered stuff we use. Am I right, Colonel?"

"We do use the imported, that's true, Paul, but I suspect what you can't identify is something else. One of Jacque's special herbs or spices. His grandfather sends him a packet every now and then from Haiti. The flavor is unusual, isn't it?"

The iron pot was seemingly bottomless, and Jacque helped Laura and Paul to second helpings, and thirds. Though Mrs. Cheney and Colonel Coulter ate sparingly, blaming their diets. More bottles of chilled wine were opened, and Jacque brought in a glass bowl of salad: endive and hearts of palm. The salad also tasted faintly of the strange Haitian spice.

As usual, the Colonel dominated the conversation, rumbling with laughter as he told them of his adventures and misadventures in the far corners of the world. Much of what he related seemed to come as a surprise to his daughter, for she reacted with as much interest and fascination as Laura and Paul. Once she said, "I never knew you had been *there,* Colonel." And once she chided him gently, saying,

"I wish you'd have told me you were going there; I'd have insisted on coming along."

Later, the table candles burning low, espresso was served, with cheese, fresh fruit, a strawberry tart, Spanish brandy.

"Who do we have to thank for this marvelous meal, Colonel?" Laura Fayette beamed at him. "You or Jacque?"

"It was a joint enterprise, dear lady," he said expansively. "Jacque loves to cook as much as I do. We're always puttering about, trying this and that. New combinations of seasonings and herbs and spices. Always something new and different. Isn't that right, Diane?"

"And I love it," she said, showing more animation than the Fayettes had seen before. "I get bored so quickly."

"Indeed you do," the Colonel said fondly.

"And I hate to cook," Mrs. Cheney said, looking at Paul Fayette. "I'm not at my best in the kitchen."

"Oh-ho!" Coulter shouted. "And none of us will embarrass you by asking in which room you are at your best! Eh, Laura? Eh, Paul?"

They nodded wildly. Both the Fayettes seemed to be feeling the effects of the wine, food, brandy. Paul had loosened his tie and unbuttoned his collar. Laura had kicked off her shoes, and insisted that Paul reach down the back of her gown and unhook her bra strap. He did, then turned to the widow.

"And may I offer you the same service, dear lady?" he said with a silly giggle.

"Sorry," she said. "I'm not wearing any."

"So I noticed," he said, a remark that seemed to him and to Laura the height of sophisticated wit.

Then nothing would do for them but to call Jacque in from the kitchen for acclamation. Laura kissed him on the cheek. Paul shook his hand fervently. Both assured him that he was a cook and footman nonpareil.

"And chauffeur," Colonel Coulter added. "And private secretary."

"And everything," Mrs. Cheney murmured.

The Fayettes insisted that Jacque have a glass of brandy. They urged him to pull a chair up to the littered table. But though he accepted the brandy, with thanks, he insisted on remaining standing.

He was a lithe willow of a man, with stretched arms and legs, tight hips, and a lilting grace. He was so black he was almost blue, and his soft, suede skin seemed to contain him as completely as a line drawing. Those handsome features were never still, but moved in secret smiles, wry grins, portentous frowns, shocked wonder. After his first swallow of brandy, he snapped his fingers with delight.

Jokes were told, anecdotes related, Penlow Park gossip exchanged, and Jacque sang a calypso ballad, improvising a verse for each of the diners. It was a bravura, and he bowed modestly and retired to the kitchen with the plaudits of his audience still resounding.

Then they were back in that gloomy living room, a fresh bottle of brandy with them to chase the shadows and hold back time.

"Got to get going," Paul said, gazing blearily at his watch. "Got to go home. What does it mean when the little hand's on one and the big hand's on nine?"

"Nonsense," Colonel Coulter said heartily. "Shank of—and all that. Right, Laura? Right, Diane?"

"Got to," Paul said muzzily. "Stay much longer, and stay forever."

"Stay forever if you like," Mrs. Cheney said.

"One more trick," Laura shouted, swaying in her chair. "Please, Paul? Please, Colonel? One more little trick, and then we'll wend our way into the—what? Please? One more little magic? I love magic, 'deed I do."

"Ah-*ha!*" Coulter said. "Excellent! Yes, I have an extraordinary trick to show you, dear lady. It's in the library. Diane, are you ready for this?"

"You know me, Colonel," she said to her father. "Always ready. Always prepared."

With much giggling and stumbling by the Fayettes, they made their way into a book-lined den adjoining the living room. Colonel Coulter flicked a wall switch. An overhead Tiffany lamp illumined the dusty room in wavery shades of rose, green, blue, yellow. A single club chair, a leather-covered cellarette with a student lamp that didn't work, a cold fireplace, and rows and rows of books by dead authors: leather-bound sets with the spines cracked and peeling.

And against one wall of books, standing upright, a spanking new coffin of stained pine. Not in the modern shape, a box, but in the old-fashioned design: narrow at the top and bottom but swelling wider a third of the way down where the corpse's arms might be crossed upon his chest.

"Marvelous illusion this," the Colonel said. "Cost me a fortune, but you'll see, you'll see. Or rather, you won't see. Hah! Now then, here we go . . ."

The lid of the coffin, facing them, was latched with a simple hook and eye. Coulter lifted it open, and swung the lid wide.

"Inspect it," he commanded the Fayettes. "Take a good look. Rap on it. Stamp on the floor. Step inside. Anything you like."

Laughing, tripping, fumbling, they did as they were told. Inspected the coffin: apparently wide planks of wood. Felt the thickness of walls, back, top, bottom, and lid. Stamped the floor around the coffin: seemingly solid. Then, to satisfy them, the Colonel tugged the whole thing farther from the wall of books and wrestled it into a new position nearer the center of the room.

"Satisfied?" he asked them sternly. "Absolutely satisfied it's solid wood? No trap doors? No swinging panels? No false bottom or top? Satisfied? Say it!"

"I'm satisfied," Laura said, giggling nervously.

"Satisfied," Paul said, blinking his eyes to get rid of a haze obscuring his vision.

"Good," Colonel Coulter said, suddenly solemn.

"We will now perform the greatest feat of supernatural mystification ever seen on this earth, or any other. My dear, will you assist me?"

"With pleasure," Mrs. Cheney said.

The Colonel held her fingertips lightly. He led her to the open coffin. She turned around and, facing the Fayettes, took two small steps backward until she was entirely within the coffin. She folded her arms across her breasts. She smiled sorrowfully at the Fayettes.

"Goodbye," she said.

The Colonel slammed the coffin lid on his daughter. He engaged the hook in the metal eye, keeping the door tightly closed. Then he stepped back. He extended his arms and hands toward the coffin, fingers spread.

"Beelzebub!" he cried. "Satan! Your son prays you, make this woman to disappear!"

He strode forward. He unhooked the latch. He swung the lid wide. The coffin was empty.

"Well?" the Colonel said, smiling coldly at the Fayettes. "Can you believe your eyes? Or would you care to make a closer inspection?"

But Laura was weeping, shoulders bent, face hidden in her hands.

"Where is she?" she sobbed. "I want to see her."

Paul, a roaring in his ears, the mist before his eyes now billowing in smoky swirls, stumbled forward and groped inside the coffin. His trembling fingers touched nothing. It was undeniably empty.

"Oh my God," he groaned, his head wagging limply. "I don't understand. My God, I don't . . ."

Coulter closed and hooked the coffin lid, then took Paul gently by the arm, led him back to where Laura huddled, still weeping, clutching herself.

"Now do you believe?" the Colonel demanded, staring at them intently. "Do you *really* believe?" When Paul nodded dumbly, Coulter turned to the coffin again, raised his arms again, fingers wide and stiff. "Beelzebub! Satan! Your son prays you, make the woman to appear again!"

He stepped rapidly to the coffin, unhitched the latch, swung the lid open. Mrs. Cheney stepped out, folded arms relaxing to her sides.

"Hello again," she said to the Fayettes, smiling strangely. "I'm back."

The seamed, blue-haired ladies sipped their dry sherries and nibbled their watercress sandwiches (date-nut bread). The mutton-chopped maître d' hovered, and the beaded fringe of the table lamp tinkled faintly when Paul Fayette touched it.

"I don't suppose you'll tell me how it was done, will you?"

Mrs. Cheney smiled. "The Colonel told you: it was an illusion."

"But I inspected the coffin," he said angrily. "The floor. The wall. Everything. There was no way it *could* have been done."

"But it was."

"Yes," he said, defeated. "It was."

"You *think* you saw it, Paul. You were more than a little drunk, you know. You and Laura."

"I know. I want to apologize for that."

"Nonsense. You were fine. No problems."

"But I usually hold my liquor better than that. May we order now? I don't mean to rush you, Diane, but I've got to get back to the office at a reasonable hour. A desk piled high."

"Of course. And I've got to get to a matinee. You didn't mind my phoning you, did you? I didn't want to lunch alone."

"I'm glad you did. Gives me a chance to find out how the Colonel made you disappear."

"Still worrying you, is it?" She laughed softly. "Let's order."

A waiter who would have looked perfectly at ease in powdered wig and knee breeches brought their martinis, and the maître d' took their orders with somber approval.

Paul lighted her cigarette, then his own. They sat

back, staring at each other. She caught his resentful
puzzlement, and laughed again.

"There are more things in heaven and earth, Horatio,
than are dreamt of in thy philosophy."

"Ain't there just," Paul said ruefully. "Well, it was
one hell of a trick."

"If trick it was," she said quickly.

"If trick it was," he acknowledged. "Listen, during
the Fourth of July weekend we always have an amateur night at the country club. All our would-be singers,
dancers and comedians get a chance to strut their stuff.
This year I'm supposed to produce it. Think the Colonel would be willing to put on a magic act?"

"He might," she said slowly.

"He'd be a sensation. You, too, of course. His tricks
and sleight-of-hand, followed by your mind-reading
act, and then the disappearance as the smash finale.
About a half-hour or so. What do you say?"

"Ask the Colonel," she said. "He makes all the de-
cisions."

"Fine," Paul said. "I'll give him a call."

"Not today," she said. "He's in Lahore."

"Lahore?" he cried. "What on earth is he doing
there?"

"Business," she said. "Ah . . . here's our food."

They waited in silence, solemn, sitting upright, while
the antique waiter served· their luncheons with the
same care he might have given nuclear material just
below criticality. Paul waited an extra moment until
she picked up a fork and probed her Caesar salad.

It gave him an opportunity to observe her hands.
He had not, he admitted to himself, really noted them
before. They were tanned, long, slender. But that was
only the beginning. They were remarkably, almost
shockingly bony. The knuckles and finger joints, seem-
ing swollen, bulged the leather skin white. And between, the fingers seemed shrunken and terse. He
could not rid himself of the notion that they were a
skeleton's hands, the whole hanging in a corner of a

medical lab, the hands a clever maze of bones and wire, articulated, dangling limply and with elegance.

Then he saw the woman herself in the same fashion. As stretched as Jacque. All of her attenuated. He could see the body so: a nude photographed by a distortion lens or seen in a funhouse mirror, ten feet tall and rippling.

But he wondered if what he saw now in her hands, in her body, did not also hold true for her personality, her character and—yes, put a name to it—her soul. He saw her as an expanded woman, pulled apart, enlarged to supernormal dimensions. But in such expansion, did not body, character, and soul become finer, more fragile? He had a fleeting image of a covered cable under stress, pulled, pulled, growing ever more tenuous. Then the break, the covering shredded, and the naked ends of steel snapping and curling up on themselves.

He found the word for it: she was *racked*. This woman was racked.

"You know, Paul," she said, looking down at her salad, forking out croutons, "I want to tell you how I feel about things."

"Do," he said, starting on his own meal.

She didn't catch the sarcasm, or ignored it.

"I've never thought of sex as just carnal desire," she went on. "Just a thing of sweat and moans. To me, sex is physical imagination. As free and creative as mental imagination, poetic imagination. Why are you looking at me so?"

"I don't believe," Paul said carefully, "that I have ever discussed the nature of sexuality while lunching on chicken sauté bourguignonne."

"You know, you're something of a prig," Mrs. Cheney said.

"*That* I agree with."

"The whole subject turns you off?" she asked. "Sexuality?"

"Not at all."

"What you people don't realize—"

He held up a palm to interrupt her.

"Whoa," he said. "Wait a minute. 'You people?' What people?"

"Oh, you know," she said vaguely. "Penlow Park."

"All right. What don't we realize?"

"I was telling you: sex as physical imagination. The whole body used as an organ of creation. Dreams and fantasies created by the body, rather than by the mind. So sex becomes more than just the pounding of two excited bodies. It becomes a means of very special communication. Do you understand? I really do believe this, Paul. It means the body is a thinking organ. A creative organ."

She looked at him calculatingly. He was frightened and inflamed.

"Interesting theory," he said, eating away. "Is this just an intellectual exercise, or are you speaking from experience?"

She said, "Ah . . ." flapping her hand, and he was aware once again of how difficult it was to get a definite answer from her, and from the Colonel. They stifled him.

"Communication," she continued, toying with her salad. "I suppose that's the key word. If we can speak, see, touch, hear, smell, taste, why not another sense of communication? Sex. A way of conveying meaning."

"Why not?" he said.

"Hidden meaning," she said, with great solemnity. "Secret significance. That cannot be conveyed by any of the other senses. In any other manner, except by sex. I think it transcends normal boundaries."

He looked at her, puzzled. "Boundaries?"

"Time," she said. "Distance. Life. Death. All boundaries. Do you think I'm mad?"

"Do you believe in UFO's?" he asked. "Little green men?"

"No," she said, not smiling. "None of that nonsense. Do you believe in ESP?"

He thought a long moment.

"I don't believe," he said finally, "and I don't disbelieve. I think the possibility exists."

"Oh yes," she nodded. "The possibility does exist. Eat your chicken."

They both ate, sipping at glasses of the house white wine she had ordered.

"Life after death," she said suddenly. "Or at least communication with the dead. Do you believe in that?"

"No," he said promptly.

"Does Laura?"

He considered. "Possibly. Laura is a very healthy, robust, out-going woman. But surprisingly, she has a strong interest in the occult."

"I know," Mrs. Cheney said. "If I arrange a seance, will you both come?"

"Oh God, yes!" he said. "That would be fun. You'll be the medium?"

"Yes. I thought I'd ask you and Laura, and Margaret and Clint Stahl."

"And the Colonel?"

"If he's in town. And Jacque. It's important to have people with a high spiritual potential. We must pool our strength. Paul, don't laugh at me about this."

"I'm not laughing," he said. "I may not believe, but I'm interested. Sincerely."

"Good," she said. "We'll do it. You may discover things about yourself you didn't know. Didn't know or recognize consciously, I mean. Does that frighten you?"

"Of course not," he said. "Why should it? Diane, I'm afraid I'm going to skip coffee and run. I've got to get back. Sorry. I'll get a cab. Can I drop you at the theatre?"

"What theatre?"

"I thought you said you had a matinee?"

"Oh," she said. "Yes, I do. But no theatre. Just leave me here."

Her smile was almost a leer, and she disgusted him.

"And you're the star?" he said, trying to stretch his mouth in an answering smirk.

"Yes," she said, looking at him with amusement. "I'm the leading lady."

When Paul Fayette went down to breakfast on Sunday morning, he found Laura sitting disconsolately at the kitchen table. Her chin was resting on her palm. She was staring at her half-empty cup of coffee.

"Morning, butch," he said.

"Morning."

"How did you sleep?"

"All right."

"The hell you did," he said, pouring himself a glass of tomato juice. "You tossed and turned all night. Kicked me black-and-blue."

"Did I? I'm sorry."

He drained the juice, then poured a cup of black coffee. He sat down opposite her. He put his elbows on the table, began to blow gently on his coffee.

"Anything wrong? You look a little puffy about the gills."

"No, I'm all right."

"Want to skip church?"

"No. I'll go."

"Laura," he said sharply, "what *is* it?"

She looked up at him, finally.

"I don't know," she said. "I really don't. It's nothing physical; I feel okay. It's just—I can't even explain it. I'm not depressed so much. It's just I feel uneasy."

"Uneasy?"

"Well, like I'm being threatened. Like *we're* being threatened. But don't ask by what or by whom, because I just don't know. When you're at work, I keep listening for strange sounds in the house. I don't like being alone anymore. It scares me. It's like I was waiting for something to happen. Don't tell me it's silly; I know it's silly. But I can't get rid of it."

"Want to go away for a week or two?" he suggested. "Take a trip. Drop in on Christine and Brian. Or go up to the mountains. Get away."

"No," she dispiritedly, "I don't want to go anywhere. It wouldn't help; I know it wouldn't. Paul, do you love me?"

"Oh God," he groaned. "First thing on a Sunday morning! Yes, I love you. Does that help?"

"A little bit," she smiled wanly. "I haven't been a bundle of joy lately, and I know it. I'm sorry, kiddo. Just a touch of the pip. I'll snap out of it."

"Sure you will," he said. He rose, took his coffee cup, wandered to the back door. He looked out at the stoop. "I see Ben's back."

"He was there when I came down this morning. I put out a dish of milk. He drank a little bit. Not much."

"Looks like he's been in another fight. God, he's ugly!"

"Maybe we shouldn't have started feeding him," she said listlessly. "Maybe he would have gone away."

He turned at the door to look at her.

"Want me to get rid of him?" he asked. "I'll call the pound."

"No," she said quickly, "don't do that. They'll put him away."

He sighed, set his empty coffee cup in the sink, ran water into it.

"I'm going up and shower and shave," he said. "You coming?"

"In a while," she said.

"I have a one o'clock golf date with Clint and the Meecham brothers."

"All right," she said.

"What will you do this afternoon?"

"I don't know," she said.

By 10:15 they were dressed for church and, on the spur of the moment, had a Bloody Mary before setting out. In the station wagon, on the way, both sucking on chlorophyll mints, Laura said, "I feel better now."

"Good," he said.

"Sorry I was such a grouch."

"You're entitled," he said, patting her knee.

"It's just—" she started, then shook her head wildly. "Ahh, the hell with it," she said angrily.

The First Presbyterian Church of Penlow Park had won an architectural award for "Design Excellence." But to most of the members, it looked like an abandoned cinder block garage topped with a Lucite cross.

The white interior was lighted by narrow cloistral windows and chandeliers more reminiscent of the Radio City Music Hall than St. Patrick's Cathedral. In the apse behind the altar, a gigantic timbered cross, round as driftwood, was secured to the wall with heavy industrial bolts. The effect was unquestionably dramatic.

Just as dramatic was the man who stood beneath the cross. Timothy T. Aiken was so obviously the benign, understanding man of God that, as Clint Stahl remarked, "That guy looks like he was sent over from Central Casting."

He stood almost six-four, and was crowned with a bushy halo of snow-white hair. His features had, obviously, once been classic. But 63 years of age had puddled the flesh, padded the bones, whiskied the complexion, and given him the unfortunate habit of spitting his sibilants as his plates slipped. The first two rows of pews were studiously avoided.

There was no denying this handsome evangelist's charm and magnetism. Some Penlow Parkers gave up their morning golf game to hear him preach. His voice rivalled the diapason of the Hammond electronic organ with which the church was equipped. His gestures were grand enough to encompass the hall and all the great outdoors. His woe was worthy of Edwin Booth and his humor of Bert Lahr. Even Clint admitted his wit remarkable for a man of the cloth, and his sheer theatricality overwhelmed and convinced. All the women, if not all the men.

This morning, the neon-lighted sign outside the

church had advertised in two lines: "'The Power of Evil.' Have a nice day!"

When the Reverend Aiken rose and came forward, the restive congregation quieted. He waited until they were silent, and a few moments longer while his light blue eyes swept the pews, face to face. Then he began to speak without notes, his sonorous voice booming off the walls, his slow pronunciation ("in-eluc-ta-ble") impressing his most dim-witted parishioners with the weighty significance of his words.

His theme was a fascinating one—especially to those in his audience still suffering remorseful pangs for their conduct on the preceding Saturday night . . .

The reverend said that evil—in novels, plays, art, and popular mythology—was invariably given an ugly visage. He said that evil was usually spoken of as an illness, a disease, a malignancy. That was comforting —to think of evil as something putrescent and disgusting, because then it was easy to abjure it when it made its loathsome appearance.

But such, sadly, was not the case, the Reverend Aiken told them. Evil frequently appeared with a laughing face, shining eyes, and a Florida tan. Evil came dancing and singing, in the guise of innocent joy. And that, too often, was its lure.

To avoid evil, the minister intoned, it was necessary to practice good. Mind, he said, *practice* good. For good was not simply the avoidance of evil: good was a course of action designed to keep evil at bay. One had to be constantly alert, for evil wore a thousand masks, and the most trivial of pleasures might be the dangled hook of a mortal sin.

During this sermon, Paul Fayette glanced sideways, smiling, thinking to see his wife as amused by this bombast as he. But he saw her leaning forward intently, gripping the back of the pew in front of them with straining fingers. Her eyes were on the preacher; her whole attitude was one of complete capitulation to his image, voice, words, ideas. Disturbed, Paul turned back to listen to more of the philosophy of the man

Margaret Stahl had once referred to, not in jest, as "Mr. Wonderful."

Just as good was not merely the absence of evil, the minister said, so evil was not merely the absence of good. But evil was a force in this world, a mode of action, and we disregarded this truth at our peril. The holocaust of Nazi Germany, the discrimination against minorities, racism, and poverty were but the grosser manifestations of the force of evil.

In subtler form, evil invaded our lives, sapped our wills, drained our strength and, like an unseen virus, if not combated, ended by conquering our immortal souls.

"Be on guard!" Timothy T. Aiken thundered. "I know it is not fashionable in our time to speak of the existence of the devil. But fashion be damned! I say unto you that the devil, that personification of evil, is everywhere at work. Everywhere! At all times! Defend your sanc-ti-ty. Protect your in-vi-o-la-bil-i-ty. Beware of the siren song of evil that lulls and beguiles. We are at war! Oh yes, my children, we are engaged in a struggle that has existed since the world began and that shall continue when you and I are dust. The force of evil is a mighty force, and it shall conquer easily if good men—and women, too, of course—simply do nothing. It can only be defeated by the day-to-day, hour-to-hour, minute-to-minute exercise of a greater force: the power of good, of light, of godliness. To the very, absolute limits of our human abilities. In Christ's name, amen . . ."

After this peroration, there were a few moments of stunned silence. The numbed congregation stared at their minister who stood with white-crowned head bowed low, his posture one of submission to God's will at the same time it reflected vigor and a desire to engage the devil in one of the Oriental martial arts. Kung-fu, perhaps. Then the Reverent Aiken raised his head slowly. He was smiling gently.

"And now for the good news," he said and, the tension broken, his audience laughed. "It gives me the greatest pleasure to announce the gift to your church of fifty thousand dollars. The donor wishes to remain anonymous, but I cannot refrain from thanking him now in public, for his charity, generosity, and goodwill. This unexpected bounty has been given freely, with no specific directions on how it should be spent, other than it be used to further the activities of your church and assist in spreading the Word of God. The Board of Governors will meet this week, and I am certain they will welcome any suggestions you might have on how this windfall might best be used. Incidentally, the giver of this most welcome contribution is present here today, and I assure him that his gift will do much to further the battle against the force of evil of which I earlier spoke. Sir, with all my heart I thank you, and I relay the gratitude of all your good neighbors who can never know your identity but applaud with all *their* hearts your act of Christian charity."

Following this announcement, the fuchsia-gowned choir sang, "Nearer, My God, to Thee . . ." and the service came to an end.

In Colonel Benjamin G. Coulter's gloomy apartment-office, carved cherubs and nymphs still struggled to free themselves from the marble mantel over the cold fireplace. The high-ceilinged room caught and held the gloom of a rainy June afternoon. No lamps were lighted, no colors glowed. The air itself seemed aged and sallow. The activity of the old hotel, muted by thick walls and carpeted floors, sounded distant and lost. Time slowed, slowed, and with it the speech and movements of the woman and man. They swam rather than walked. They drifted with a weary languor. Gestures floated, expressions congealed. Speech took on a rhythm of pauses, and timbreless voices had the prolonged drone of hums.

Later, Mrs. Diane Cheney sat upright in an armchair pulled up to a dark refectory table. She had put on an old-fashioned bathrobe of a blanket-like material in an imitation tartan pattern. The robe was closed high on her neck, cinched about her waist with a worn cord. Her iron-gray wig, uncombed, hung damply loose about her shoulders.

"Sonny?" she called, in a strained, querulous voice. "Now where can that boy be? Sonny, are you playing jokes on your poor auntie again?"

In a dark corner, crouching on hands and knees behind a high-backed wing chair, Clint Stahl bit his lower lip to keep from giggling aloud. Cautiously he peeked around the corner of the chair to watch the stringy-haired woman in the sleazy bathrobe. She turned her head to peer about the murky room.

"Sonny?" she called again. "Now you stop this foolishness and come out here at once. You hear me?"

She moved restlessly. The robe fell open, a bit. Her naked calves and knees gleamed whitely.

"Where can that boy be?" she asked fretfully.

Slowly, with infinite care, Clint Stahl crawled from his hiding place. He scuttled across the rug. She was looking here, there, everywhere, but apparently she did not see him.

"Sonny," she said again, "stop this foolishness at once."

Hidden beneath the table, beginning to feel the same fire that had engulfed him forty years ago, Stahl began moving stealthily toward those white knees. They drew him forward, beacons in the gloom.

"Sonny," she said, her voice lower now, throaty, "what are you doing? You naughty boy! Oh, you're going to get it. Wait till your auntie catches you; you'll be sorry.'"

They played their roles solemnly in the remembered dream. She spread her legs wider; the robe fell open, exposing naked thighs, smooth, and the shadow between.

"Sonny," she said coarsely, "behave yourself. You naughty boy."

Breath thick and clotting in his throat, he moved to her in slow motion, a beast on stalk. Sweat dampened his face, ran in rivulets down temples and chin. His mouth opened; he began to gasp.

"Oh sonny," she said, and now her voice was deep and endearing. "What a naughty boy he is. Shame on you, sonny. Aren't you ashamed?"

He had crawled close to her now. He reached out timorous fingers to touch one cool knee.

"Naughty," she said, and jerked her knee aside. But in the movement, her thighs opened wider.

He touched again. This time she suffered his fingers to remain. Then his hot palm.

"Naughty," she breathed. "Naughty, naughty boy. Just wait till I tell your mother and father, sonny. You'll get it."

But he was lost, unable to resist, the memory so sharp that he could smell the camphor and hear the tick of the grandfather clock on that long-ago day.

"Naughty boy," she murmured. "What are you doing to your poor auntie?"

Sobbing, he pressed forward. His mouth was open, his eyes wet with tears.

"Oh sonny," she whispered. "Oh sonny, that feels so good. Don't stop, sonny. Don't stop."

4

Paul Fayette sat at his desk, reading for the third time the confidential memo from the home office of Fourth National of Boston. They didn't want the distasteful task of firing Clint Stahl, but the memo made it obvious they expected Fayette to swing the ax.

"Of course," the memo concluded, "final solution of this unfortunate problem will be left to your judgment."

"Final solution." Fayette pondered that phrase and wondered if it had been deliberately selected or used through inadvertence. He was still pondering when his phone buzzed twice, sharply, indicating an interior call from his secretary.

"Yes, Marie?"

"Mr. Raeburn is here, Mr. Fayette."

"Fine," he said. "Send him in and hold my calls while he's here."

"Yes, Mr. Fayette."

He rose from behind his desk and moved to greet Raeburn at the door. He led the way to the leather couch. Raeburn was carrying a thin manila folder. He sat down, placed the folder on the glass cocktail table.

"Cigarette, Eddie?" Fayette asked, proffering his pack.

"Thanks, Mr. Fayette."

They both took cigarettes. Paul reached for his lighter, but Raeburn was there first with a book of matches.

He was the youngest investigator in the Research Department and, in Fayette's opinion, the best. To the routines of financial and personal examination and inquiry, he brought energy, meticulousness, and, best of all, a freewheeling imagination the other investigators lacked. And he enjoyed challenges; Fayette knew that.

He was a short, sharp-faced man with gingery hair and a pale face sprinkled with freckles. His boyish features were a great aid in his detective work; people said more than they should before they realized the boy-face masked a first-rate mind. Raeburn could put two and two together and, like as not, come up with twenty-two.

"All right, Eddie," Paul said, "what have you got?"

"First of all, Mr. Fayette, I want to make sure I have the spelling right. It's C-o-u-l-t-e-r—correct?"

"That's correct. Colonel Benjamin G. Coulter, U.S. Army, Retired."

"No, sir," Raeburn said definitely. "I checked U.S. Army rosters of retired officers. No one by that name. I also checked active duty lists. He's not on those. Graves Registration never heard of him. Then, remembering the Marine Corps and Air Force also have colonels, I checked them. He's not theirs. You're certain he was U.S. Army?"

Fayette thought about that a moment.

"Jesus Christ," he said finally, "he never said he was U.S. Army. I just assumed it."

"Well, they don't know him," Raeburn said. "British armed forces?" he asked.

"I can't believe it," Paul said. "He uses a lot of what he thinks is British slang—stuff like 'chin-chin' and 'toodle-oo.' It would get him laughed out of every club in London. Like he learned how to speak English from reading Wodehouse."

"Wodehouse, sir?"

"Forget it. Before your time."

"Well, he *could* be British," Raeburn said, flipping open his file. "It would explain a lot. For instance, you said he does a lot of traveling. But there's no U.S. passport issued to a man of that name and description. The other possibility, of course, is that 'Coulter' isn't his real name. He's using a passport in another name."

"What about his banks?"

"He hasn't any."

"What?" Fayette said, startled. "No banks at all?"

"No, sir," Raeburn said, pleased with the sensation he had caused. "No American banks, that is. And no-credit cards. No charge accounts. And he's never paid taxes to the IRS or New York State or New York City tax bureaus. He's not registered to vote. As far as American paper goes, the guy just doesn't exist."

"Damn it to hell," Fayette said, almost angrily, "he's real enough. Eddie, there must be *some* record of his financial dealings."

"No, sir, there isn't," Raeburn said stubbornly. "If there is, I haven't found it."

"Well, how the hell does he pay his hotel bills? I gave you that address."

"He pays in cash," the investigator said triumphantly. "On the dot. In crisp, new bills."

"And who signed the lease for his Penlow Park house?"

"His daughter."

"Well, what's the name of the export business he runs? Earth-moving equipment, and so forth?"

"No one at the hotel knows," Raeburn said. "No one anywhere knows. The only mail he gets at the hotel is addressed to him personally; no company name. I bribed a chambermaid to let me into his office-apartment. Only there's no evidence it *is* an office. No files, no typewriters, no letterheads, no brochures. Nothing. It's just a big, old-fashioned apartment with some crazy clothes hanging in the closets."

"Crazy clothes?"

"Women's clothes. Costumes. Wigs. An old, shabby bathrobe. Slinky evening gowns from fifty years ago. High-button shoes. A laced corset. A feathered neg-

ligee. Something made out of black leather. I couldn't
figure out what the hell *that* was. Shoes with heels
five inches high. Weird stuff."

"Weird is right."

"But nothing to indicate the place is ever used as
an office. He gets a lot of phone calls there, and
makes a lot. Long distance. All over the world. Some
months his phone bills run in the thousands. He pays
up promptly."

"In cash?"

"Right. Always in cash. His two cars are leased.
Also paid for in cash."

"Surely he had to give a bank reference for the
cars?"

"Well—uh—yes, he did," Eddie Raeburn said,
blushing and looking down at his file. "He gave
Fourth National of Boston."

"The hell he did!" cried Paul Fayette, and burst
out laughing. "Well, he did tell me he was buddy-
buddy with Bernard Stiffens, Chairman of the Board,
but I thought he was putting me on. Maybe he
wasn't."

"That's about all I've got, Mr. Fayette," Eddie
Raeburn said, closing his file. "And that's not much.
Sorry. I've never been up against one like this before.
Apparently he's never written a check in his life. Not
a bit of paper anywhere with his name on it."

"Did he give the hotel any permanent address?"

"Sure he did," Raeburn said, with a sour grin. "His
daughter's place in Penlow Park. You want me to
keep digging on this, Mr. Fayette?"

"Like what?"

"Look into the British angle. I could check with
their embassy in Washington. Or I could run a paper
chase on his daughter."

Fayette considered a moment.

"No," he said finally, "just drop it, Eddie. Many
thanks for your time and trouble. You did a good,
thorough job. As usual."

"Thank you, Mr. Fayette."

After Raeburn left, Paul went back behind his desk and buzzed Marie Verrazano.

"Would you get me Boston, please?" he asked her. "I want to talk to Betty Mather. She's executive assistant to Mr. Stiffens."

"Yes, Mr. Fayette."

He hung up and stared blankly at the home office memo, not seeing it. When his phone rang, he plucked it up quickly.

"Paul?" she said. "How are you, darling?"

"No complaints, Betty," he said. "How's life in the salt mines?"

"Shitty as ever," she said cheerfully. "When are you going to brighten a gal's life by coming up here and taking me out to dinner?"

"One of these days," he promised. "Listen, Betty, the reason I'm calling, did you ever hear of a man named Coulter? That's C-o-u-l-t-e-r. Benjamin G. Claims to be a retired colonel in some army or other."

"Coulter?" she repeated slowly. "No, it rings no bells with me. Why do you ask?"

"He claims he knows the Old Man and gave Fourth National as a bank reference.

"Oh-ho," she said. "A con?"

"Could be," he said. "I just don't know."

"Want me to ask Mr. Stiffens?"

"Could you do that for me, Betty? This guy is so slippery. I can't pin him down. Just ask if Mr. Stiffens knows him. Okay?"

"No problem."

"Many thanks, dear. How's the Old Man feeling, by the way?"

There was silence on the other end of the phone. For a moment Fayette thought they had been disconnected, and he said, "Hello? Hello?" When she spoke her voice was low, hushed. He thought she might have a hand cupped around her mouth and the receiver.

"What have you heard?" she whispered.

"Nothing," he said. "Nothing except what this man Coulter said."

"What did he say?"

"That Stiffens didn't have long to go. That he didn't have a chance. Then he tapped his chest."

"Jesus," she breathed. "When was this?"

"A few weeks ago. Maybe a month."

Silence again. Then: "I don't understand it. He only told me about it last week."

He started at the phone, shocked.

"Betty, you mean it's true?"

"Not a word of this Paul, to *anyone*."

"I understand. But is it true?"

"Lung cancer. Inoperable. How could this Coulter have known?"

"I don't know," he said desperately. "I don't know anything. What the hell's happening?"

"Got to go," she said swiftly, speaking now in a crisp, business voice as if someone had just come into her office. "I'll try to obtain the information you requested, sir, and get back to you as soon as possible."

"Thank you," he said faintly.

Laura and Paul Fayette had been invited, and Margaret and Clint Stahl. Jacque would be there but, regrettably, Colonel Coulter could not be present since he was spending a few days in Kinshasa. The women had agreed the seance would begin at 9:00 p.m., after dinner. Diane Cheney said it would take no more than an hour. Afterwards, if they cared to, they might have a rubber of bridge (although she herself didn't play) or just sit around, have a few drinks, and visit. It seemed like a pleasant way to spend a summer evening; the promised seance gave it a special lure.

The sitting was planned for the dining room in the Cheney home. Extra leaves had been removed from the table so it was perfectly round. It was uncovered, showing an oak finish stained with spills and pitted with cigarette burns. In the center of the table was placed a three-branched, wrought iron candelabrum with white tapers.

The guests assembled at the appointed hour and

were served one round of drinks by Jacque, wearing his black chauffeur's livery. They were then ushered into the dining room and directed to their chairs by Mrs. Cheney. Clint Stahl sat to her left, Paul Fayette on her right. Margaret Stahl was seated next to Paul, and then Jacque, Laura Fayette, Clint, Mrs. Cheney, and the circle was complete. The hostess explained what was to happen.

Jacque would light the three candles, then turn off the electric chandelier and draw the drapes. He would then take his place at the table. They were all to clasp hands, left and right. They were to stare fixedly at the burning candles. They were to breathe deeply, inhaling through their noses and exhaling through their mouths. They were to try to relax completely, utterly.

"Try to wipe your minds clear of everyday concerns," Mrs. Cheney told them. "Think of your mind as a blackboard, and the moment a conscious thought appears, erase it. Try to make your mind blank, receptive to any unexpected images or memories that might appear, even if they seem to make no sense to you. There will be no trumpets sounding or tambourines rattling or the table tilting or anything like that. What we will attempt to do, first of all, is delve into the past, to recall moments in your lives long forgotten. These are events of which I know nothing, so I cannot say with certainty to which of you the memory belongs. It may concern someone long dead. It may be an event in your childhood."

"I hope it won't be too embarrassing," Margaret Stahl said, with a nervous giggle. "There are some things in my life I don't *want* to remember."

"I will name no names," Diane Cheney said. "If I can achieve clairvoyance, visions will come to me as dim images, as they will come to you. No person will be recognizable, but objects will be, and details of dress, surroundings, and so forth. Now I must warn you, if this session is successful, if we are able to generate enough psychic power to recall the lost and forgotten past, there may be physical effects. You may feel a tingling, the sensation of a slight breeze in the room, perhaps even a kiss on your cheek, like the touch of a feather. Do not be alarmed. You will not be hurt. Those who have passed over have no desire to injure the living. Do you have any questions? No? Then, Jacque, will you light the candles, please."

The three white tapers began to flicker. The overhead light was extinguished. The drapes were drawn. Jacque took his seat, and the circle clasped hands. There was silence.

The candles cast a globe of wavering light. Only expressionless faces were illuminated, and the clenched hands on the tabletop. Eyes widened, staring at the flickering flames. Unconsciously, all leaned forward slightly, to the fire and to each other.

"Try to relax," Mrs. Cheney said in a low voice. "Try to breathe deeply. Open yourselves. Become receptive to the spirits. Relax. Breathe deeply. Do not break the chain."

They sat in silence for moments, watching the candle flames steady and grow higher. Then it seemed to them the three blazes bent and quivered, all in one direction, as if from an invisible breeze.

Mrs. Cheney had closed her eyes. Lips were drawn back from white teeth. When the flames guttered, her body stiffened. Her head went back slowly until she seemed to be staring upward into the darkness.

"What do you see?" she asked. "What do you feel? What is in your mind?"

Her voice sounded hollow, deep, echoing. Her voice boomed in the black room; they heard her questions as commands.

"I see a clock," Laura Fayette faltered. "A grandfather's clock. The pendulum is swinging. I can hear the tick."

"Nothing," Paul Fayette said. "I see nothing. I feel nothing."

"Like mothballs," Margaret Stahl said wonderingly. "I can smell it. Like camphor. Something old. Stored away."

Clint Stahl made a sound, a strangled noice.

"An older woman," Jacque said in his soft drawl. "Oh yes. I see a gray-haired woman. This woman now she sits at a table. Long gray hair. Down to her shoulders. Oh yes."

"The boy," Mrs. Cheney said. "Do you see the young boy? What is he doing? No, no, I cannot hold it. It is fading, fading. I am losing it."

Clint Stahl made a sudden movement, scraping back his chair. But the clenching hands held him fast.

"Do not break the chain," Mrs. Cheney intoned. "Keep the circle complete. We will try again. Relax. Breathe deeply. Stare at the flames."

They were silent again. The taper lights steadied. Their hands, still clasped, relaxed, and it seemed to them a tingling ran through their fingers, a current that pulsed, growing, diminishing, growing, but finally waxing, becoming intense, until their fingertips burned.

"My God!" Paul Fayette blurted. "I see a room. A child's room. Toys."

"No, sir, no," Jacque said in his lilting voice. "We are outside, sir. A little girl, and little boys pushing her away."

Then the images were coming fast, and they were all chiming in. All except Laura Fayette.

Mrs. Cheney: "The boys are pushing her away."

Clint: "They will not let her play. What? A game? Baseball?"

Margaret: "She is in tears. I see her, I see her! She is crying."

Mrs. Cheney: "Rejected. They are her brothers and their friends. They reject her. Laugh at her."

"Paul: "Yes! She goes to her room. The room I saw! What is she doing?"

Clint: "The doll! Do you see the doll?"

Margaret: "A sweet doll. A little girl's doll."

Mrs. Cheney: "With long, blonde hair. Blue eyes. A white dress..A beautiful doll."

Clint: "What is she doing?"

Margaret: "She's breaking the doll!"

Clint: "She's smashing the doll!"

Jacque: "The little girl is breaking the doll, smashing the doll, *killing* the doll."

Paul: "Holding it by the feet, cracking the head open on the floor, pulling off the arms, yanking——"

"Stop it!" Laura screamed. "All of you! Stop it! Stop it! I can't stand any more. Please, please! No more! No more . . ."

Her frenzied shriek startled them all back to the present. Their sweated hands fell open. Paul pushed back his chair, moved swiftly to his wife. Jacque rose quickly to switch on the lights. Margaret and Clint Stahl turned slowly, blinking, to look at Laura. Mrs. Cheney lowered her head, opened her eyes, stared sightlessly at the candlewicks, no longer burning but black, twisted, smoking oilily.

Paul could not comfort Laura. Nor could any of them comfort her. They clustered about, patting, touching, attempting to hold her. But she threshed about in uncontrolled hysteria. Paul tried to grip her flailing hands. Jacque took her about the waist, from behind. Margaret and Clint hovered, trying to speak to her calmly, reaching to her. Her wildness increased.

It was not until Mrs. Cheney rose, moved to her quietly, took her in a strong embrace that Laura's madness began to diminish. Her jerky, bone-cracking convulsions eased, her stretched mouth closed, the strained muscles of jaw and throat softened. Then suddenly she collapsed, weeping, gasping, coughing, her face in Mrs. Cheney's shoulder, her body pressing close. Inchoate sounds came from her: sobs, groans, but mostly moans of anguish in a regular rhythm as if a raw nerve end was being scraped, again and again and again.

Jacque brought brandy. They made her drink, and then they drank. Clint Stahl downed two shots as fast as he could gulp. Then Mrs. Cheney led Laura away to an upstairs bedroom. The others mooned about, drank more, talked feverishly of the weather, the old

Barstow place, the new tax on cigarettes—anything but what had happened, and why.

They drank more, too rapidly, Jacque at their elbows to make certain their glasses never emptied. It was almost a half-hour before Laura made her entrance again with Mrs. Cheney. The widow's arm was about her waist. She looked at them, bright-eyed, trying to smile.

"Well," she said, "my first and last seance. Sorry for making such a scene."

Paul went to her, took her in his arms. He assured her—they all assured her—there was no reason to feel shame or remorse. It was an emotional thing. They were all guilty. Everyone had been carried away. It was the darkness, the spooky darkness. It was the flickering candlelight. Those mesmerizing flames. Forget it. She should forget it. They intended to forget it.

Nothing was said of a young girl, rejected by young boys, smashing the skull of a beautiful girl-doll against the floor.

The liquor helped, and when Mrs. Cheney mentioned a bridge game, they were eager to play. Anything. Mrs. Cheney suggested Laura and Jacque team up against the Stahls while she and Paul observed. In moments, the round seance table was covered with a green baize cloth; cards, scorepad and a pencil were provided; the players were crying, "I can't believe it!" and "Who dealt this mess?"

Mrs. Cheney took Paul's arm, drew him away from the lighted circle. Carrying their drinks, they strolled into the darkened living room.

"What happened?" he asked in a hesitant voice. "To Laura?"

Mrs. Cheney shrugged.

"A memory," she said. "Hidden. Too painful to endure."

"How did you know?" he asked. "She's never mentioned it."

She took her arm from his, gazed at him stonily.

"I?" she asked. "How did *I* know? We all knew. You and the others. All joined in."

"Yes," he said, frightened, "that's true."

"Do you have sleeping pills at home?"

"What? No. Nothing like that."

"I'll give you two. Have Laura take them. Tomorrow it will seem like a bad dream, nothing more."

"Well . . ." he said doubtfully, "if you say so." He paused a moment, then . . . "Is the coffin still in the library?"

She laughed softly. "Why do you ask? You want to examine it again?"

"The thought had occurred to me."

"No, sorry, it is gone. The Colonel moved it out. He wants to show it off somewhere else."

"In Kinshasa?"

"Why not? They are closer to magic there than we are here. But I can see you don't believe me. All right, you unbeliever, come into the library; I'll show you it's gone."

He followed her down the short, unlighted corridor into the book-lined chamber. She switched on the overhead Tiffany lamp.

"Well?" she said

He sighed. "It's gone. I thought the entire back might swing away on hinges. Was that how it was done?"

"Oh Paul, Paul," she said, touching his cheek with cool fingers. "With you, everything must have an explanation. Isn't it better to wonder?"

"No," he said shortly, and she laughed again.

They stood a moment, sipping their drinks, alone in the gloomy room. From far away they heard the faint cries of the card players. They looked at each other.

"Well . . ." he said uncertainly.

She took the drink from his hand. She placed it on the leather-covered cellarette and put her own glass beside it. Touching. She took him by the hand.

"Diane," he said, his own voice sounding to him hoarse and alarmed.

She did not answer. She led him from the library, back toward the living room. In the dark hallway she paused before the shut door of a closet.

"Please don't," she said.

"What?" he said, stunned.

"Please, Paul," she said. "Don't."

She opened the closet door. Still holding his hand in her bony fingers, she stepped within. She turned to face him.

The closet was crowded with coats, jackets, mackinaws, rain gear, cloaks. There were boots and galoshes on the floor. Umbrellas leaned in the corners. Above her head, on a shelf, were hats, caps, gloves, scarves. The Colonel's brown bowler.

She flung hanging garments to both sides. She moved farther back into the closet, pulling him after her. When he was within, she closed the door. Darkness was absolute.

He smelled harshness of wool coats, dampness of rubber overshoes. Rough fabrics rasped his face. He heard his own hard breathing, her quiet sigh. He could not rid himself of the fantastical notion that she had stepped again into that trick coffin, and pulled him after. The Colonel would call upon Beelzebub, and in an instant the two of them would disappear—where?

But she was corporeal enough, releasing his hand to grip his arms, draw him close. She was wearing a thick, cloying scent; he couldn't draw a deep breath or see or hear anything now but a deep, throbbing hum that threatened to become a roar. Then he felt her breath on his lips and knew how near her face was pressed.

"Paul," she whispered wildly, "we shouldn't—I can't— Please don't make—"

Her soft submission inflamed him. He brushed her grasp aside, moved forward to take her fumblingly in his arms.

"Don't hurt me," she murmured. "Please don't."

He stabbed his mouth forward in the darkness, found her lips. His thrusting tongue pressed until, sighing, she yielded her open mouth. All of her fell slack against him.

"I can't—" she breathed. "Do anything—Whatever you—I don't care."

He reached downward and discovered she had raised her skirt on naked thighs, was holding her dress bunched about her waist. He heard the shuffle as she spread her legs wider. A plastic raincoat fell about his ankles; he kicked his way through a forest of boots.

"Feel me," her voice came in a throaty gasp. "So hot. So wet. Feel me, feel me. Ah lover, lover . . ."

Disordered, anxious, he uncovered himself, grappling with her, with his own flesh. He found her hand, guided it to him, heard her pant as those skeleton fingers closed around. They were of a height, and she steered him cunningly, biting his tongue, his ear, her hungry lips sliding over his face.

"You're driving me crazy," she said, louder now. "*You* are. *You,* Paul. Oh, what a lover you are. I can't hold back. I can't stop. Love me! Love me!"

Awkwardly, stooping, then lurching upward, he penetrated, shuddered, stood still. He gripped her buttocks, feeling satin skin over hard muscle. She began to move, standing astride him, her whole body throbbing as he pressed her back into the black, back, back, until the wall supported them both.

Then, faint, frantic, desperate with the doubt, excited by the mystery, he sought to wound her, pierce her through, and thought he heard them both wail and howl like beasts in the hot darkness.

"I had no idea it was going to be so warm," Laura Fayette chattered on. "The radio said cool and cloudy, so naturally I wore a sweater. And by the time I got here . . ." Her nervous voice trailed away.

"Margaret can't make it," Diane Cheney said lazily. "A sudden stomach cramp, or something like that. She called me. She may drop by later if she's feeling better."

"She's too embarrassed to face me," Laura said

miserably, stiffening her fingers to stop the tremble. "After the way I behaved . . ."

Mrs. Cheney lifted up to put her palm on Laura's bare back.

"Ah sweetheart," she said, "don't pick at it so. We all love you; you know that. No one's blaming you for anything."

"I'm so ashamed," Laura said, her voice muffled as she dug her face into her folded arms. "So ashamed."

They were both lying prone on beach towels spread over faded mattress pads, on two of the redwood lounges alongside the Penlow Park Country Club swimming pool. Away from them, at the shallow end, one other lounge was occupied by a young blonde girl with a gifted body. She was wearing a knitted string bikini. Flesh-colored. They had noticed her.

Laura was wearing a black nylon maillot, cut low in back, high on the thighs. Mrs. Cheney wore a two-piece white suit, a modest bikini, brief enough to expose her navel but ample enough to cover breasts and hips.

"How do you think it happened?" Laura asked, turning her strained face toward Mrs. Cheney. "I never mentioned it to *anyone*. Not even Paul."

"I can't say how it happened," Mrs. Cheney said. "But is it so shameful? When you were a child, you smashed up a doll. Is that so awful?"

"It was," Laura said. "Awful. I was always a tomboy. Three brothers. But they wouldn't let me play with them. Kept pushing me away. Told me I was a girl, to play with my dolls."

"I know," Mrs. Cheney murmured. "You've never forgotten, have you?"

"No. Never. It was like I was destroying myself. The doll was me."

"Yes, yes," Mrs. Cheney soothed. "I understand completely. I now believe, sweetheart, that a nice, cold gin-and-tonic would do us both a world of good."

"I'll get them," Laura said, starting to rise.

"No, no," Mrs. Cheney said quickly. "Let me wait on you, dear."

She went away. Laura closed her eyes and began counting slowly backwards from 100 to 0—anything to keep from brooding again about her behavior at the seance. When she opened her eyes, she saw Mrs. Cheney, drinks in both hands, standing alongside the young blonde in the string bikini. The girl was smiling vacantly. Mrs. Cheney turned away, came back to Laura. She walked barefoot with a strange, gliding stride. Her posture was good—head up, shoulders back—but it seemed to Laura that the widow was *slinking*.

Mrs. Cheney's body was extraordinarily slender. Almost sleek. Long arms and legs. Small head. Elevated neck. The body of a thin dancer, with shield breasts, articulated feet with apostolic toes. All of her lengthened, pulled. Above the top of the bikini pants, hip bones pressed tight skin. Her thighs were hard, taut arms muscled. The rib cage showed.

She came flowing up to Laura, sat cross-legged on her own lounge, handed over one of the drinks. Laura turned onto her hip, took the glass gratefully, swallowed deeply.

"Oh God," she said, "that's what I needed. Thank you. Who's the sex object?"

"The blonde child?" Mrs. Cheney said casually. "I didn't find out. I just asked if she'd care to trade her tits for my legs."

"Diane, you didn't."

"Why not? Her breasts are delicious."

"What did she say?"

"She said, 'No way!'" Mrs. Cheney laughed. "Can't blame her." She looked down at her crossed legs, touched one thigh. "Scrawny, aren't they?"

"Oh Diane," Laura said, "you have lovely legs. Your whole body is lovely. I wish I was as thin."

"I'm glad you're not," Mrs. Cheney said. "I love you just the way you are."

She fished in her canvas beach bag, brought out a pair of mirrored sunglasses with wide silver frames.

She put them on, poking the earpieces into her hair, beneath a wide-brimmed straw hat. When Laura stared at her, she saw only her own reflection, repeated, distorted by the curvature of the mirrored lens.

"I never burn," Mrs. Cheney said. "Never. Just get darker. But let me get some stuff on you, darling; you're beginning to redden."

Laura rolled over on her stomach. Her head and arms were stretched above the lounge. She held her drink on the grass with both hands.

"Young girls seem to be maturing so fast these days," she said. "Vitamins, or the pill, I suppose. How old do you suppose that girl is? The blonde?"

"She's fifteen," Mrs. Cheney said.

"I didn't have breasts like that until after Christine was born," Laura mused. "When I was fifteen, I kept looking in the mirror, hoping. Nothing."

"I know," Mrs. Cheney said. "Try some of my lotion."

She spilled a little puddle of white into one palm.

"I'll take down your straps," she said. "You'll be wearing off-the-shoulder things this summer."

"Will I?" Laura said, taking a sip of her drink. "Maybe I will. But the flouncy, romantic styles look like stage costumes on me."

Mrs. Cheney pulled Laura's shoulder straps down. She began to smooth the lotion onto Laura's neck, shoulders, back. Her palm moved in long, slow strokes.

"That feels good," Laura murmured.

"Yes," Mrs. Cheney said. "But I don't think you dress for yourself. I think you dress for Paul."

"I never thought of that," Laura said. "He likes pantsuits, tweed skirts, flannel jackets—things like that. And I do, too, I think. Man-tailored shirts, for instance."

"Do you?" Mrs. Cheney said. "Really like it? Odd. I see you in softer things. Not frilly. Oh no, nothing fancy. But soft, flowing. Very feminine. Are you getting hungry, sweetheart? Can I get you a sandwich?"

"Not yet, thanks. A salad later maybe, but not a sandwich. I watch every ounce."

"Nonsense. You have a beautiful, womanly figure."

"Womanly?" Laura said. "Do I?"

Mrs. Cheney rubbed suntan lotion onto her shoulders and back, then started on her legs.

"Cigarette?" she asked.

"That would be nice," Laura said sleepily. "Mine are in my bag."

"A joint?" Mrs. Cheney said. "I have some with me."

"No, I don't think so. Just one of mine. You go ahead."

"Not if you won't."

"Well, maybe some day. Not right now."

The widow lighted a cigarette, then handed it down to Laura.

"Now a little more behind the knees," she said, "and you'll be covered."

Laura drowsed, feeling the smooth palm gliding over her calves. She took a slow drag from her cigarette, sipped her drink.

"I feel better now," she said. "We *are* going to swim, aren't we?"

"Of course," Mrs. Cheney said. "Later."

"Are you good?"

"Yes," the widow said unexpectedly. "I can't play tennis or golf, but I do swim well."

"I wish I could. I just go plowing along."

"Ever swim naked?"

"Once," Laura said. "In the sea. Alone."

"At night?"

"No. Very early in the morning. The family was on vacation in South Carolina."

"Enjoy it?"

"Glorious!"

"You should try it at night. Not alone."

"Sometimes here in the pool, after parties, people go skinny-dipping. Or so I've heard."

"It's not the same," Mrs. Cheney said.

They sunbathed, together, for almost an hour, hardly speaking. Once Laura said, "I feel so good. Comfortable. Like I'm melting." Mrs. Cheney murmured something, but Laura didn't hear.

The sun rose higher. The morning breeze faltered and died. The hot afternoon quiet was broken only by the smack of tennis balls from the nearby courts, the calls of the players. Two men came to swim, puffing side-by-side, then hauled themselves out and departed, dripping and laughing. The young blonde turned over onto her stomach, unhooked her bra strap. Her long, lithe back gleamed golden.

"I'm going in," Mrs. Cheney said finally. "Join me?"

"In a minute," Laura said. "When I wake up."

She turned onto her side. She watched Mrs. Cheney step out on the diving board, bounce twice, do a perfect, careless header. She hardly made a splash. Laura waited for her to reappear. But she didn't, until she was at the shallow end. Then her flowered red cap came bursting above the surface. She lurched up, took a deep breath, turned, surface-dived, swam back underwater. She came up near Laura, leaned her arms on the pool edge, shook water from her face.

"Marvelous," Laura called enviously. "I wish I could do that."

"Come on in," Mrs. Cheney said. "I'll show you how."

In the pool, they swam slowly, together, down toward the shallow end until they could stand, the water slicing their throats.

"You *can* float, can't you?" Mrs. Cheney asked.

"Of course," Laura gasped. "But not for long. I don't like to put my face in the water."

"Try it. A belly float. Just relax, I'm here; I won't let you sink. Spread your arms and legs wide. Spread-eagle."

Obediently, Laura went face down into the water. When she felt she was beginning to sink, there were strong arms and hands across breasts and thighs. She bobbed higher, lifted her head to take a breath, put her face back into the water. Mrs. Cheney's hands supported her, touching her liquid torso, her glossy legs. Then she was tilted upright.

"Good," the widow said. "Now take a deep breath and try to touch bottom with your fingertips. Then kick off to the other side of the pool. We'll go side-to-side for starters. It's all in the legs. Keep swimming forward and down. Use the breast stroke. But remember the kick. Always the strong kick."

They practiced for almost an hour. Mrs. Cheney was attentive, tireless, patient. She moved Laura's legs about gently, showing her the frog kick. She supported Laura's body in the water, one hand grasping her waist lightly, the other circled about a sleek thigh. Skin brushed, occasionally their legs became entangled, arms went twining about neck and shoulders. Once they collided underwater, socked into each other, and then came spluttering and laughing to the surface, Mrs. Cheney's hands beneath Laura's arms.

Toward the end, tired, amused with their own antics, they merely sported, shouting with glee. They dunked each other, splashed, grappled underwater. Shiny limbs slid. Flesh drifted along flesh. Fingers touched breasts by accident, and once Laura found herself clamped between Mrs. Cheney's strong legs, and turned and twisted to free herself. What fun they had!

Finally, weakened, gasping, they both came to the surface. They clung to the edge of the pool.

They shook their faces clear of the water. They looked up to see the young blonde in the knitted string bikini. She was sitting up on her lounge, knees raised. She was watching them with cool, unblinking eyes.

Paul buzzed Clint Stahl's office on Friday morning. "Can you make lunch today?" he asked.

There was silence a moment, then Stahl said, "A hearty last meal for the condemned man?"

"Something like that," Fayette said, relieved that Clint knew what was going on.

"Sure," Stahl said. "How about one o'clock?"

"Fine. At Reggie's. See you at one."

But Stahl didn't show up until 1:25. Fayette was into his second martini, sitting at their usual corner table, when he saw Clint come in. He was moving with the careful deliberation of a man who's had too much to drink and knows it. Just before he reached the table, he drew aside cautiously to allow a large, handsome, wondrously coiffed woman sweep by with her escorts—two fags and a Chihuahua.

Stahl slid into the chair next to Fayette. He was still staring after the woman.

"What I really need," he said with drunken solemnity, "really, *really* need, is a beautiful woman with a dick."

"What you really, really need," said Fayette, "is a new brain. Your old one has turned to Silly Putty. How many have you had?"

"Not enough," Stahl said. "Never enough." He looked around for a waiter and snapped his fingers. When a waiter sauntered over, he ordered a double martini. Then he looked at Paul owlishly. "I snapped my fingers," he explained, "because I know how much you hate it."

"I know," Fayette said, thinking with dread of what lay ahead. "I also hate luncheon partners who pass out. You're not going to do that, are you?"

"Me?" Clint said indignantly. "Not me. I'm in the pink."

"The gray," Paul said. "You're in the gray."

He was, too. Ashen-faced, with a shaving scar on his chin. His lapels were spotted, his tie yanked awry. All of him rumpled and soiled. But it was the eyes that disturbed Fayette, the burning, desperate eyes. And a loose mouth with lips that had become unhinged. The tremor of the hands was even more noticeable.

"Listen, Clint," Fayette said slowly, "you're going to get canned. You know that, don't you?"

"Yes."

"I wheedled a month for you. Give you a chance to look around while you still have a job. It's easier that way. And, of course, all the bullshit reference you want. But screw the job; it's you I'm worried about. Can I help?"

"No."

"Can anyone help? A doctor? A shrink? *Anyone?*"

"No," Stahl said miserably. "You ever hear the old bromide: 'Know thyself'? Implying that if you know yourself, everything will be hunky-dory. That's a small boat owned by a Polàck. But there's not a word of truth in it, Paul m'lad. Know thyself, and you wind up slashing your own throat."

"How about some food?" Fayette said hurriedly. "You look starved. Have a rare steak and baked potato."

"Whatever," Stahl said.

Paul ordered for both of them. While they waited, he watched Stahl slug his way through the double martini and order another. Stahl never looked up. But his trembling fingers plucked at the tablecloth.

"How's Laura?" he asked suddenly.

"Fine. You'll see her tonight at the club dance. You know that crazy cat who adopted us? Ben? The ugly job on the back stoop? Well, Laura finally let him into the house. He stays in the kitchen when he does come in. Just long enough to gobble some food. Then he scratches the door to get out again. At least he's getting sleeker. Doesn't look so moth-eaten now."

"What?" Clint Stahl said.

"Here're our steaks," Fayette said. "Let's eat."

Stahl fumbled his knife and fork. He tried to cut a slice from his sirloin. But the knife turned in his nerveless grasp, the fork slipped from his fingers and clattered onto the plate.

"Take it easy," Paul said gently. "Wait a minute."

He cut up his own steak and baked potato, then exchanged plates.

"Thanks," Stahl muttered. "Think they'll let me make baskets? Maybe I'm not capable of that. But I'll bet I can do fingerpainting."

"Clint," Fayette said, "don't. You're going to be all right. Cut down on the booze. Eat a decent meal occasionally. Sleep. Get some exercise."

"Thank you, doctor," Stahl said. "and while we're on the old bromides, try this one on for size: 'Physician, heal thyself.'"

Paul looked at him, puzzled.

"That one went right over my head," he said.

"You know what I mean," Stahl said. "Or *who* I mean."

"I swear I don't know what the hell you're talking about."

Stahl raised his eyes, stared at him.

"Jesus," he breathed. "I think you're telling the truth."

"Of course I'm telling the truth," Paul said angrily. "What *are* you talking about?"

"When I asked about Laura, I meant the seance. Did she get over that?"

"Oh sure. We never mention it. She's forgotten it."

"Don't bet on it, buster. You remember before we got to the business of the smashed doll? You were all talking about a gray-haired woman, a grandfather's clock, the smell of mothballs."

"I remember. But I got no image on that one."

"Thank God for that. But that one was mine."

"Yours?"

"The memory, man! It belonged to me. Happened to me when I was a kid."

"What happened?"

"Ah," Clint Stahl said. "What happened? You haven't a clue, have you?"

"A clue about what?"

"About *whom*, you dummy. The widow lady. She knows."

Fayette put down his knife and fork, pushed his unfinished plate away.

"All right," he said. "The light dawns. You're talking about Mrs. Cheney. You're claiming she knew about Laura's memory of the smashed doll and your memory of whatever, and she put the ideas in our heads, the images. Is that what you're saying?"

"Yes," Stahl nodded violently. "Except for Jacque. That black devil. He's in on it, too."

"In on *what?*" Fayette said furiously. "Assuming Mrs. Cheney can put thoughts in other people's minds —which I will never admit as long as I live—why would she? What's the point? Just to make us recall old memories? For what reason?"

"They're secrets, you see," Stahl nodded wisely, with a ghastly wink. "She knows the secrets. Where the bodies are buried. She knows your secret, too. You'll see, you'll see."

"I have no secrets," Paul said shakily.

"Everyone has secrets. She knows them. Paul, she *knows!* And Jacque. And the Colonel. The three of them know."

Fighting it, losing, Fayette was moved by the man's fervor, his intensity.

"But why are they doing these things?" he asked. "What do they want?"

Stahl took a deep breath. He looked down at his empty plate. Then raised his head to stare around the room with lost eyes.

"What do they want, what do they want, what do they want?" he mumbled drunkenly . . .

"They want *us*," he said.

The entrance hall of the Fayette home was floored with slate. An open staircase led to the second floor. At the head of the stairs was the master bedroom, with an interior bathroom and small dressing room. Then, down the hallway toward the rear of the house, were Christine's bedroom and Brian's. These rooms remained much as they had been when the children left for college: cluttered with their favorite pictures, souvenirs, phonograph records, sports equipment— and clothes they would never wear again.

At the rear of the hallway was a spacious guest room, with its own bathroom. And finally a small storage room with a ladder to a trap that led to the attic.

Having showered and dressed first, Paul Fayette left the master bedroom to his wife. He paused to light a cigarette, then wandered down the hall, into Christine's bedroom. He didn't switch on the light, but even in the semi-darkness he could see the posters on the walls (Che Guevara and Robert Redford), the collection of stuffed animals, a dusty violin case in the corner marking the death of a short-lived dream and five hundred dollars in lessons.

Looking down from the window, he could glimpse a corner of the back stoop. He thought he saw a darker mass that could be Ben, the cat, lying on its side with thin legs extended. But then his focus changed; he was looking into black window glass that gave his reflection back: a wispy, white-haired man languidly smoking a cigarette in fingers that trembled slightly.

He had told Laura little about his bewildering luncheon with Stahl. Only that Clint had accepted the news of his dismissal stoically. Paul reported nothing of Stahl's comments about the seance, about Mrs. Cheney.

Now, staring at his own ghost image, he realized how his relationship with Clint Stahl would change. The man might remain a neighbor, a Penlow Parker, but inevitably there would be a cool awkwardness between them. That saddened him. He acknowledged how much he would miss Stahl's despairing wit and sour iconoclasm.

He could not rid himself of a dim sense of dread. Those besotted notions of Stahl's—that, somehow, Mrs. Cheney knew his "secret," all their secrets, and was using them in an unknown manner for reasons unexplained—all that could be nothing but drunken maunderings. But still . . . But still . . .

He smelled again the sharp damp of winter clothes and rubber overshoes in that black closet. Then, when he quizzed his own response, his fervid acquiescence, the glory he felt in his masculine dominance—My God, it was almost a rape!—then his mind slid away, veered off, went hurtling on to something else. Anything else.

It turned out to be a dreary evening for Laura and Paul Fayette. The Stahls did not attend the Penlow Park Country Club dance. Nor did Mrs. Cheney. The Fayettes sat by themselves, drank sparingly, exchanged wry grimaces when Sammy Lobo and the Lamplighters played "Say It Isn't So."

"Cheap irony," Paul said.

"Isn't it," Laura agreed. "You down?"

"Yes. You?"

"Sort of."

"Firing Clint is my excuse," he said. "What's yours?"

"I don't know," she said. "Everything. Let's go home."

"Let's," he said.

She took a double martini up to the bedroom. He had his final drink downstairs, alone, a darkened house between them. Finally, he locked up, went upstairs without courage. Laura was already in bed, the lights out.

He undressed, slid in alongside her. She was on her side, facing outward. He did the same. Both were naked, and after a while both bowed slowly into the fetal position. But the top sheet was tucked between them. As if the slightest touch of their bare backs would be offensive to them both.

5

"Farewell!" the minister cried, throwing wide his arms. "Farewell, Bernard Stiffens, servant of God!"

The organ in the old Boston church immediately launched into sonorities that vibrated the stained glass windows. Mourners rose respectfully to their feet as the family of the deceased left their front row pews and exited slowly, sadly, up the aisle. A veiled widow, supported on both sides by middle-aged sons. And following, daughters, daughters-in-law, sons-in-law, a train of grandchildren, solemn, with slicked-down hair.

Paul Fayette glanced at his watch as he moved out into the crowded aisle, calculating which shuttle he could catch back to New York. A hand clutched his arm.

"Paul," Betty Lanahan gasped, "I've got to get out to the cemetery. Lots of things to see to."

"Betty," he said, "I wish we could have—"

"Paul, *please,*" she said. "Come with me. An hour. I promise. Only another hour. I've got to talk to you."

"I wish I—"

"Please, Paul. An hour. I'll take you to the airport after the burial. It's car eight."

She disappeared.

He moved onto the porch. When chauffeured limousine eight was announced, he stepped down and opened the back door. A woman was sitting in the corner of the seat, dressed in black, a heavy veil obscuring her features.

"I beg your pardon," he said hastily. "I thought Betty Lanahan was—"

"This is it," a gravelly voice said. The black veil fluttered. "Climb in, buster."

Obediently, he climbed in. Betty came hurrying up. The door was closed. He found himself sandwiched between the two women. Car eight moved off, then stopped again while the funeral cortege was completed.

"Thanks, Paul," Betty said gratefully, picking up his hand. "I appreciate it. Paul, this is Marya Dubek. Marya, meet Paul Fayette."

"A pleasure to meet you," he said, trying to peer through the thick veil.

"Hi," she said in that hoarse voice.

"Are you a relative of Mr. Stiffens?" he asked.

"You could say that," she nodded, and Betty Lanahan clutched his fingers tightly.

Betty was a rangy woman who moved with a forward tilting slouch. It was the neck and head that fascinated Paul: of equal width, the neck a thick, smooth column, the egg-shaped head set atop it at an angle, with a tight cap of blonde curls. The neck and head of an Apollo. Or, he thought, one of Hitler's heroic young men.

Now, looking out the window, her face was turned, and he caught a quarter-view of crisp jawline, sculpted lips, deepset eyes. The skin as unwrinkled as creamed marble.

Outside, smoky clouds closed them around. Mist drifted steadily, gathering in droplets on the limousine's hood, fogging the windows. The air conditioner purred; the chilled air was clammy, clinging. It smelled faintly of sulfur.

"What the Irish call a 'soft day,'" Betty Lanahan said.

"Soft, my ass," the veiled woman said harshly. "It's bloody wet. Anyone want a belt?"

She fished inside an enormous black alligator hand-bag and brought out a new pint of California brandy. She unscrewed the cap, then proffered the bottle. Paul and Betty shook their heads. The woman shrugged, thrust the neck of the bottle beneath her veil. Fayette caught a glimpse of heavy chin, seamed neck. She was not young.

She took a deep gulp, then leaned forward, bottle gripped between spread knees. She twisted to look at Betty Lanahan.

"You sure he didn't leave anything?" she demanded. "A letter? Envelope? A package? Anything?"

"I told you," Betty said patiently. "He left nothing for you."

"Well . . ." the woman said, "what the hell. I did all right. But I thought maybe he'd want to surprise me. He did that once—surprise me."

She sprawled back in her corner. She thrust out her lumpy legs. She clutched the brandy bottle to her bosom. She belched softly.

"He wasn't a bad asshole," she muttered.

The funeral cortege moved slowly through crowded streets, then picked up speed. They rode in silence, hearing the snick-snick of the windshield wiper. Occasionally Marya Dubek took a small sip from her brandy bottle. Paul saw enough of her chin, cheeks, mouth to guess her age in the forty-five to fifty range. She appeared to be full-bodied, ungirdled, with pendulous breasts, sausage arms, swollen thighs.

Outside, the grayness deepened; they moved over slick pavement through a landscape torn to a dream by the fogged windows. Sodden trees drooped along-side the highway. They saw a few hooded figures hurrying along, bowed in plastic. Neon lights glimmered through the mist.

Betty Lanahan pulled Paul Fayette to her. She was shivering. She put her lips close to his ear.

"That man you called about," she said in a low voice. "Coulter?"

Paul nodded. "Benjamin G. Coulter. Says he's a colonel."

"He wasn't in the files. Not in the private files either. About a week before he died, I asked Mr. Stiffens about him. He said he'd never heard of him."

"All right," Paul said grimly. "The man's a fake. I thought so. Thanks, Betty."

"No, no," she said urgently. "I got a look at the will. Stiffens left a hundred thousand cash to a Benjamin G. Coulter, colonel, retired."

Fayette's head turned slowly. He stared at her, expressionless.

"A hundred thousand?" he repeated. "Cash? To Benjamin G. Coulter?"

"That's right."

"Any address given?"

"Your town," Betty Lanahan said. "Penlow Park. Who is he, Paul?"

He tried to laugh.

"Who is he? Good question. I ran a trace on him. He doesn't exist."

"Doesn't exist?"

"No record of his existence. Nothing on paper. Not a scrap. Anywhere. But I've talked to him, had dinner with him. I've smoked his cigars and drunk his whiskey. But I don't know who he is."

"What does he look like?"

"Short, stout, very jolly. Does incredible magic tricks. Betty, he *looks* like a retired colonel. White hair. Military mustache. Fake British accent."

"Why did Stiffens leave him the money?"

"Who the hell knows?" he said angrily. "Nothing about him makes sense. Or about his daughter either."

"Daughter?"

"A widow named Cheney. Diane Cheney. Does that name mean anything to you?"

"No."

"She wasn't mentioned in the will, was she?"

"No," Betty Lanahan said. "Coulter was the only

one outside of family, servants, business associates, and so forth. Paul, you think it's a con game? A fraud?"

"Could be," he said, shrugging. "If it is, it's working. Coulter will get the bequest, won't he?"

"I don't see why not," she said. Then added furiously, "He left *me* five thousand."

The limousine turned slowly through the cemetery gate. The cortege circled down a winding road, stopped at the foot of a low, plump hill fanged with wet gravestones. Near the crest, a striped awning had been erected over an open grave. The doors of the black limousines opened. Black umbrellas popped out. Groups began trudging slowly up the hill.

Their chauffeur held the umbrella.

"Paul, I've got to run," Betty Lanahan said breathlessly. "I'm in charge of things—you know?"

"Of course," he said. "You go ahead. I'll follow, with Mrs. Dubek.'"

"Miss Dubek," she said. "Thanks, Paul. I don't know what I'd have done without you."

She moved closer. The chauffeur maneuvered the umbrella over them, his body turned away. He stared up vacantly at the murky sky.

"I'll drive you to the airport," Betty Lanahan whispered. "When it's finished. Okay?"

"Fine.'"

"Wouldn't like to stay over, would you?" she asked swiftly. Then she saw his face. "That's all right," she said. "Sorry I asked."

"As a matter of fact, I *would* like to stay over. But I can't."

"I know," she said. "The happily married man."

"Something like that," he said. He swooped suddenly to kiss her cheek. "Better go now."

She and the chauffeur moved off, huddling under the umbrella.

"Another umbrella in the front seat, sir," the chauffeur called back.

He nodded. He turned up the collar of his black

silk jacket. He opened the back door of the limousine, leaned in.

"Would you care to go up to the service now, Miss Dubek?"

"No," she said. "I don't think so. I think I'll sit this one out. I'll just watch from here."

He considered a moment.

"Mind if I join you?" he asked.

She waved her brandy bottle.

"Be my guest," she said.

He climbed in, closed the door behind him. He ran the electric window down a few inches. A cool, wet breeze came billowing in.

"Would you like a cigarette?" he said, offering his pack.

"I heard what you were talking about," she said in her harsh voice. "You two. About Coulter. Bernie did know Coulter."

He leaned forward. He raised her veil to look at swollen features, roadmap cheeks, wattled neck. Thick pancake makeup didn't hide the discoloration around her right eye: blue, purple, yellow, red.

"Bernard Stiffens knew Colonel Benjamin G. Coulter?" he inquired in a stiff, precise voice.

"Sure," she said. Her laugh was sudden, hard, knowing. "Ben introduced us. Bernie and me."

Paul Fayette sighed, sat back, lighted his cigarette.

"If the offer is still open," he said, "I'll have a drink of that brandy now, thank you."

It was a drizzly morning, too wet for jogging. But by the time Paul left in the station wagon, to drive to LaGuardia for the Boston shuttle, the rain had turned to a fine mist. By 10:00 a.m., when Mrs. Raskin arrived for the semi-weekly house-cleaning, the sun was beginning to stab through. And at noon, when Mrs. Raskin departed, the sky was bluing, the sun was blurred, the air smelled of new steam.

Laura Fayette made herself a Bloody Mary, lighted a cigarette, mooched around the kitchen, doing this and that. She saw Ben yawning and stretching on the back stoop. She opened the door, and the cat came stepping delicately in, placing one foot directly ahead of the other, hips swinging. He acted like he couldn't care less if he was in or out.

She poured him a saucer of milk, and he sipped tentatively for a few minutes, then sat back and cleaned his face and long, white whiskers with his paws. His wounds had healed; his ribs no longer pressed the skin. He had filled out, become sleeker, glossier. He seemed to move with an elegant languor, and, occasionally, suffered Laura to pat his head a few times or scratch his ears.

Now he went back to the door and waited, not turning to look at her. She opened the door, and he stalked out again, haughty, uncommitted.

Laura, wearing her jogging shorts and a Penlow Park Country Club T-shirt, wandered barefoot into the living room and puttered about. Things had been displaced during Mrs. Raskin's dusting. Laura moved them back to their usual positions. She wondered if she should call Diane Cheney, call Margaret Stahl. Call Christine, perhaps, or call Brian. Watch a soap opera on TV. Shower. Cut her toenails. Wash her hair. Read a book. Make a stew. Make a sandwich.

She had decided to make another Bloody Mary when she heard a car pull into the driveway. She rushed to the front window, peered out. Diane Cheney in her red MGB sports car. The widow slid out, then reached back for a long, flat box tied with a pink ribbon. She came toward the front door. She was wearing her white gabardine pantsuit. Laura hurried to greet her.

"I know I should have called first, but I took the chance that you might be in."

"Glad you did."

"Not interrupting anything, am I?"

"Of course not. Paul's gone to Boston for the day."

"I know."

"You know?"

"Bernie Stiffens' funeral, isn't it? The Colonel was supposed to go, but he was called away at the last minute."

"Baghdad?" Laura asked.

"No," Mrs. Cheney smiled. "Moscow, as a matter of fact."

Laura made them both vodka martinis. They sat in the tidied living room, sipping their drinks, pleasantly relaxed. They talked about the Stahls.

"It's getting worse," Mrs. Cheney told Laura. "She came over last night, in tears. You don't suppose he beats her, do you?"

"Of course not."

"I'm not so sure—he's very disturbed. And worse after losing his job."

"Oh, you know that, do you?"

"Margaret told me. She's frantic."

Laura Fayette considered Margaret Stahl her best friend, and wondered why she hadn't come to cry on *her* shoulder.

"Been shopping I see," she said, jerking her chin toward the long, flat box tied with a pink ribbon. "Something nice?"

"I hope so," Mrs. Cheney said. "It's for you."

Laura looked at her in astonishment. "For me?"

"The moment I saw it, I thought of you. Knew you *had* to have it."

"What on earth is it?"

"Heavens," Mrs. Cheney said, with mock solemnity, "where *has* my drink gone? Very high rate of evaporation in here. May I have another?"

"Of course," Laura said, draining her own glass. "Paul won't be back until this evening. Let's have a drunken afternoon."

"Splendid idea," Mrs. Cheney said.

The widow's gift to Laura was a long-sleeved blouse of white chiffon, with a high, ruffled neckline of white lace, a choker collar, tied with a narrow black velvet ribbon. White lace ruffles down the front and on the cuffs. With this revived antique came a soft dirndl skirt of white crinkle cotton, sheer as a breeze. The whole had a maidenly effect: a young woman of the early 1900's in a tintype portrait or sepia photograph.

Laura shook out blouse and skirt, stroked the gossamer between her fingers. She looked at Diane Cheney with wonder.

"Beautiful," she said. "Just beautiful. But *why?*"

"I told you," Mrs. Cheney said. "I saw it, and thought you'd like it. I could see you in it."

"I've never worn anything like this. You think . . . ?"

"You'll see."

"Thank you. Thank you so much. Shall I try it on now?"

"In a while," Mrs. Cheney said casually. "Let's finish our drinks first. Then we'll have dress-up time. When you were a little girl, did you dress up in your mother's gowns and go tumbling about in high heels?"

"Of course. With circles of rouge, and lipstick smeared on, and my hair . . ."

Then they were gone, exchanging memories of dress-up times, prom gowns, wedding gowns, favorite suits and inherited fur coats. They finished their drinks, and Laura mixed two more.

"God, I'm happy you dropped over," she told Diane Cheney. "Oh, not just for the marvelous gift," she added hastily. "But I was at odds and ends, ready to climb walls."

"I hope it fits," the widow said. "I guessed at sizes. But you can always exchange it. Try it on now?"

They carried their drinks up to the master bedroom. Mrs. Cheney sat on the bed. Laura took her gift into the dressing room.

"I really should get a wig to go with this outfit," she called nervously. "A bun or chignon. Something like that."

"Why not let your hair grow long?" Mrs. Cheney said. "I think you should."

Laura came out a few minutes later, laughing self-consciously, blushing, smoothing the long skirt over her hips. She was a virgin.

"Well?" she asked. "With my big feet, should I be running through the heather shouting, 'Heathcliff! Heathcliff!'?"

She stood stiffly before Mrs. Cheney, arms at her sides.

"Well?" she asked again, timidly this time. "What do you think?"

"Lovely," Mrs. Cheney breathed. "Just lovely."

"Honestly?"

"The dress. You. Everything . . ."

Mrs. Cheney, still seated on the bed, put her arms about Laura's hips. She pulled her close.

They were caught, frozen in the moment. Hazy sun filtered through white curtains. White walls. White counterpane on the bed. Mrs. Cheney's white pantsuit, Laura's white blouse and skirt. A high-key photograph, caught and frozen. The air itself seemed milk; motes of chalk danced in the air . . .

"Diane . . ."

Whispered entreaty.

"Lovely girl, lovely girl. So soft, so sweet. Sugar and spice, and everything nice."

Their voices were white, too. Disembodied. Floating.

"So soft, so soft. Dear girl. Sweet girl."

She was naked beneath the long, sheer skirt. Tanned thighs, taut and quivering. She lay back, a knuckle at her teeth, eyes swollen with innocent fright.

"Diane . . ."

"Dear girl. Sweet girl."

Cool fingers were at her, stroking, prying gently. The drawstring of the blouse was loosened, the neckband of velvet untied.

"Let me," Mrs. Cheney kept murmuring. "Let me." And: "Dear girl. Sweet girl."

Laura closed her eyes. Sensed her own melt, a thaw. Knew eager submission, warm surrender. Felt slide of blouse from tight breasts, glide of skirt from smooth legs. And through her eyelids saw the white sunglow.

"Dear girl. Sweet girl."

All murmuring and fluttered fingers. Strong on hers. Snake tongue darting. A hard knee between her strengthless thighs. She was slowly moved, easily shifted, twisted, maneuvered, and she could not resist, could not, but gave herself up. Eyes still closed. Swollen lips parted.

Her flesh was set aflame, burning with a white flicker, and it would not stop, would never stop, but she would be consumed, from out to in, and in to out, until the fires became one. Something she had never known before: herself given totally with delight. Penetration. Joy. Dominion. Bliss.

"Ah!" she shrieked.

"Dear girl. Sweet girl."

Everyone said the Fourth of July celebration at the Penlow Park Country Club was the best party of the year. Everyone planned their away-from-home summer vacations so as not to miss it. Everyone said the party was a time for discarding diets and falling off the wagon. Everyone said there was always a rash of unexpected pregnancies following the July Fourth festival, and you know why. It was a bash, a riot, an orgy. Really one hell of a good time. Everyone said.

Festivities began early in the morning with a golf tourney and championship tennis matches. The clubhouse bar opened at noon, and a salad buffet was set up alongside the swimming pool. Sammy Lobo and the Lamplighters appeared in the main dining room at dusk for a cocktail-hour dansant. Dinner was served until 9:00 p.m. Then, on a makeshift stage at one end of the long room, the Penlow Park Country Club Annual Amateur Night was presented.

There was no curtain or public address system. Amateurs were introduced by master of ceremonies Paul Fayette. They then walked onto the bare stage, performed—frequently interrupted by groans, drunken

catcalls, applause, or the impatient stamping of feet—
and retired to make room for the next act.

Fayette, with the assistance of Sammy Lobo, had
planned the program artfully. It opened with a frenetic
Charleston by Helen Cantor. This was followed by a
barbershop quartet, followed by Babs Feldman and
Tom Spencer doing a tango to "Jealousy." Next came
Eileen Rabinowitz singing an aria from *Tosca*. Then
Billy Hawkins did his well-known impressions of sev-
eral dead movie stars. Veronica Bates performed a
solo ballet entitled *Ode to Spring,* and Dr. Henry
Forsythe demonstated how his wire-haired fox terrier
Trixie could dance on her hind legs—and, unfortu-
nately, defecate at the same time.

The final act . . .

"And now, ladies, gentlemen, and drunks," Paul
said loudly, "to wind up this remarkable cornucopia of
beauty, wit, charm, grace and talent, it is my very
great pleasure to introduce two newcomers to our midst
who will puzzle, amaze, and astound you with a dazzling exhibition of fantastic legerdemain and mind-
blowing magic. Let's have a big round of applause
for Mrs. Diane Cheney and Colonel Benjamin
Coulter."

The Colonel, wearing a silk top hat and long black
cloak lined with crimson satin, bounded onto the stage,
beaming. Following him, smiling softly, came Mrs.
Cheney. She was wearing a man-tailored dinner
jacket, starched dickey, black bow tie. She was also
wearing brief black velvet shorts and black pantyhose
that made her legs seem enormously long and shapely.
Whistles greeted her appearance.

With a minimum of patter, Coulter began ten minutes of rapid prestidigitation, trick following trick so
swiftly that his audience scarcely had time to applaud
before he was on to something new. Playing cards
flashed and disappeared; lighted cigarettes apparently
went down his throat; a rabbit materialized in an
empty box; he found a bowl of live goldfish in his
top hat; a newspaper torn to shreds became whole

again; a length of rope cut into pieces was tossed in the air to become complete; coins were plucked from nowhere, disappeared, appeared again; he slammed a cleaver down on his wrist—to horrified screams from the ladies—only to wave his undamaged hand blithely at the fascinated spectators.

Paul Fayette, standing at one side of the stage, marveled at how rapidly the Colonel worked, and how skillfully Mrs. Cheney moved props on and off; dexterously caught coins and scarves tossed to her; provided stands, boxes, cages, wands; removed rabbit and goldfish; anticipated the Colonel's wants. Fayette realized, of course, that those slim, curved legs moving smartly about the stage provided a good part of Coulter's needed misdirection. But the act went so smoothly, so professionally, he was certain they had done it before, together, many times.

The Colonel concluded his sleight of hand by tossing his top hat into the air. When it descended, it was a brown bowler which he cocked jauntily atop his head. He then winked at the flabbergasted audience.

The applause was still pounding widly when he stepped to the front of the stage.

"Ladies and gentlemen," he said, holding up a hand for silence, "what you have seen so far I am certain you have seen many times before. Although not so well performed!" (Laughter.)

"What you have seen is legerdemain. Prestidigitation. The use of misdirection. And, of course, illusion. It's all illusion. But now, let us depart from the realm of mere mechanical tricks and enter the kingdom of true magic. Diane, will you assist me, please?"

The Colonel and Mrs. Cheney then went into their mindreading act. She sat on a straight chair, her back to the audience. She was blindfolded. The mask was closely inspected by three eager volunteers from the audience. The Colonel then moved about the dining tables, requesting he be furnished small personal items which Mrs. Cheney would identify.

"What am I holding?"

"A ballpoint pen."

"And what is this?"

"A lady's wallet."

"What have we here?"

"A handkerchief—and not too clean."

Laughter.

"And now what do I have?"

"A pocket watch."

"And this?"

"A wilted flower. A rose."

And so on . . .

This portion of the act ended to amused applause. But Colonel Coulter raised his hand again.

"It has been brought to my attention," he said solemnly, "that there are some unbelievers among you who actually doubt that my daughter is capable of reading minds, that the exhibition you have just witnessed was accomplished by some sort of code between Mrs. Cheney and myself, the wording of my question being the clue by which she identified the object selected.

"Very well. To convince you once and for all of Mrs. Cheney's supernatural powers, I will now ask one of you to select and hold up the objects, and to ask each question in the same words: 'What is this?' You agree this will rule out all possibility of chicanery or fraud? Good. Now let's see . . . who shall we slect to enter into spiritual communication with this remarkable seer?"

He turned his head slowly, inspecting the audience. There were a few short laughs, then silence.

"Mrs. Fayette," Colonel Coulter boomed suddenly, "would you be willing to assist in this extraordinary exhibition of the supernormal? Of course you would! Come on, Laura, step right up here. Let's have a little encouragement for Mrs. Laura Fayette."

There was a splatter of applause. Laura rose hesitantly, smiling nervously. She came forward. The Colonel took her hand and patted it.

"Now don't be frightened, dear lady," he reassured

her. "It won't hurt a bit! As you and everyone else can see, my daughter's back is turned and, in addition, she is tightly blindfolded. Now just request personal items from your friends here, concentrate on each one, and ask, 'What is this?' in a loud, clear voice. You do understand, don't you?"

"Yes, Colonel," she said faintly.

"Good," he said. "And Mrs. Cheney will tune her incredible psychic sensitivity to your spiritual emanations and identify exactly what you are thinking. All right, dear lady, you may begin."

Laura looked around, somewhat dazed. Someone thrust a dinner fork into her hand. Laura held it, stared at it. Then she turned toward the stage.

"What is this?" she called in a faltering voice.

"A dinner fork," Mrs. Cheney said firmly.

"What is this?"

"A woman's compact."

"What is this?"

"A ring of keys."

"What is this?"

"A driver's license."

As Laura proceeded, the audience grew quiet, puzzled, uncertain. There was restive stirring, an exchange of troubled glances. The Colonel let the doubt and mistrust build for a few moments, then stepped in to take control again.

"Thank you, dear lady," he said, leading a shaken Laura back to the dining table where she had been seated with Margaret and Clint Stahl. "I think we have convinced all the skeptics of the reality of extrasensory perception. Ladies and gentlemen, that concludes this part of our act. I thank you for your close and kind attention."

There was applause, but it was perfunctory and unsure. Colonel Coulter went back onto the stage, removed Mrs. Cheney's blindfold, and led her to the apron of the stage where she bowed gravely. This time the applause was more enthusiastic.

"And now," Coulter said when they had quieted,

"we would like to climax this little exhibition of the unknown and the unexpected with one of the most devilishly clever illusions ever presented on any stage anywhere. To assist my daughter and me in bringing you this incredible feat of magic, I require the assistance of my faithful companion, Jacque. Will you come forward, Jacque, please?"

Jacque, dressed in a somber black suit, white shirt, black tie, stepped out onto the stage. He was carrying a bundle of cloth. He shook it out and held it up, turning it this way and that. It was apparently a large square of black velvet, approximately 4′x4′. He then handed it down to the occupants of a front row table for closer examination.

"You agree is is merely a large square of black cloth?" Colonel Coulter asked them. "Good. Now, Diane, will you take your position, please?"

The straight chair was turned to face the audience. Mrs. Cheney sat down, crossed her arms so her fingers rested on her shoulders, bowed her head.

With Jacque's assistance, the Colonel draped the black cloth over the seated Mrs. Cheney. It concealed her and the chair completely, the edges piling up on the floor. Jacque quietly left the stage.

The audience watched these preparations with some trepidation. They stared, almost breathless, as Coulter stood beside the muffled figure of his daughter. He gazed at them sternly.

"Do not doubt the evidence of your senses," he instructed them. "Even if what you are about to see and hear contradicts reason, logic, and rationality. It *will* happen, and you will see it happen. It is magic, and *magic conquers all!*"

He stepped back. He extended his arms and hands toward the shrouded figure, fingers spread.

"Beelzebub!" he cried. "Satan! Your son prays you, make this woman to disappear!"

As he spoke the final words, he strode forward, whipped the cloth away—and the chair was empty.

There was a gasp from the audience, a small

scream from a back table, then silence. A sprinkle of
applause began, grew hesitantly, became louder, until
the entire room was clapping, roaring its approval.

"Thank you, thank you, thank you," Colonel
Coulter said, showing his porcelain teeth. "A charming illusion, is it not? And now to make the lady reappear." He paused a moment. "Goodness," he said
with pretended confusion, "I certainly hope I remember how this is done!"

Reassured by the professional magician's innocuous
patter, the audience laughed and relaxed.

The Colonel flapped the black cloak high, like a
bullfighter swinging his cape. As the velvet settled
lower, Coulter muttered words no one could hear.
But as the cloth came to rest, it was apparent someone sat in the chair.

"Presto!" the Colonel shouted, and flicked away the
cloth again. And there was Jacque, white teeth gleaming, smiling slyly at the astounded guests.

There was a yell of surprise, more laughter, then
applause louder than before.

"Whoops!" Coulter caroled merrily. "A slight mistake! We'll have to fix that!"

He swirled the cloth again to cover Jacque, murmuring his incantation. The velvet shroud rose,
hovered, swooped like some great bird. It settled into
place. The Colonel whisked it away again, and Jacque
was gone. In his place, Mrs. Cheney sat quietly in the
chair, arms crossed, head bowed.

Then they did cheer! And rushed up from their
tables to cluster around, inspect stage, chair, velvet
cloth, and back wall. To congratulate the Colonel,
Mrs. Cheney, and even Jacque on a marvelous per-
formance.

"A great illusion!"
"Best magic trick I've ever seen!"
"But how did you *do* it?"
"Completely mystifying!"
"You fooled us all!"
"Magnificent trick!"

Coulter accepted their plaudits with pleasure. Mrs. Cheney smiled and said nothing. Jacque folded the square of cloth, began to pack up the Colonel's props.

Paul Fayette, standing to one side, lighted a cigarette with trembling fingers. A few club members stopped by to tell him what a great show he had produced—"Best Amateur Night ever!"—and he, too, smiled tightly and said nothing.

Finally, Clint Stahl came weaving up, glassy-eyed, tripping over his own feet.

"She's quite a medium, isn't she?" Paul said.

"She's quite a medium, isn't she?" Clint mumbled. "Lucky I'm wearing my seersucker suit."

He went stumbling away, pushing through the crowd on the stage. Paul Fayette searched about for Laura. He finally found her in the bar, alone, drinking frantically.

Never had their home seemed so close.

"That act," Paul Fayette began. "I've never seen—"

"Please," Laura said. "I don't want to talk about it."

He went into the kitchen. He made a pot of instant coffee. He brought it back to the family room and poured them each a cup, black.

"Brandy?" he asked.

She didn't answer. He brought her a snifter of brandy, a heavy one, and a glass for himself. They sat in the gloom, shaken, sipping coffee, brandy, coffee, brandy.

"Do you love me?" she spoke, into the air.

"You know I do."

"Say it."

"I love you."

"Yes, but do you *really* love me?"

He didn't answer that, or sigh. The darkness pressed them around.

Something brushed his leg. He jerked nervously, looked down.

"Did you let him in?" he demanded.

"What? Who?"

"Ben. He's here. In the room. Did you let him in?"

"No. Maybe. I don't remember."

"I'll put him out," he said.

"Let him stay," she said. "Tomorrow I'll buy a pan and some litter."

He leaned down, stroked the cat's long, supple back. He thought he heard a purr.

"All right," he said. "Let him stay."

The windows were wide. A damp midnight air came puffing in. And between, periods of still, stifling heat. Blasts.

"We should go to bed," she said.

"I suppose," he said.

But they could not move. They were drained. The single lamp flickered once, then steadied.

"Storm somewhere," he said vaguely.

He leaned down to pet Ben again, but the cat was in Laura's lap, curled, licking its own fur.

"He likes you," Paul Fayette said. "You're the favorite."

"I feed him," Laura said. "Should we go up?".

"In a while."

Their words dropped, pebbles in a pond. Ripples went out.

"What would you have done?" she asked. "If we had never married?"

"Die."

"Seriously. I mean if we had never met?"

"How can I answer that?"

"You can't," she said. "I can't—if I had never met you. That's what I mean."

"I don't understand."

"Well . . ." she said, "it's all chance, isn't it? What we do, what we are. Isn't it chance, Paul? Accident?"

"I suppose," he said cautiously. "In a way."

"That's what I'm getting at," Laura said. "We have no control, do we?"

"Oh," he said, "I see. No. I guess we don't. Up to

a certain point—day-to-day things—but the big things are beyond our control."

"That's what I meant. Scary, isn't it?"

"Scary? No, it's—interesting. I mean—waiting. More brandy?"

"Please. And coffee."

"It's lukewarm."

"That's all right."

He served her, and himself. He slumped in his chair again, across the room from her. Separated. The cat had disappeared.

"Where's Ben?" he asked.

"Gone," she said. "Prowling somewhere. The kids are old enough to take care of themselves—aren't they, Paul?"

"I suppose. Why?"

"Just wondering."

"Do you want to fuck tonight?" he asked her desperately.

"No," she said. "Do you?"

"No," he said. "What's happening?"

"I don't know," she said. "Something's happening. Like my legs."

"Your legs?"

"You don't shave them anymore."

"I didn't know you needed it."

"Liar," she said sadly. "But that's not the worst of it."

"What's the worst of it?"

"I don't want you to," she said.

"Oh," he said, relieved.

"It's her," Laura said. "Isn't it?"

He reflected a moment.

"Yes," he said. "It's her."

She made a sound, rose from the chair. She came over to him, not steady, leaned down and embraced him. It was an awkward posture. He was yearning up to meet her lips. She was bending from the hips, trying to hug him. It didn't work. Their teeth clinked.

"Good years," she gasped.

"What?" he said. "Oh God, were they ever."

"Goodby," she said.

"Goodby?"

"I'm going up to bed."

"Oh," he said. "Yes, go along. I'll be up in a while."

"Paul . . ." she said.

"What?"

"Nothing."

She took her glass of brandy. She left the room. He watched Ben come out of the shadows, pad silently after her. The woman and the cat disappeared. Paul Fayette watched them go. He hoisted his glass.

"Hello, Beelzebub," he said aloud. *"Hello,* Satan."

The drapes had been thrown wide, windows opened. Afternoon sunlight came flooding in; the lumpy living room of the old Barstow place seemed almost cheerful.

"Damned good of you to come," Colonel Coulter sang out, bustling about. "Would have popped over to see you, padre, but the press of business, you know. Things to do, places to go, people to see. Been rushing around like a madman."

"Not at all, sir, not at all," the Reverend Timothy T. Aiken said genially. "I welcome this opportunity for a chat. Just a bit of water, please, and not too much ice."

"Of course, of course," Coulter said happily. "Exactly to my taste. We're two of a kind, we are."

He constructed the highballs carefully, brought one to the reverend, and stood by hopefully while he sampled it.

"All right?" the Colonel asked anxiously. "Not too much water? Too much ice?"

"Just what the doctor ordered," Aiken said benignly, tasting his lips. He sat back comfortably, crossed his legs. He was wearing a leisure suit of black alpaca, with a crimson sport shirt open at the throat. His snowy hair seemed elaborately coiffed; the stern, heavy features—somewhat pendulous—were almost cordovan-covered. "Excellent Scotch, sir, ex-cel-lent."

"Glad you like it," Coulter said. "Happy to hear it. Special brand, you know. Oh yes. I have a small interest in the distillery. In Perth, it is. Lovely spot. Get you a case if you like."

"Colonel, you're too kind."

"Not a bit of it! A man in your position needn't shun the good things in life. What? What?"

Aiken nodded benevolent agreement, sipping his just-right Scotch highball, at home in the world.

"Colonel," he boomed in his diapason voice, "I must tell you that your generous gift to the church has caused more problems than I anticipated. The members of the Board and I have already held several meetings on the subject, and it seems each individual has his own ideas on how best the fifty thousand dollars might be spent. For instance, it has been suggested we build a youth center, install a stained glass window, endow a small church in Zambia, and so forth. I had hoped to present you with a firm plan before this, but I trust you'll be patient awhile longer."

"No rush, no rush," Coulter said, waving a hand. "As a matter of fact, it's in regard to the money that I asked you to stop by."

"Oh?" said the Reverend Aiken, slightly uneasy. "No, ah, problem, is there? No, ah, temporary difficulty perhaps?"

"Aw no, no," the Colonel said laughing heartily. "Nothing like that. No problem at all. What I wanted—"

But then Mrs. Cheney came into the room, smiling brightly. Both men immediately rose to their feet.

She was wearing a short, pleated skirt of white silk, a middy blouse loosely tied with a light blue scarf. Knitted knee-length hose partly covered her bare legs. White sneakers. And a honey-blonde wig, long and full, concealed her dark hair.

"My dear," Timothy T. Aiken said, bending gallantly over her hand, "you look as fresh as a daisy today."

"Oh Reverend," Mrs. Cheney giggled, "how *sweet* of you. I just wanted to dress for the day; it's so lovely and sunny."

"Not as lovely or as sunny as you," the old man chortled, holding her hand. "You're a delight for these dim eyes."

"Another highball, sir?" the Colonel asked softly. "I see our glasses are empty."

"Well . . . perhaps one more. Will this beautiful child join us?"

"Oh, nothing for me," Mrs. Cheney protested. "You big men go on with your talk, and I'll just sit over here in the corner, and I promise to be quiet as a mouse and not say a word."

Coulter turned his back to mix two more drinks. Mrs. Cheney dropped sighing into a deep chair directly across the room from the Reverend Aiken. She drew up her feet prettily, sitting sideways. The short skirt pulled up over her bare, tanned knees. She cocked her head charmingly, began to wind a tendril of blonde wig slowly around a forefinger. She smiled at the reverend.

"As I was saying," Colonel Coulter said loudly, "about the gift . . . The reason I asked you to drop by, Timothy—may I call you Timothy?"

"My dear sir!" the reverend cried. "But of course you may. Delighted!"

"And may I call you Timothy, too?" Mrs. Cheney caroled innocently, then clapped a hand to her mouth. "Oops! I'm sorry. I promised not to say a word."

"Of course you can call me Timothy," the old man beamed. "I'd consider it an honor. And a pleasure."

Colonel Coulter glanced at his watch.

"Grief," he said, "it's getting on, and I must dash. What I wanted to say, Timothy, is that I wish to increase the amount of my gift. I've had a bit of a windfall, and can think of no better way to invest it than in the future of the church. So here you are—" He tugged a fat envelope with some difficulty from his inside jacket pocket. "—An additional fifty thousand. In cash."

Reverend Aiken jerked forward in his seat, mouth working.

"Colonel?" he said. "Fifty thousand more? Colonel?"

"Yes," Coulter said blithely. "In cash." He rose to thrust the envelope into the reverend's trembling hand. "But anonymously, you understand. Just between the three of us in this room. Our secret. I hope that's understood, Timothy?"

"A hundred thousand?" Aiken said, unbelieving.

"You and the Board discuss it. Decide what's the best thing to do. I'll abide by your decision. Yours in particular, Timothy. I trust you, you see. Have great faith in your judgment and good sense. As I said, we're two of a kind."

"It's so much," the reverend said, still stunned. He opened the envelope flap, ran this thumb over the edges of the crisp bills. "Such a great deal of money."

"It is indeed," Colonel Coulter said promptly. "Think of it—a hundred thousand dollars! What a man could do with that, eh? Change your entire life. Start a new life, for that matter. Interesting idea. A whole new life. Being born again. Starting over. Make your dreams come true. A man could do all that with a hundred thousand dollars. But why am I blathering on like this? It's not one man's money, of course. It belongs to the church, to further God's work on earth."

"Ah, yes," Aiken nodded vigorously. "To be sure. Exactly. And may His blessings be granted to you and yours, Colonel, for this splendid testament to your faith and love."

"I thank you," Coulter said, looking at his watch again. "Well, I really must run. Please stay, Timothy, as long as you like. Diane, entertain the padre like a good girl, will you?"

"Of course I will," Mrs. Cheney said.

The Colonel rose, and Aiken stood up with him.

The two men shook hands warmly. Then suddenly the reverend embraced Coulter. They hugged.

"God bless," Aiken said throatily. "God bless."

The Colonel left the room, dabbing at his eyes with the end of his paisley ascot.

The Reverend Aiken took out a pocket handkerchief. He blew his nose thunderously. Then he walked to the table where the bottles were set out. He poured a generous Scotch.

"Something for you, my dear?" he asked hoarsely, looking toward Mrs. Cheney.

She shook her head, blonde curls swinging.

The old man sat down heavily again.

"Your father is a remarkable man," he said. "Remarkable."

"He surely is," Mrs. Cheney said.

She uncoiled lithely from her chair. She trotted over to stand before the reverend. Her feet were apart, her hands clasped behind her. She swung back and forth from the waist, twisting.

"You need some ice, Timothy," she said. "Let me get it for you."

She brought two cubes from the ice bucket, plopped them into his drink.

"Excuse my fingers," she giggled.

He caught up her hand, kissed the wet fingertips.

"Any time, my child," he said feelingly. "What a delight you are! Ah youth, youth!"

She stood close to him, stroked his white waves softly.

"What beautiful hair you have," she said. "Just beautiful!"

"Well, I . . ."

Her warm hand fell to the nape of his neck.

"I do like older men," she said dreamily. "I really do. They're sooo understanding."

"Ah well," he said, "we have lived and, hopefully, learned a little about life. No drink for you, dear girl? Nothing at all?"

"Well . . ." She considered, pouting sweetly, then

biting her underlip. "Maybe I'll just have a teensy-weensy sip of yours."

"Of course," he said eagerly, "Of course," and he held the glass to her lips as she bent over.

"Ooh!" she breathed. "That tastes so good."

"More," he urged. "Have more!"

"Well, maybe just a wee bit. You don't want me to get silly, do you?"

"Of course not," he said, showing his gleaming plates. "Of course not, dear girl. Sweetums."

She held the glass with both palms, like a child, and drank deeply. His arm hung over the side of his chair. His hand dangled. His fingers touched her calf lightly, the stockinged calf. Then moved up to stroke the satin backs of her bare knees.

"Goody?" he asked in a strangled voice. "Tastes goody?"

"Marvy," she said. "Just marvy."

"Why don't we share it?" he suggested. "A sip for you, and a sip for me."

"That's nice," she sighed. She handed him the glass. "Let me sit in your lap. Okay, daddy?"

"Okay," he chuckled. "My, my, yes, okay. A-okay. Oh my."

She slid softly onto his lap.

"Not too heavy, am I, daddy?"

"No, no," he said, writhing. "Just right. Just fine. Now . . . a sip for you, a sip for me . . ."

She squirmed about, and the old man clamped a shaking arm around her boneless waist. They traded the drink, back and forth. Then, after a while, they both tried to drink at the same time, giggling. Aiken's face grew redder and redder.

"Isn't this awful?" Mrs. Cheney whispered. "What we're doing?"

But the Reverend Timothy T. Aiken could only grunt. One hand was beneath the pleated skirt. One hand caressed the long blonde wig. And he just didn't care.

"Daddy," Mrs. Cheney moaned. "Ooh, daddy."

Printed on the Oiija board were numbers from one to ten, letters of the alphabet. "Yes," "No," and "Good Bye."

"If we're really going to get messages from outer space," Stahl said, "why in hell doesn't it say, 'Hello'?"

"Clint," his wife said, "if you're just going to make jokes about it, I don't want to work it with you. The directions say that if you poke fun at it, you get "underdeveloped influences.' That means the spirits won't speak."

"How much did you pay for this thing?" he demanded.

"Laura bought it," Paul Fayette said. "Five bucks."

"Oh God," Stahl groaned, "that's a bottle of vodka. And speaking of vodka . . ." He held up his empty glass.

"Get your own," Laura Fayette said crossly. "I made the first round; my duties as a hostess are over. All the fixings are in the kitchen. Help yourself."

"You, Paul?"

"Sure, I'm ready."

Stahl took their glasses into the Fayettes' kitchen. The others, sitting around a bridge table in the family room, read again the instructions on the back of the carton.

"Best results are obtained with two people facing each other," Laura recited. "Lady and gentleman preferred."

"That lets Clint out," Margaret Stahl said. "Why don't you and Paul give it a try?"

He slid the Indicator around on the board, peering through the little round window.

"All right," he said. "Come on, Laura, let's see if we can get a message from the Great Beyond."

Clint came in with the vodka martinis.

"Any bets that the first message received won't be 'Fuck you'? Don't tell me you adult-type people believe this crap?"

Margaret said, "Babs Feldman said the Ouija board told her where she left her cigarette lighter."

"Did it tell her where she left her husband last Thursday night?" Clint asked. "I know, but I ain't telling."

"Come on, Paul," Laura urged, "put your fingertips on the Indicator."

They sat opposite each other, leaning forward. They placed their fingers lightly on the planchette.

"Now what?" Paul said.

"Ask a question," his wife said nervously.

"*You* ask a question," he said.

"Paul hasn't got any questions," Stahl said. "He knows all the answers."

"All right," Laura said, "I'll ask a question: What color is the new dress I bought?"

"Oh for God's sake," Margaret said. "That's not the way to do it. Everyone knows that stupid dress is white. You're supposed to ask a question you don't know the answer to."

"All right, all right," Laura said. "Is Christine going to get married this year? Is that a good question?"

"That's more like it," Margaret said. "Now you must wait a few minutes until the answer comes back."

They waited, staring at the board. The Fayettes' fingers were motionless on the Indicator.

"Come on, you mother, *move*." Clint said.

As if in reply to his exhortation, the planchette began to slide slowly about the board.

"Paul, you're pushing it," Laura said.

"I'm not. I swear I'm not."

"Well, I know *I'm* not."

The Indicator moved faster and faster, then stopped. Through the little window they could see the word "No."

"Thank God for that," Clint Stahl said. "No wedding gift to buy this year."

Laura sat staring at the board. She raised her head to look at Paul.

"Are you sure you didn't push it?" she asked suspiciously.

"Oh for God's sake, Laura, I already told you I didn't. Now ask it if Brian is going to get married this year."

Laura did, and they waited a few moments. Then the Indicator started, stopped, started, stopped . . . It spelled out BPLXFGT.

"Good heavens," Clint Stahl said, "Brian is going to marry Gertrude Bplxfgt. Who'd have thought they had anything in common? I'm going to build another drink. Anyone else ready?"

The ladies handed him their empty glasses. Then the Fayettes bent over the Ouija board again.

"I'm going to ask a question," Paul said, "but I'm not going to tell you what it is. I'm just going to think it."

They waited in silence for what seemed like five minutes. Clint came back with the drinks.

"What's the question?" he wanted to know.

"Paul won't tell us," his wife said. "He's thinking it."

"I'll bet ten dollars the board says, 'Good Bye.' "

But the Indicator began to move slowly. It stopped over letters, then moved on. It had spelled out C-H-E, when suddenly it jerked onto the numbers and began sliding back and forth.

"I thought it was working there for a minute," Margaret said. "It spelled C-H-E."

"Cheney?" Laura asked, looking at Paul. "Was your question about Diane?"

"No," he said quickly, "I was testing the board. I asked what poster hangs over the bed in Christine's room. It's Che Guevara."

"My God," Margaret said. "Well, the spirits got the first part right."

"Yes," Paul said. "I need a drink. Clint, take my place."

"Not me, old buddy. The only spirits I want to commune with are ninety proof."

"Let me try it," Margaret said. "There are a lot of

questions I want the answers to. Like where is our next mortgage payment coming from?"

"Isn't she sweet?" Clint said. "My wife—I'd take her anywhere. Once!"

"Oh shut up," Margaret said angrily. "Get pissy-assed drunk if you want to, but just keep your mouth shut."

The two women worked the board. Margaret asked, "Will I meet a tall, dark, handsome man?" The Indicator moved about, then stopped over "No."

"Now ask the spirits if you'll meet a tall, dark, handsome woman," Clint Stahl said.

His wife whirled, glared at him.

"What's that crack supposed to mean?" she demanded.

"Our little secret, honey," he smiled coldly. "Why look, I must have a hole in my glass."

He wondered off to the kitchen.

"He's got a hole in his head," Margaret grumbled. "Ask the board a question, Laura."

"I'm going to try what Paul did," Laura said. "I'm going to think a question. Now concentrate . . ."

They waited, fingertips on the planchette. It began to slide slowly. It spelled out C-H-E, then jerked wildly about the board.

"That poster again?" Margaret said softly, looking at Laura.

In the kitchen, Paul leaned against the sink, smoking a cigarette. He watched Stahl splash a martini together, lift it with a shaking hand, drain it off.

"Why don't you take it easy, Clint?"

"Why don't you go fuck yourself, Paul?"

Fayette sighed. "All right, go ahead. Drink yourself to death."

"Quicker ways than that," Stahl said. He glanced around, picked up a long chef's knife from the cutting board. He began waving it about. "How's this? Make my quietus with a bare bodkin."

"Don't be a goddamned fool. And put the knife down."

"I could do it," Stahl said. "I really could. Look . . ." He held the knife edge at his throat. "One quick slash. You could never stop me. Where would you put the tourniquet—on my neck?"

"Clint, will you—"

"Maybe my wrist," Stahl said, holding the sharp edge to his bared wrist. "Press and draw. Make a hell of a mess on your linoleum."

"I don't like this talk. Make yourself another drink, and let's go back—"

"To the spirits," Stahl said. "Let's go back to the spirits. C-H-E. That was quick thinking, old buddy."

"I don't know what you're talking about."

Stahl tossed the knife back on the counter. It slid, clattered to the floor. Fayette picked it up, put it into a drawer.

"Want me to tell you what I'm talking about?" Stahl asked.

"No."

Paul went back into the family room. In a moment Stahl came lurching after him. He was holding a half-full quart of vodka by the neck, drinking out of the bottle.

Margaret stood up. "I better get him home."

"Home!" Stahl shouted. "Great idea! I'm going home!"

He stumbled drunkenly toward the hallway, still carrying the bottle. Fayette grabbed for him, but Stahl twisted away. He ran giggling down the hall to the entrance.

"Let him go," Margaret called. "I have the car keys."

Stahl banged open the outer door. He rushed out into the night. Fayette stood in the open doorway, watched him go. Then he closed the door, came back inside.

"Maybe I better go after him," he told the women. "He's liable to get in trouble."

"Let him go," Margaret repeated coldly. "A night in jail would do him good."

"I'll put some coffee on," Laura said. "He might come back."

But then they heard a car start, the squeal of tires. All three hurried to the front windows. They saw the Stahls' white Buick accelerated down Chancery Lane, take a screaming turn, and disappear.

"Oh my God," Margaret said. "The son of a bitch must have taken the keys from my purse."

"Paul, he shouldn't be driving," Laura said. "He'll kill himself, or someone else. Go after him. Please."

Fayette got his car keys and went out to the garage. He backed out, turned slowly into Chancery Lane. He knew exactly where to go.

The white Buick was parked crazily on the lawn of the old Barstow place. The driver's door was open. The car was vacant, the empty vodka bottle discarded on the grass. Fayette parked across the street, in the shadows, and killed his lights. He sat there a long time, smoking three cigarettes. The lights were on downstairs in Mrs. Cheney's home. Fayette thought the lights might go out, but they didn't.

He drove home slowly. The women were waiting anxiously in the entrance hall.

"Couldn't find him," he reported. "I checked your home, Margaret, but he's not there."

Margaret burst into tears. Laura put her arm about her, led her back to the kitchen.

"Coffee, Margaret. Sit down and have a cup of hot coffee. Paul, do you think we should call the police?"

"No," he said. "I don't think that's necessary. Maybe he just went for a drive. Maybe he's parked somewhere, sleeping it off. He'll be back tomorrow morning with a bad case of the guilts."

"You really think so, Paul?" Margaret said tearfully.

"Sure."

"Oh God," she said in a low voice, "I don't know what I'm going to do."

"Margaret," Laura said, "why don't you stay here

tonight? Sleep over. I don't think you should be alone. Paul, don't you think that would be best?"

"Aren't the kids home?"

"No," Margaret said, "they're at camp and visiting."

"That settles it," Fayette said. "You stay here. We have plenty of room. He may come back here. Or if he gets into trouble, he'll call here first. I'll drive you home in the morning."

"Sleep with me," Laura said, her arm about Margaret's shoulders. "Paul can use the guest room. All right, Paul?"

"Of course."

"It's only for one night," his wife said.

Paul lay naked on the hard bed in the guest room, wide awake staring out at the moonlit night. After a while, he rose, pulled on a robe, went paddling barefoot down the hall. He paused outside the closed door of the master bedroom. He put his ear close to the panels. He could hear nothing.

He went downstairs as quietly as he could. He put on a corner lamp in the family room. He sat down at the bridge table. He placed his fingertips on the Indicator on the Ouija board. He whispered his question. The planchette began to move. . . .

6

Supersaturated air closed them around, a gray smoke. Droplets gathered and ran down the hood and fenders of the white Buick. Inside, it was damply cool; the air conditioner had been going full blast until they parked. But the air coming through the slightly opened windows was moistly hot, clinging. It smelled of the woods about them, of jelly earth, fern rot. A steamy place of reaching vines, barbed creepers, roots beneath and swamp around. The sun was blocked.

Mrs. Stahl and Mrs. Cheney slumped in the front seats, Margaret behind the wheel. They thrust out long legs. They lighted cigarettes. Margaret held the lighter.

She told Mrs. Cheney what had happened at the Fayettes.

"That was last Friday," she said. "Clint came home on Saturday morning like Paul said he would."

"Did he say where he had been?"

"No."

"Did you ask?"

"No, I don't care anymore. Diane, I've made up my mind; I've got to get away from him."

"Did you talk to Dr. Terhune about this?"

A short, harsh laugh. "Terhune? I gave him up weeks ago, when Clint lost his job. It's the groceries I'm worried about now."

"If you leave him, how will you live?"

"I 'don't know; I haven't even thought about it.

First things first. I suppose my father would help out. He hasn't got much, but he'd do what he could. I know he would."

"What about the children?"

Margaret leaned forward to stub out her cigarette.

"Oh God, Diane, I need answers, not more questions."

Mrs. Cheney continued smoking slowly when Margaret leaned toward her.

"There's a snap behind the top button," she said.

"Yes, all right," Margaret said nervously, fumbling. "I'll get it . . . There . . ."

"Slowly."

"Yes, dear, I will."

"Margaret, I think you have two problems, personal and financial, all mixed up together."

"That's right. Diane, this is beautiful. New?"

"Yes, do you like it?"

"Gorgeous. The lace is so fine."

"Alencon. It unhooks in front. Put out my cigarette like a dear."

Mrs. Cheney settled back, took a deep breath, lifted her chin.

"Oh," Margaret breathed. "Oh, Diane . . ."

"Your fingers are so hot."

"But knowing my problems are, one, personal, and two, financial, doesn't solve anything."

"Oh, I don't know," Mrs. Cheney said dreamily. "Maybe. Perhaps I can help."

"How? What? Anything!"

"Not me personally, but I could talk to the Colonel."

"How could he help? Do you like this?"

"Love it. But just a bit slower. The Colonel has so many things going. All over the world. He's always looking for new people to help out. Talented people."

"That lets me out," Margaret said. "I can't type, and I'm no good with figures, or anything like that. I'm not very talented."

"Oh, I don't know," Mrs. Cheney said lazily.

"You're anxious, eager to learn. The Colonel could teach you."

"Oh, God, I'd work my ass off."

"Well, that might be necessary. All right, dear, a little lower now."

"Like this?"

"Very good. You're a quick learner. Shall I talk to the Colonel then?"

"Would you? Please? I'll do anything. It's so steamy in here."

"Yes, isn't it wonderful? Like we're floating. Oh yes, do that again. That's your own idea, isn't it?"

"Yes. Good?"

"Marvelous. Yes, I think the Colonel could find a job for you. You wouldn't mind traveling, would you?"

"I'd love to travel. Could you lift up a bit? No use getting it wrinkled. There . . . that's better."

"Light me another cigarette," Mrs. Cheney commanded.

Gray fog came swirling in. Far off, they heard traffic sounds on the highway, and once the thunder of a plane passing low overhead. But they were in their own world, shut away. Their scent hung in the closed space, a still coffin for two.

"Wait a few minutes," Mrs. Cheney said, "then begin again."

She put her head back, closed her eyes. She smoked slowly.

"All right," she murmured finally. "You can begin again. Yes, there. You remember what I taught you?"

Margaret made a sound deep in her throat.

"This job," Mrs. Cheney said, "with the Colonel . . . it may involve very confidential work. Top secret. You can keep your mouth shut, can't you?"

Margaret raised her head.

"Of course," she said. "If the man's going to give me a job and save my life, I'll be loyal. He can depend on that."

"Yes," Mrs. Cheney said, "that's what I thought. Are you getting out, dear? Forgetting your worries?"

"Am I ever! Am I going too fast?"

"No, but we have all afternoon. Perhaps we should get in the back seat?"

"Not now, please, Diane. Later maybe. I don't want to stop now."

"All right, greedy," Mrs. Cheney laughed, opening her eyes. "Don't stop then. But put my cigarette out first."

Margaret stabbed out the cigarette butt quickly, turned back.

Mrs. Cheney stared at the fogged window. Her eyelids fluttered.

"You're getting good," she whispered. "Very, very good."

"I'm not hurting you, am I?" Margaret asked anxiously.

"Of course not, silly. And what if you were? Deeper, dear. Go deeper."

"Like this?"

"Just like that. Oh, yes. Now do what I showed you. That's it, that's it . . ."

She looked down at Margaret's head. She patted the wig of tight blonde curls Margaret was wearing.

"It's a whole new language, isn't it, dear?"

The head bobbed once.

"I tried to tell Paul Fayette," Mrs. Cheney said thoughtfully. "Some of it. I don't think he believed me. He'll learn."

She stretched out her arms, smiling, listening to Margaret's sobs.

They had become strangers, speaking to each other savagely and with suspicion. Neither knew the cause of their discord: neither had the will to search. But both grew grumpier; hostile silences lengthened. Ben had something to do with it.

The cat, stealthy and aloof, moved about the house like the first owner. Paul resented him, Laura did not. Both had an incomprehensible perception: the cat grew silkier as their marriage grew tawdrier. Ben was long, limpid, smooth as a leg. How he prowled! Upstairs, downstairs. Scraping against edges with a purr, stretching his beauty with a yawn. Accepting a caress or scorning a stroke, according to his mood. Black as night, shiny as rain, he lurked, hid, pounced, or strolled out coolly, hips swinging.

"Please," Paul said, "keep him out of the bed, at least."

But Laura would not. Paul, finding his excuse, moved into the guest room, bringing along his toilet articles, then more and more of his clothes. There was unspoken agreement that the move was permanent; they slept in separate beds with two locked doors and a long hallway between them.

No more the shared breakfast at the start of the day, a shared drink at the close. They looked on each other with chilly indifference, wondered what had kept them together so long, and decided it was merely habit, damnable habit. Now they were fettered, and to each a vision of life alone, free, seemed less grim with each passing day.

"Do you want to go away?" he asked her.

"Go away? Where?"

"Anywhere. A trip. A vacation."

"No," she said. "I want to stay here."

"Suit yourself," he said, and began planning how he might transfer funds from their joint checking account to one in his name only.

They did an excessive amount of entertaining, at home and at the club. In the presence of friends, they treated each other with glacial politeness and used such terms as "Dear" and "Darling," thinking thereby to maintain their image of the loving Fayettes. They did not catch the puzzled glances, the whispers exchanged. Everyone agreed: something was happening to the loving Fayettes. What was happening?

They had known each other for more than a year before they were married. Dissolution was speedier; estrangement accelerated. She saw his weak chin, faded hair, effete manner. He saw her thick waist, thumping stride, a coarseness of feature he had never noted before. They looked for imperfections, and they found them.

The word "divorce" was never uttered, but each found it increasingly easier to face the possibility. There was an emptiness now in their life together, a lack. They had glimpsed something more intense. They had each found an unknown capacity. It had charged their lives. Beside it, habit, damnable habit, left them insensate brutes.

"Do you want to go to the club tonight?" he asked her.

"No. You go if you want to."

"All right."

Or . . .

"I'm going for a drive," she told him.

"All right," he said, not looking up from his book.

"I'll be late getting back."

"All right."

Or . . .

"I'll be working late tonight," he said. "If it's very late, I'll stay in the city."

"All right."

They lived within themselves, sharing only a roof and a cat. And waited, disinterested, while the blood of their marriage ran out.

It burst. The whole thing burst.

Clint Stahl thought he could contain it, hold it in. The booze helped, and the corrosive wit. But in the end they weren't enough, and he knew who he was. Worse, his shameful needs seemed to him clownish. The world saw his fright wig, bulbous nose, baggy pants. People snickered at him: a man without dignity. He could not endure that: the scoffer scoffed.

When the explosion came, he was not unusually drunk or abnormally despairing. It was, for him, an ordinary night, and nothing triggered his outburst but that: the realization that this dead night was routine;

there was nothing in his future but a silent parade of
similar empty nights.

Resolve came not from a hot flush of courage, but
from cold desperation. He felt the need to act, not
caring what he might do. It would be something dumb
—he was convinced of that—but the need to do something, *anything,* to regain control of his own destiny
was overwhelming. He could no longer be a victim.

"I can no longer be a victim," he said aloud, and it
sounded so melodramatic that he laughed gleefully,
wondering from what old movie that line came.

He drove aimlessly through the drizzle for almost an
hour, drinking steadily from a bottle of Scotch. He
held it with one hand on the empty seat beside him.
He was aware of passing the homes of friends and acquaintances in Penlow Park. Passing the church, the
fire station. All the places he knew. Passing, even, his
own home. The windows in Margaret's bedroom were
lighted, but he didn't want to think about that.

It was almost two in the morning when he parked
at the foot of the hill. He looked up at the old Barstow
place. At first he thought all the lights were out. Then,
on the upper floor, he thought he saw a flickering
glow. No brighter than a candle flame. He rolled down
the window. Rain came misting in. He peered,
squinching his eyes. The light behind the drawn shade
was reddish, and it was fluttering.

He wiped his wet face with his palm and stared,
stared, trying to make it out. A dark figure passed behind the shade. A brighter light, also flickering. Like a
religious procession. Flaming candles, and beyond a
stronger blaze. Everything moving, wavering: crimson
and pink, black smoke and drifting shadows.

He stumbled from the car, leaving the door open.
He struggled up the wet lawn, slipping, sliding, falling
once to his knees. There he rested, shaking his head
like a wounded beast. Rose to his feet again. Lurched
up to the house. Stood swaying beneath that lighted
window.

His first impression had been correct; there was a

fire burning in the room, on this hot, muggy July night. And the occupants of the room, more than one, passed back and forth behind the shade, holding candle flames aloft.

Stahl went fumbling around the ground floor, rattling doors and windows. In the rear, at the kitchen door, infuriated by the lock, he clenched his fist and smashed through one of the small panes of glass. Then reached in and turned the key, feeling it slip in his bloodied fingers. He wiped the slashed hand on his shirtfront, but a trail of red bubbles followed him across the kitchen, down the hallway to the staircase. He paused and listened, the bannister becoming slick under his dripping hand.

He heard the beat of a drum. He thought the pounding was in him. But the deep thumping became clearer as he mounted the stairs. He heard muffled cries now, yelps of triumph, a harsh braying. And a curious wailing whistle that rose and fell, a keening that kept rhythm with the hollow boom of the drum. Fast, faster, came wail and drumbeat, rising to a louder crescendo. With animal sounds: barks and whines, snorts and bellows.

He staggered down the darkened hallway, propping himself with gory hand against the wall, leaving a long, wavering smear. He stood swaying outside the closed door, head lowered. Drum and whistle were deafening now, vibrating walls, ceiling, floor. And the animal sounds had become grunts and whimpers. He fell against the door, turned the knob with blood-wet hand, pushed in.

Fireplace roaring. A dozen candles guttering. Set now in twisted iron holders. The heat of the room struck him like a blow. Everything swimming, floating.

He saw a tape unreeling, heard the shattering pound of drum, the cutting whistle wail. Sound pulsed in this secret room as if the air itself was alive. Sound beat like flame, the true fire dancing in time.

And the two naked bodies: white woman, black man. Bodies gleaming with sweat, rubbed raw and bitten. Both wearing masks. Rough hair and animal features: pig snout, boar tusks, dog ears, cat eyes. False teeth slick, wet tongues lolling, stained nostrils stretched, necks arched.

The white woman bent, hands on knees, spine curved, beast head up and grinning, her long slender legs spread wide. Behind her, tight to her, the black man bucked deep, hands splayed, tearing slimed buttocks open, ebony loins driving. His animal head was down, shaking its mane from side to side.

Deep, guttural cries came from these two in rut, and grunts of lust, moans of anguish and love screams of sharp delight. They plunged about, masks wagging, shiny skin catching the fire's red glow, the candles' flicker.

Stahl fell into the room, smelling the heat, smoke, the bodies' spermish stink, and something else. Something that stung his eyes and seared his throat. He made one loud, fevered cry. He rushed at them, catching up an iron candlestick in his blood-oiled hand.

Then he was on them, flailing the two-backed beast with all his strength, hearing bones crack, seeing the spurt of red. It hung in the heated air like a mist, a rain of blood. And when they reached up to stop him, he beat them down, crushing, pounding, stained iron rising and falling.

The three went lurching about, candles overturned, flames dying, then spurting. Curtains caught. The scented wood in the fireplace was scattered onto the rug. Then the entire room was aflame, three blazes that jerked about, cries lost in the fire's roar, everything burning bright, the snap of blackening wood drowning drum boom and whistle wail, until the only sound that could be heard was the flames' crackle, and the three sank down, melted down, all in a heap, intertwined, masks flaring up then glowing down, real hair catching and going, Stahl's clothing burned away, naked flesh crisping, eyes cooked, tongues fried, the room a rumbling holocaust, floor, walls, ceiling blue and billowing, then bright as the sun, the house itself beginning to shudder, groan, crack. And finally, the drum stopped, the whistle faded out, flames engulfed all, and when the outer wall was breached, the faint rain came hissing in. . . .

Paul Fayette had always enjoyed heavy, satisfying sleep—until about a month ago when his sleep became thin, fretful, thronged with vague anxiety dreams he could not remember when he awoke. Previously, he had always looked forward to a good night's sleep with anticipation and gratefulness. Now the suspension of consciousness filled him with dread. He was beginning to resist sleep; he didn't know what might happen.

He had tried heavy drinking and pills. They solved the problem of insomnia, but didn't make his sleep any more restful or fulfilling. And they resulted in morning-after headaches and nausea. So he went undrugged to bed each night in the great room and tried to calm his churning thoughts, tried counting backward from a hundred, tried self-hypnosis, tried anything to relax, to forget, to drift off to a deep and dreamless slumber. Nothing worked; his sleep continued to be a tenuous doze: tossing and turning, punching the pillow, sudden moans and weak cries that brought him wide awake and trembling.

On this night he was drifting in a light and bitter sleep, conscious of all the noises of the dark, when he was alerted by the distinctive scream of Penlow Park police sirens and the hoot of fire-engine buffalo whistles. They seemed unusually loud, and he tensed, fearing they might growl to a halt outside his home. But they wailed on past. He wondered what was happening, and where. He glanced at the illuminated dial of the digital clock. It was after 3:00 a.m. He sighed, rolled over, closed his eyes determinedly.

But that was not the end of it. He heard more sirens, more whistles. These sounds he could not identify as belonging to Penlow Park police or fire vehicles.

Then, after while, all these interruptions seemed to be ended. He dozed, grinding his teeth.

He came awake again when he heard the telephone ringing. Heard it dimly because there was no extension in the guest room; the nearest phone was in Brian's room, next door. Paul slid out of bed, bemused to realize he had a stiff erection. He pulled on a robe, clutching it loosely about him. He unlocked the door, then stopped, suddenly aware that the ringing had ceased. Either the caller had given up or Laura had answered on the phone in the master bedroom. Paul went back to sit on the edge of the bed. He lighted a cigarette. He bent forward, elbows on knees. He smoked slowly, eyes closed, thinking of nothing.

He heard Laura running down the hallway. A hard rap on the door.

"Paul! Paul!"

"Come in. It's open."

She stood, riven. She was wearing one of the maidenly nightgowns she had recently affected: all eyelet cotton, pink ribbons and bows.

"Paul, it was Margaret. The police are there. They want her to go to the Barstow place, to Diane Cheney's. It's burned down. Margaret was hysterical. I don't understand. Their car is parked there. Someone's dead."

He wasn't surprised.

"All right," he said. "I'll get dressed."

They weren't the only ones standing silent and bewildered at the foot of the hill. Others had gathered, drawn by the fire, the sirens, the searchlights of police and fire vehicles from Penlow Park and surrounding suburbs. Men and women huddled in the drizzle, wrapped in raincoats thrown over pajamas and nightgowns. Some were barefoot. All stared dazedly upward at the smoking shell.

The brick chimney still stood, blackened and steaming. And the ground level wall in the rear was intact. But all the rest was gone, crumpled in on itself, a sodden mass of rubble, still snapping occasionally, shifting, falling. The steel mist fell steadily, shining on the firemen's helmets and the cops' black slickers, fizzing on hot metal and charred timbers. The searchlights were all focused upward, crisscrossing; the wreck shone dismally in lemon light.

"Yes, it's our car," Margaret Stahl said over and over. "Yes, it is. No, I don't know what it's doing here. No, I don't. Where is Clint? Has anyone seen Clint? Has anything happened to Clint?"

Chief Michael Bird of the Penlow Park Police Department looked about helplessly. He saw Laura Fayette, motioned to her. Laura went swiftly, put her arm about Margaret's shoulders, led her away. Both women were sobbing.

"What is it?" Paul Fayette asked.

"We got three bodies," Chief Bird told him. "Two men and a woman."

"Is one of the men Clint Stahl?"

The Chief shrugged. "Who knows? They all look like unwrapped mummies. Shrunken—you know? What a mess. Cinders. You know who Stahl's dentist is?"

"I can find out."

"Would you? Thanks. Let me know. What a mess."

Chief Bird stalked back up the hill to the ruins. Paul stood, hands in raincoat pockets. His fine hair was plastered wet to his skull. His slippered feet were soaked. But he was aware only of that smouldering shell atop the hill. Three bodies. Unwrapped mummies. Cinders.

A uniformed cop, young, earnest, began urging people gently to return to their homes. They started moving away slowly, looking back over his shoulders.

"Nothing to see, folks. It's all over. Go home and get some sleep. It's finished. Good-night, folks."

But Paul didn't move. He watched the firemen rolling up their hose lines, watched three canvas bags being loaded into a waiting ambulance, watched men poking about the debris moving cautiously, clambering over snapped beams and broken walls.

"Paul," Laura said.

"What?"

"I'll take Margaret home. To her place. I'll stay over with her."

"All right."

"Was it Clint?"

"I don't know. They don't know. Probably."

"And Diane?"

"I don't know," he shouted furiously. "God damn it, I don't know!"

Shaken, she stared at him, then moved away. He was conscious of her leaving with Margaret. But still he stood, staring up the hill, waiting to feel something.

Chief Michael Bird came down to him slowly.

"A wild one, Mr. Fayette," he said, shaking his head. "We found bones and tusks. Big animal teeth. Stuff like that. Near the bodies. I don't get it."

"I don't know," Paul said dully.

The Chief looked at him queerly, then walked off, still shaking his head.

Paul stood there rooted, while the pumpers and ladder trucks retrieved their equipment, loaded their crews, pulled away with a low growl of sirens. Finally, finally, there was a single policeman ·left on duty, walking around and around the destruction.

Then, suddenly, to one side, almost hidden in the heavier darkness of a drooping copse of maples, Paul saw a short, chunky figure standing motionless. He walked up slowly to Colonel Benjamin G. Coulter. The Colonel was wearing a fawn poplin raincoat— and a brown bowler set squarely atop his massive head. The hat glistened with moisture. Coulter lifted it gravely as Paul came up.

Paul stopped close. The two men looked at each other. They shook hands solemnly.

"Colonel," Paul said in a low voice, "my condolences on your loss."

Still holding Paul's hand, Coulter reached out with his left hand to grip Fayette's arm and squeeze it.

"Aw, yes," he said. "Thank you. She was one of the best."

"And Jacque? It was Jacque, wasn't it?"

"Yes. It was."

The Colonel dropped his hands, thrust them into his raincoat pockets. Paul put his hands away, too. Together, they stood there under the dripping trees, staring again at the demolished home on the hilltop. The slickered police guard made his slow rounds. Wisps of smoke struggled up into the misty night air. They could smell the scorch, and the ash.

"Will you be staying on in Penlow Park, Colonel?" Paul asked finally.

The Colonel turned his head. Paul turned. They looked into each other's eyes again. It seemed to Paul that even in the darkness he could see the focus of Coulter's stare change. It grew more intense, blacker, until the Colonel wasn't looking at him at all, but was looking into him, through him, beyond, at something or somewhere else.

"Stay in Penlow Park?" Colonel Coulter said. "No. I'm finished here."

The fiery destruction of the old Barstow place, and the deaths of Mrs. Cheney, Jacques and Clint Stahl, provided conversation enough in Penlow Park for the next several days. In fact, the story was featured in New York City newspapers under such headlines as "What Happened?" and "Destroyed Mansion Said to Be Haunted." A TV crew came up from the city to film the ruins.

But within a week the puzzle had lost its fascination. Penlow Parkers went away on summer vacations. Children departed for camp. People returned with peeling sunburns. Outdoor barbecues were held. The Friday evening dances at the country club were well-attended. It was said that Babs Feldman and the waiter Carlos were discovered fornicating at midnight on the tennis court.

"Love game," someone said.

The main topic of conversation became the anonymous gift of a hundred thousand dollars to the First
Presbyterian Church, and what should be done with
it.

Paul Fayette moved through this period as in someone else's dream. He was at once participant and
observer, listening to the clatter of life, hearing, seeing, smelling, but detached. He was outside himself,
peering down on Paul Fayette and watching the alien
creature function with the same wonderment he might
bestow on a caged tiger in a zoo or a bewildered fly
caught between screen and window.

He began to have deep, deep thoughts about fantasy and reality. He remembered the perplexing things
Mrs. Cheney had said about sex as physical imagination. The whole body an organ of creation. Sex as a
special means of communication. Sex transcending normal boundaries. He wondered if she had told the same
things to Clint Stahl, and if Clint had believed.

He began to see life in Penlow Park not so much
as a dream, not a charade, but as theatre, a dramatic
production. All knew their roles and recited their
lines. Some better than others. But all responding to
cues, moving about in rehearsed patterns, trying not to
bump furniture or drop a prop.

And beyond all this, hidden by curtain and sets,
was the machinery of the stage: lights and flies, ropes
and rafters, a big, echoing place that could never be
shown. Because . . . well, because it was of no interest
to anyone. Nothing was there, backstage. There, at
night, the audience gone, a man might howl, and no
one would hear his pain or see his anguish.

He knew such thoughts were reaction to Clint Stahl's
death. Depression. There was enough of Clint in him
that the poor bastard's frightful end clamped a cold
fist of fear around his heart. At times he wondered
what, exactly, had happened. But then his thoughts
slid away, simply veered off to something else: the
identity of Colonel Coulter or his growing alienation
from Laura. Anything to keep from reflecting on Clint

and Mrs. Cheney. Stahl's entrapment. That was how
Paul saw it: entrapment. Perhaps in that same black
closet among the musty winter garments and damp
rubber overshoes.

He was well free of her, Paul assured himself. Oh
yes, he had been the lucky one. It was over now.
Finished. And yet . . .

At night, sleepless on the hard bed in the guest
room, his thoughts, swerving from the tragedy, settled
on her. Mrs. Diane Cheney. He felt again those
supple thighs (squeezed from tubes, were they?),
smelled her heat, tasted the salty liquor of sweated
lips. Her body was real to him; he heard the gasps.
He felt the damp friction, knew again the harsh
scrape and punishment release.

But more than the erotic details of that coffined
love, he relived his own splendid role: the master, the
sexual vandal, the Hun. He wondered that it had
come so easily, so pleasurably, this foreign language.
Just as an untrained child might suddenly babble ancient Greek, so he had magically become the wanton
despoiler as if he had been practiced to the part. It
lifted him, that moment. He soared. And what had
she said? Such things as: "Don't hurt me. Please
don't. You're driving me crazy. Oh, what a lover you
are. I can't hold back. I can't stop." And: "Love me!
Love me!" This last in piteous pleading, unable to
resist his strength, surrendering to his force, overcome
and raped.

Head whipping side to side on his sodden pillow,
he remembered, heard it all again—and she came to
him. He saw her! It was not memory, nor dream, nor
hallucination. It was Mrs. Cheney, returned.

He stared, spreadeagled naked on rumpled sheets,
and saw white curtains suddenly flutter inward on a
windless night. He watched, breathless, as she, wraith-
like, appeared. Not in swirls of fog or billows of
smoke as some fictional ghost. But taking form
slowly, almost timidly, as if she was resisting this

transmutation, feared it, but was compelled by a force she could not resist.

She coalesced before his eyes. The scene, wavering waterily, was a sheet of blank photographic paper floating in clear developer. Grays appeared, blacks darkened, whites grew more intense. The image took on definition, became one and whole. Mrs. Cheney stood faltering, one trembling hand raised to brush the long, black hair back from her temple. Her burning eyes sought his, then lowered. Her posture was unassertive, almost shy.

She was wearing the white satin dress she had worn the night of the seance. The full, pleated skirt swung lazily as she moved hesitantly into the shadowed room. Eyes still lowered, head bowed in sweet submission, she came to stand alongside the bed.

Paul lurched upright, grabbed to touch. Beneath his frantic fingers was cool satin, warm flesh. No delusion this, but corporeal; she had the substance, scent, and sighs of a living woman.

"I told you, Paul," she said in a voice so faint he could scarcely catch the meaning of her words. "Of sex so strong it can transcend the boundaries of time and place."

"And death," he said wonderingly, holding her hand, staring at her.

"Yes," she said, raising her eyes to his. "Of death, too. I didn't want to come back. I fought against it. But you brought me back. Your strength . . . Your passion . . ."

Then he was standing close to her. His arms went about the slithery satin and the pliant body within. She stood limply, arms at her sides, all slack surrender.

"I have never let a man do to me what you did," she whispered. "Never before. I don't know what happened. I couldn't think. I couldn't hold back. I couldn't stop."

·He groaned, pulling her closer. He felt her naked beneath the cool stuff, probed cleft of buttocks, soft

pad of breasts, the springy mound between her legs.
As his fingers pried, she began to shiver, to sway in
his embrace.

"Don't make me wait," she begged. "Don't tease
me, lover. Oh lover, lover!"

Inflamed by her complaisance, he became increasingly brutal. His hands pushed beneath her fluted skirt
to grip suede skin. His teeth fastened on her lower lip.
He punished her with his caresses, bruising, twisting,
as her weak cries and soft moans kindled his lust, and
he thought nothing in his life would be as winning as
that limpid flesh yielding beneath his body's blows.
Eyes closed, he could see her strained supine on the
glittery remnants of her ripped dress, her long, black
hair a tangled net across wet lips, the eyes swollen,
brimming with tears, as he would buck and lunge and
pound himself upon her as her gentle white arms and
legs floated high and she sobbed, "Lover, lover,
lover . . ."

He went to that ancient hotel. He walked back and
forth in front. He marched the entire block three times
before deciding to go in.

"Colonel Coulter, please," Paul Fayette said sternly.

The desk clerk had teeth as curved and yellow as
salted cashews.

"I'm sorry, sir. Colonel Coulter is not in residence."

"He's given up his room?"

"His suite, sir."

"He's given up his suite?"

"Oh no, sir. Colonel Coulter maintains his suite. I
merely meant that, at the moment, the Colonel is not
here."

"Do you know where he is?"

"No, sir, I do not."

"This is very important," Paul said desperately.
"I've got to get in touch with him."

"Ah, sir?"

"You don't have a forwarding address?"

"No, sir."

"A telephone number?"

"Not, sir."

"May I leave a message for him?"

The cashews gleamed.

"Never mind," Paul said.

He decided to lunch at the hotel. So he did, the only man in a roomful of blue-haired ladies nibbling their watercress sandwiches and sipping dry sherries. Paul had three martinis and something to eat. He thought it was chicken, but it might have been veal.

He was certain he was considered a stranger, a lonely businessman from out of town who had strayed into the wrong restaurant. But when he paid his tab and was leaving, the mutton-chopped maître d' touched his arm.

"How sad about Mrs. Cheney, sir," he murmured.

Paul looked at him blankly.

"Yes," he said finally, "it was sad."

"You have my deepest sympathy," the old man said.

"Thank you," Paul nodded, convinced that madness was engulfing the world.

Back in his office, on his desk, was a message asking him to call Madge Cunningham. She was the receptionist-secretary-bookkeeper at the Penlow Park Country Club."

"Yes, Madge?"

"Mr. Fayette, about Colonel Benjamin G. Coulter . . ."

"Yes? What about him?"

"You sponsored him?"

An accusation.

"Yes, Madge, I did."

"Mr. Fayette, he filled out his application. His three personal references were a United States Senator, a monsignor of the Catholic Church, and a bank president in Chicago."

"Well . . ." Paul said dully, "he couldn't have done much better unless he had the President and the Pope. What's the problem?"

"The problem is," Madge Cunningham said, with some asperity, "that I sent all three the form letter for references. And all three letters came back. The addressees are all deceased. Mr. Fayette? Are you there, Mr. Fayette?"

"Oh, I'm here, Madge," he sighed, "I'm here. Just looking for paper and pencil. What were the names of the senator, the monsignor, and the bank president?"

She gave him the information, spelling the names carefully. He wrote them down just as carefully.

"Thank you, Madge. I've got them now."

"What should I do, Mr. Fayette? I mean about Colonel Coulter's application? Should I ask him for more references?"

"No," he said hastily. "Don't do that. Just forget it."

"Forget it?" she said suspiciously. "You mean just forget about getting personal references?"

"Tear up Coulter's application," he told her. "Just destroy it. He's moving from Penlow Park. I don't think he's really interested in joining the club."

"Oh?" she said doubtfully. "You mean—?"

"After the tragedy," Paul Fayette said quietly. "His daughter. You understand?"

"Oh, of course," she said. "Naturally. I'll just cancel the whole thing."

"Yes," he said, "do that. Just destroy the application. It's no longer valid."

He hung up. He sat staring at the list of names. Three prestigious men. Then he called Eddie Raeburn, the young investigator in Research.

"Eddie, how are your contacts at local newspapers?"

"City newspapers, Mr. Fayette? Pretty good. I know some guys on the staffs. I've done some favors for them, and they've done some favors for me."

"Would they do a little digging in their morgues for you?"

"Sure," Raeburn said promptly. "What do you need?"

"It's three men," Paul said. "All dead. Take this down."

He recited the names and titles of the three personal references of Colonel Benjamin G. Coulter. Raeburn read the information back to him.

"Have I got it right, Mr. Fayette?"

"That's fine, Eddie."

"What is it you want, Mr. Fayette?"

"I want to know how they died."

"Cause of death?"

"That's it. How long do you think it'll take?"

"An hour. Maybe two. Later this afternoon."

"Fine."

"You want a written report?"

"Oh no. Nothing like that. Nothing in writing. I'll be in all afternoon. Just give me a call when you've got it."

"Right. I'll get back to you as soon as possible, Mr. Fayette."

He replaced the phone softly. He sat there, swinging slowly back and forth in his swivel chair. After a while his secretary, Marie Verrazano, came in to empty his Out basket and bring him a sheaf of correspondence, reports, memos. He watched her move about his desk.

"Would you like a drink, Marie?" he asked suddenly.

She looked at him, startled.

"A drink?" she said. "You mean a coffee? A Coke?"

He was silent a brief moment.

"Yes," he said, "that's what I meant."

"No, thank you, Mr. Fayette," she said. "I just had lunch. But thank you anyway."

He nodded. He watched her sway out of the office. Clint Stahl had been right: she was something. He saw it for the first time.

He locked the outer door. He took the bottle of Scotch from his lower drawer, poured himself a drink, added some chilled water from his desk thermos. He took the glass to the wide window and stood staring out. Everything he was doing seemed commonplace. Ordinary. But everything seemed significant. The dichotomy puzzled him. He was seeing everything anew. Fresh eyes.

"I have fresh eyes," he murmured.

Below him, the summer sun made an abstract of the city's profile: warm stone and cool shadow. There was a harsh jerkiness there, jagged, broken. Cars moved, people rushed. He was above it all.

He received several phone calls, and told Marie to tell the callers he'd call back. He was on his third Scotch-and-water, the cityscape below him beginning to ripple and waver, when the phone call he had been awaiting came through.

"Mr. Fayette," Eddie Raeburn said, "those three guys you gave me, the dead guys . . ."

"Yes, Eddie?"

"The senator got racked up on graft charges. He was facing criminal indictment, and did the Dutch. A shotgun in his mouth. The church fellow, the monsignor, that one's a little fuzzy. The clips say he died in a car accident. But the guys I talked to said there was more to it than that. No one really knows. But there was gossip about him and—uh—well, a young priest. Just gossip, you understand. The two of them died. Drove into an abutment at high speed. The car was totaled. And the two of them, of course."

"Uh-huh. And the bank president?"

"A crook. No doubt about that. Embezzled almost two mil. Got caught and sent to Joliet. There was some kind of a prison uprising there, the cons took over for a few hours, and this guy got knifed."

"Did they recover the money? The two million he embezzled?"

"No sign of it, Mr. Fayette. Not a penny recovered. Slow horses and fast women, I guess."

"I guess. Thanks very much, Eddie."

"You want any more on this?"

"No," Paul Fayette said slowly, "that's enough."

He hung up and considered the devilish impertinence of an applicant who would give the names of three such men as personal references. It was two or

three minutes before Paul Fayette began to laugh, and
perhaps five minutes before he began weeping.

Laura Fayette, virgin bride in white nightgown,
ribbons at neck and wrists, lay on the lonely bed and
waited. Propped on a bolster, hands clasped behind
her head, she stared through the dimness across the
room to the rag rug where Ben sprawled indolently.
He was grooming himself with long, loving licks of his
pink tongue. When he had finished his gleaming body,
he licked his paws and began on head, ears, face.
Completed, he yawned, put his head down, returned
Laura's stare thoughtfully.

There was no sound from the end of the corridor
where Paul slept. No sound in the house. No sound in
all the night. Silence closed in, pressed in. Laura
looked away from Ben, up to the ceiling. Ceiling,
room, home, family. The words had a strange and
foreign ring. They did not concern her.

The pills and water sat ready on the bedside table.
But Laura was not yet willing for dreamless sleep. She
waited, for what she could not have said. But all her
recent days seemed a time of anticipation. Great
events loomed, she was certain. Expectation inflamed
her like a fever. Her life seemed to her to be opening
up, unfolding. Within the bloom, floating on a breathless scent, lay what had been missing from her life so
long: mystery and wonder.

It was not that her life had been unhappy or without
mirth. But, children grown and gone, she had a dulling
sense of finitude, all done and ended. Penlow Park was
a closed circle, and the charmless routine brutalized
her soul. She felt small and without hope. Is this all
there was? Her world seemed limited, life miniatur-
ized, spirit scorned and brought low.

Until Mrs. Cheney . . . Then the remembered past
became meaningful, the present sordid, the future
chanceful and without limit. What Mrs. Cheney meant
was: *it was not over.*

When she came, as Laura knew she would, a nylon

curtain billowing in from a window to the world signaled her arrival. She materialized, a hazy outline hardening. She grew, gathering form, filling. Until she stepped toward the bed, white gabardine pantsuit gleaming, all of her complete and serene.

"Sweet girl," she said to Laura Fayette.

It was a dream recalled: the cool, mischievous eyes, witchy face, a look at once aloof and masterful. She sat on the bed, took Laura's hand into her own skeleton fingers, leaned down to press hard lips lightly on Laura's fingers.

"Dear girl," she said.

"I've been waiting for you," Laura breathed. "I knew you'd come to me."

"Yes, yes," Mrs. Cheney soothed. "Of course you knew. Miss me? Did you miss me?"

Laura nodded violently, lower lip pressed in her teeth. Mrs. Cheney laughed softly, stood, arched her back, stretched her arms wide.

"Where is he?" she asked.

"In the guest room. At the end of the hall. The doors are locked."

"Yours and his?" Mrs. Cheney asked.

"Yes. Both."

"That's nice," the widow said lazily. "To be alone. We have all night then, don't we? And there is Ben. Hello, Ben darling. Behaving yourself, are you?"

The cat rose immediately, shambled over to rub itself purringly against Mrs. Cheney's ankles. She bent to touch its head, tweak its ears. The beast twisted under her hand, groaning with content.

"Go away, Ben," Mrs. Cheney said, and after a moment the cat stalked off into the shadows.

Laura watched her, a knuckle to her lips. She saw Mrs. Cheney prowl the room slowly, picking things up and putting them down, opening closet doors and bureau drawers.

"Lovely," Mrs. Cheney said. "You have so many lovely things."

"Thank you," Laura said faintly.

Mrs. Cheney turned to face her. She unbuttoned her white jacket, took it off, let it fall. She was naked above the snugly fitted pants. She raised her hands, combed fingers through her long, black hair, splayed it out over sleek shoulders and back.

"We must do something about him," she smiled at Laura Fayette. "Paul, not Ben. Do you mind my being jealous?"

"No."

"Because I want you all to myself, you lovely girl. I want you for my very own."

"Oh yes," Laura cried. "Yes!"

Mrs. Cheney sat on the edge of the bed. She began to loosen the ribbon about Laura's neck. She did this tenderly, with slow fingers.

Laura's eyes grew wider. Arms and hands floated back until her upturned palms were alongside her head on the bolster. Mrs. Cheney leaned forward to kiss one of those palms. The tip of her wet tongue traced a cabalistic design.

"Don't," Laura whispered. "Please don't."

"Don't?" Mrs. Cheney said, smiling. "You mean, 'Do. Please do.'"

"Yes," Laura said. "That's what I mean."

"Shh," Mrs. Cheney said. "I know, I know. How sweet you are to me, how dear. Look at those great eyes, that tempting mouth. Ah now, the ribbon's opened, and now the buttons. Ooh, how soft and tender, all pink and white. Let me; I'll do it. Are you shivering, dear? Are you frightened? Don't be. I won't hurt you, you know that. Well, maybe just a *little*. There— is that good? Do my nails hurt? Of course they don't. So white she is, so pink. All soft and ready. Just let me—there, like that. Ah, look at her, look what's happening. All hard and glistening. I can feel your heart. How it pounds! My heart, my heart, too. Don't pull away. Don't reject me. Come to me, sweet girl, just as I've come to you. That's better, that's nice. No, no, let me do it. I love it. Now here, here's something you'll like . . . Ah, you do! I knew you would. And this. Raise up a bit, there's a dear girl."

"Don't," Laura moaned. "Don't."

"Do," Mrs. Cheney laughed. "Do. And so. And so. Ah, darling, do I hurt you? Only to love you more; you know that. Has Paul ever loved you like this? You know he hasn't. Can't. But I can. Oh sweet. Open to me, dear girl. There, ahh there. Ooh, ooh. She smells of daisies, so she does. All fresh and green and new. Don't fight me, dear, don't put me away; you know you can't. That's it, that's better, that's my sweet, dear, loving girl. Oh yes. Pull me close. That's better. Isn't that better? How lovely. How divine. Yes, yes. Surrender, dear. Just surrender. Give yourself up. All of you. Like this. And this. Is that right for you? A little higher? There? Of course, there. Like that. Right *there*. I know, I know. *There*. Don't stop, don't stop. Yes, yes. Sweet girl Dear girl."

"Please," Laura begged, "don't leave me."

"Oh darling," Mrs. Cheney said lightly, "you already have a husband."

"Don't ever leave me," Laura pleaded.

7

It was hurtfully hot that night. The sixth of August. Lowery sky. Squalid sundown wind. They took their drinks into the family room, the only air-conditioned area in the house. Laura and Paul Fayette put Margaret Stahl between them. She wasn't wrapped too tightly.

They were appalled by her appearance. Her natural hair, wigless, was plastered damply to her skull. Without makeup, her complexion had a waxy look, sheened: the face of a department store mannequin. The body was a mannequin's, too: elbows and knees ajar, a stiff, contorted twist to her torso. With pluckings at lips, rubbing of eyes, sudden moves, constant blinking, giggles and groans.

She wore a wraparound housedress, stains down the front. And she was not clean. Chokers of smut encircled her throat. Her bare ankles were punky, and toenails rimmed with black. She smelled of defeat.

"I thought—" she started. She stopped. Barked laugh. "Well, I thought, frankly, there would be more. I didn't know. Clint handled the money end. I should have— But I didn't. I knew about the mortgage, of course, and children *are* expensive. But still . . . So I didn't, really know quite what to do, and I think possibly slicing my wrists wide open might be the most efficient solution for me—don't you, dears?" And she smiled brightly at them.

"Come on, Margaret," Paul said. "Things will work out."

"Of course they will," Laura said stoutly. "Insurance?"

"Fifteen thousand," Margaret said. "Practically nothing in the bank. And that's it. That-is-it."

"The house," Paul said. "You could sell the house."

"But of course I could," she said with a dazzling smile. "And that's the first step down, isn't it? Sell the house, sell the furniture, sell the car, sell my clothes. Could I sell the kids? How's the market for teenagers these days?"

"Margaret," Paul said, "for God's sake!"

"Don't you see?" she pleaded with them. "I *like* the way I live. I like the house, the car, the clothes, the club. I even liked Doc Terhune. I don't want a ratty apartment with a stained tub, roaches in the sink, and no fondue set. Jesus, that's not me. Can't you understand? It's just not *me.*"

She looked at them back, and forth, and it would have helped if she had wept. Then they could have hugged her, conforted her, brought Kleenex and murmured. But they could not handle the dry desperation in her eyes.

"That bastard," she said, beginning to pant. "That cocksucker."

"Margaret," Laura said, trying to push back the tide, "don't—"

"He was infatuated with her," Margaret said, nodding her head furiously. "Oh yes, he went running after her. You knew Clint. After anything in skirts, wasn't he? The mad lover. Always trying, never succeeding. The Penlow Park lothario. The lover boy who could never quite make it. Oh yes, I know. Listen, I was married to the maniac for almost twenty years, wasn't I? Think I don't know what he was? So he had this thing for Diane, and she kept putting him off. I'm sure of it. Maybe she laughed at him. You remember Clint pawing all the women at the club when he was drunk enough to try it. Probably tried it with you, didn't he, Laura? Of course he did. I knew. I saw. But Diane just laughed at him. Probably told him to act his age. Behave. He was a married man. She told him something like that. So he got drunk, went up here to try his luck again, and found her and Jacque in the house alone. So, you know Clint. Poor, stupid Clint. He immediately jumped to the wrong conclusion. Diane and Jacque? Ridiculous. No way. I happen to know. She didn't swing that way. So he killed them, or burned the house down and they all died. That's how I see it. Isn't that how you see it?"

She looked at them, broken. They were silent. Both Fayettes bent forward, heads bowed. They held their glasses between their knees. Finally . . .

"I'll get us some fresh drinks," Paul mumbled.

He took the three empty glasses, went into the kitchen. He ran the cold water, but it wasn't cold enough. He took the plastic bottle of chilled water from the refrigerator and soaked the dishtowel. Then he slowly swabbed his face and the back of his neck. He pressed the cold cloth against his forehead. Then he dried off with paper towels. He mixed fresh drinks and carried them back to the family room. He was surprised to note that his hands weren't trembling.

Laura was standing behind Margaret Stahl. She had found a short, black comb somewhere and was trying to comb the snags out of Margaret's hair.

"—the day after it happened," Margaret was saying. "I'm talking about Colonel Coulter, Paul. He came to see me the day after it happened. Couldn't have been nicer. Such a sweet man. Never a mention that it was all Clint's fault. Asked me if I needed any money."

"Do you, Margaret?" Paul said. "If we can help out, just say—"

"God bless," she said. "But why? Pissing in the ocean. So you give me—notice I say *give* and not *loan,* because I could never hope to pay it back—say you give me enough to live for a week, a month, a couple of months. Then what? You see?"

"Well . . ." Paul said lamely. "Still . . ."

"Anyway," Margaret chattered on, "after he left I remembered—I thought maybe he could really help me by giving me a job. I mean, he's a very successful businessman—isn't he, Paul?"

"Apparently."

"Well, he's always traveling, and he certainly seems to have money, so he must need people and, oh God, I'll do anything, you know that, go for coffee if that's what he wants. But tonight I realized—and that's why I came over—I suddenly realized I don't know how to get in touch with him. No phone. Not in New York; I looked it up. How do I contact him? Do you know?"

"Paul?" Laura said. "Do you know?"

"I have no telephone number for him," he said, with a great show of briskness. "But he keeps an apartment-office in a hotel up on Madison Avenue. You might try him there, Margaret. I'll write out the name of the hotel and the address before you leave."

"Thank you, Paul," she said humbly. "I know I'm being a pain in the ass. I *know* it. But I'm clutching—clutching at straws. Anything. Maybe he can do something for me. Paul? Do you think?"

"I wouldn't be a bit surprised," he said.

"Margaret," Laura said, "did you have anything to eat today?"

"What? Well, of course. I think. I don't know."

"Why don't I make you a sandwich? And then, maybe you'd like to stay the night. We have room. The kids are away, aren't they?"

"Thank God for that. No sandwich, no, thanks anyway. The thought of food is enough to make me scream. No, I'll just finish this drink and then I'll go home. I'm still going through Clint's papers, hoping I'll find some buried treasure. Like an insurance policy I don't know about, a bank account in his name. Something like that. So far, zilch."

"He got a hefty severance settlement," Paul said, suddenly guilty. "When he was terminated. You knew about that?"

She laughed nervously. "What do you think I've been using for the frozen macaroni-and-cheese? But that won't last long when the kids come back and start eating. My God, do they eat. That son of a bitch!" she shouted suddenly. "That bastard! A loser to the last. Widow and three kids starving to death. Practically. All because he went chasing after a woman who had the great good sense not to have anything to do with him. Oh God! Forgive me, Diane, forgive me! She must have been disgusted with him. Disgusted! But he kept smelling around, and probably trying to feel her up, you know how he was, and maybe she told him off, I'm sure she told him off, and his fucking macho ego just couldn't take it, and I don't blame her for one minute. I know she couldn't stand him. An animal. She thought him some kind of dirty animal, oh God, and then he had to go and—but she wasn't interested at all in—so beautiful, she was so beautiful. I'd kill him!" Margaret screamed, jerking to her feet. "If he was here, alive, right now, I'd kill him, the bastard, for what he did to her. I'd drive nails through his skull if I could, and I'd cut off his balls and make him—"

But then she was completely gone, tears finally starting, teeth grinding. They pressed about her with alarm, patting, stroking, soothing. But she ranted on: what he had done, what she would do, what had happened to Mrs. Cheney.

Until finally, at last, she collapsed in a splintered heap, wailing, "Diane, Diane, Diane," and they did what they could.

Which wasn't much.

The shade of Mrs. Cheney didn't appear every night he willed it. Then he was left empty and bereft feeling his loss. Other nights he could summon her with a sigh. She appeared, the billowing white curtain heralding her coming.

He asked why she could not be with him every night or, for that matter, every minute. She put a soft

finger on his lips to stop his protestations. He was so
inflamed by this sweet gesture that he popped the
finger into his mouth and sucked it greedily, glorying
in her moan of delight.

When she did come to him, she arrived demure,
hesitant. She was fighting a passion she could not resist; that was evident in her demeanor: downcast
eyes, shy surrender. Each coupling was a new seduction. Never once did she lead him or hint of lust
in her dress or manner. The costumes were reserved,
behavior modest.

It was only when he began his rough, masculine
ministrations that she, slowly, became engorged beneath his hands. He never ceased marveling at this
exciting transformation: the glitter of her eyes, sweat
pearls across her upper lip, panting breath, limbs flung
wide and floating, and a rhapsody of sobs, groans,
cries. Best of all: whimpers and pleading.

He had never felt such a sense of power. Sexual
power. She tried to withstand him, but could not. The
touch of his mouth was a sharp spur, his hands
were burning brands, the smell of his skin was pep-
per. Once surrendered, she was lost in a paroxysm
of love, and there was nothing he might not do. To
her. With her. She became his creature. His hot, gasping servant. He might drink her blood.

It was this enticement and temptation of Mrs.
Cheney that consumed him. Their union had the
structuring of a formal ballet, a religious ceremony.
She appeared fully clad, groomed, lightly scented.
His first attentions were soft and courtly. She responded modestly. He became more insistent. Her
agitation grew. He pressed his wooing with increasing
vigor. She tried to fend him off, but was no match for
his masculine strength.

It ended, always, with ripping, tearing, shredding
of her costume. And then the grunting rape itself
when he threw himself upon her in an agony of lust,
all but howling in his need to penetrate and rend that
long, cool body, rip it wide, and spend himself in the

hot heart. Most satisfying was her weeping, her head turned aside. Then he might comfort her with magnanimity and pride.

He tried his power, pushing it farther and farther, and found no limit. He had her on her knees, groveling, and was convinced it had become an addiction to her; she could not oppose him. He despoiled her, humiliated her and only once, fleetingly, paused to wonder which might be slave and which master.

One night, before their ritual began, he saw the green eyes of Ben gleaming from a dark corner of the guest room. He moved to put the cat out into the hallway. But Mrs. Cheney objected so prettily, putting a beseeching hand on his arm, that he relented and allowed the cat to stay. It was amusing, in a way, to have a dumb witness.

Then, later, when he rolled from her swollen flesh, he found the cat sitting solemnly at the foot of the bed, regarding him gravely. Paul winked at Ben, and could almost swear the animal winked back. From then on, the cat was present during Mrs. Cheney's visits.

He never wondered that he might be dreaming or hallucinating, that the tender tissue beneath his questing fingers was wraith, ghost, or apparition. This writhing body was real, and he knew it. Did wraiths gasp in sexual anguish? Did ghosts sweat? Did apparitions grasp his buttocks in lubricious frenzy to pull him closer, deeper? Did disembodied spirits, lost in lust, perform such frantic acrobatics and then later huddle weeping in shame and dismay? No, no, it was all real enough, the most *actual* experience of his life.

It seemed to him that rather than dream or fantasy, his hours with Mrs. Cheney were a world of new significance and heightened intensity. All that had gone before—his marriage to Laura, his children, his career—these things were the dream and fantasy, an insubstantial fairy tale of smoke and spiderweb without meaning or lasting moment.

He urged her, always, to return more often, to return and never to depart. But she put him off gently, again and again. Finally, when he persisted, she told him what came between them. It was Laura, their marriage, and she could not compete with that.

"Do you blame me?" she faltered. "For being jealous?"

"Of course not," he groaned, embracing her naked shoulders. "But there is nothing left between Laura and me. No love. No sex. We're strangers living in the same house."

"I want you for myself," she said timidly, hugging him. "The two of us, alone. Is that so awful?"

She seemed so young, tender. She seemed so innocent, inexperienced. His fancy soared. She was a maiden, untried. She was a virgin, waiting and anxious. A caress might bruise her or a kiss turn her to a beast. She was all trembling unknown. Between her thighs she gripped a moist mystery. And only he had the power to unlock it all.

He dallied with her, teasing. And as he played, fingers straying almost idly, he thought of what she had said: his marriage between them. He plotted how he might rid himself of the encumbrance. How he might set himself free, and she could come to him forever, and they would . . . and she would . . . and he would . . .

But, as always, sense and reason fled when she was beneath his hands. Her whimperings excited him. He put his teeth to her flesh, and as his passion grew, and she writhed and twisted, and he tasted her liquor, and she matched his rage, and he wrenched slippery limbs, and all of her was opened to him in eager surrender, and he plunged, and she shrieked in bliss, he wondered if, by pleasure, he might kill a woman already dead.

It began with a senseless disagreement. Laura Fayette had prepared a boneless roast, a sirloin tip, and Paul carved. He used the ten-inch chef's knife—the same blade Clint Stahl had presed against his own throat. He grumbled to Laura, not for the first time, that it was not the correct knife for the task, and one of these days they'd have to buy a proper carver.

"You're cutting against the grain," she told him.

He paused and looked up at her.

"Does that slice look like it was cut against the grain?"

"Yes," she said.

"You don't know what you're talking about," he said, slicing away. "I've been carving since I was twelve years old. My father taught me how. I'm slicing this roast the way it whould be cut."

"It's crumbling," she said. "You're ruining it. You're making a mess of it."

He threw the chef's knife and carving fork down with a clatter.

"Carve the goddamn thing yourself," he said stonily, and stalked out.

Later, she brought the sliced meat and the rest of the meal into the dining room. They ate in silence, except for one short exchange.

"The roast is tough," he said.

"You're chewing one of the slices you cut," she said.

He flung down his napkin, jerked to his feet. He slammed out of the house, through the kitchen door, into the backyard. He marched about, smoking cigarettes furiously. He threw the burning butts into the scraggly, untrimmed lawn. After a while Laura came out. She sat on the stoop. She lighted her own cigarette. She huddled, smoking, hugging her knees and staring at him.

It was a thin night, the sky shredded. Weak moonlight poked through torn clouds. A hot breeze blew fretfully from everywhere. Far off, to the west, the dark blazed occasionally with lightning. Thunder rumbled like distant guns. There were bugs about, winged things that flew in and out of the glow from the kitchen window. A few dashed themselves against the screen and fell twitching.

"Did you read Christine's letter?" she asked in a loud voice.

"What?"

"Christine's letter," Laura repeated. "Did you read it?"

"No."

"She wants to transfer in the Fall."

"Transfer? Where to?"

"Yale, if she can get it."

"Yale?" he said. "They take women?"

"Where have you been?" she asked him. "Well, what shall I tell her?"

"Tell her to stay where she is," he said.

"You tell her that."

"Ahh, the hell with it. Let her do whatever she pleases."

"Don't you care about your children?"

He thought a moment.

"No," he said, surprised, "I don't care about my children. Let them make their own mistakes; they're old enough."

"That's what Diane Cheney said."

"What?" he said. "When?"

"One of our first talks. She said to let the kids make their own mistakes."

"This lawn looks like shit," he said. "Everyting needs trimming and pruning."

"So do it," she said.

"Hire someone," he said. "I've mowed my last lawn."

"You just don't care anymore, do you? About anything."

"That's right. I just don't care."

His hard statement came as a judgment. It stunned them both. She lighted another cigarette with shaking fingers.

"You've got someone else, I suppose?" she said, examining her burning cigarette.

"No, I haven't got someone else," he said, mimicking her cruelly. "Do you?"

"No."

"That's what Clint Stahl thought. Margaret was screwing anything that moved."

"You think Clint was a saint? He didn't strike out as often as Margaret thinks. He did all right."

"You're speaking from personal experience?"

Again there was a stunned silence. What began as senseless disagreement had regressed to rancorous quarrel. It seemed to be neither her fault nor his fault. The night had a bitter momentum of its own. They could not hold it back. They could not end it.

"I never went to bed with Clint Stahl," she said, her voice quavering, a little, "if that's what you're thinking."

"Bed?" he said, with what he thought was a scornful laugh. "With Clint it could be a phone booth, standing up in a hammock, or the green on the sixteenth hole. I don't give a damn whether you did or not."

"And you never got it off with Margaret?"

"Margaret? Holy Christ! No, and I never got it off with Donald Duck either."

"You say," she said. "I don't believe you anymore."

"Tough titty," he said.

"Brilliant," she said. "Really a brilliant riposte."

She hadn't moved from her perch on the back stoop. He paced back and forth, into the gloom at the end of the garden, into the weak, orangy light from the kitchen window. They didn't look at each other. They both looked at the ground.

"Do you want a divorce?" he said roughly.

Pause.

"Do you?" she asked tonelessly.

"I don't want any more nights like this. A clean break is better than this bullshit."

"My," she said, "our language is elegant this evening."

"You've heard worse," he said, "I'm sure."

"What about the kids?" she said.

"What about them? They're always talking about 'Doing your own thing,' aren't they? All right, we're doing our own thing. And the last time Christine was home and had a date, I heard her tell him she 'was into self-awareness.' That's me, kiddo, I'm into self-awareness. Listen, we brought them into this world, fed them, clothed them, taught them. It's time to kick them out of the nest. Let them fly."

"I'll go along with that," she said unexpectedly. "I'm not about to devote the rest of my life to putting on Band-Aids. I'd like to do a little living myself."

"I'll bet," he said. "Well, what the hell . . . they'll live. You want to see a lawyer?"

"Jake Davidson," she said promptly.

"No way," he said. "He's *my* lawyer. He can't represent us both. Get your own."

"I will," she said. "A smart lawyer who'll . . ."

Her voice trailed off.

"Who'll pound nails in my skull and cut off my balls?" he finished for her.

"Something like that," she agreed.

"Lots of luck," he said. He paused to light another cigarette. "The one thing I *don't* want is a friendly divorce. None of this 'Can't we still be friends?' crap. No Christmas dinners and meetings at the kids' birthday parties. A complete break. Fini. Everything legal. Everything through the lawyers."

"Suits me," she said. "I'm warning you, I'm taking half. At least."

"It's worth it," he said.

"God," she said, "I thought I knew you. I don't know you."

"I could have told you that," he said.

The lightning to the west had ended. There was no more rumbling of thunder. But the cloud had clotted; the moon was hidden. The air had grown oppressively humid. It clung to skin, soddened them, pressed them down.

While they were silent, both trembling with their

anger, Ben came stepping jauntily from the bushes
and picked his way across the lawn. They watched his
passage. He paused to sniff the earth, inspect the
blackening sky. Then the cat stepped daintily into the
undergrowth on the other side of the yard. They saw a
flip of tail before he disappeared from view.

"I get Ben," Laura said firmly.

"We'll talk about it," Paul said. "Our lawyers will
talk about it. I'm going up."

"So go," she said.

"That was a lousy roast," he said.

"Fuck you," she said.

The fourth time Mrs. Cheney appeared to Laura
Fayette, she came striding forcefully, clad in skin-tight
jeans and a T-shirt that had *NEXT?* printed across the
bosom.

Laura greeted her in an embroidered dirndl skirt
and peasant blouse, ribbons in her hair and on her
pumps. She told Diane that she had started divorce
proceedings. She looked for approval, and saw only
resignation.

"I thought you'd be pleased," she said in a low
voice.

"Oh I am, dear girl," Mrs. Cheney said. "But these
things can drag on for years."

"It won't!" Laura cried. "My lawyer said not. As
soon as possible. He understands that."

"If you say so," Mrs. Cheney sighed. "It's just that
I can't stand being apart from you. I want you for my
very own; I told you that. Come sit on my lap."

The master bedroom was in darkness. Not even the
gleam of Ben's avid eyes. Mrs. Cheney sat in a
cretonne-covered armchair, Laura on her lap. They
traded one cigarette back and forth.

"Am I too heavy?"

"Of course not, sweet girl. Give us a kissy-poo."

Moist lips touched lightly, then harder. Wet mouths
pressed. Mrs. Cheney's agile tongue pried, flickering.

"Ah don't," Laura breathed. "Please don't."

"Sometimes it's nice just to kiss," Mrs. Cheney said. "What did you call it when you were in school?"

"Necking, I suppose. Petting."

"Did you do it a lot?"

"Oh no. I didn't have many boyfriends. Oh, I did, but they were just that—friends. When they took me out, it was to tell me their problems with their real girlfriends. I was always one of the boys. Always had a weight problem. Legs · like a fullback. Wide shoulders. Muscles. I played a lot of field hockey. I was really strong. That's how I lost my cherry. I was Indian-wrestling with this boy. A neighbor. It was a summer vacation; I was home from school. Anyway, we were Indian-wrestling, and I guess we got carried away."

"Did you enjoy it?"

"Not really. It was the first time for him, too. Very awkward amd fumbling. Very unsatisfactory. Indian-wrestling! Can you imagine? That's funny, isn't it?"

"Touching," Mrs. Cheney said. "Very sweet and young."

She brushed cool lips over Laura's neck, chin, up to her ear. The tip of her tongue screwed wetly inside the ear. Sharp teeth nipped the lobe. Laura closed her eyes.

"I was happy at home," she said dreamily. "My mother died when I was six, and my father raised me and my three brothers. All older. A happy home. We did things together. Went camping together, fishing together. Things like that. And we played cards and word games. We were very close, all of us. I kept up with them. I mean hiking and riding and running. Baseball. I wore jeans and shirts, just like theirs. It was like my father had four sons."

"And all the time . . . ?" Mrs. Cheney murmured.

"All the time I was hoping to meet someone like my father or brothers. A strong man—you know? A very masculine man. I never met anyone like that."

"Not Paul?"

"Especially not Paul."

Mrs. Cheney's lips drifted slowly over Laura's closed eyes. She kissed temple, brow, the tender corners of Laura's mouth. One hand slid to encircle a soft breast. A fingertip traced languid circles.

"It wasn't bad with Paul," Laura said. "I mean at first. I knew from the start he wanted a strong woman. He liked to wait on me. Shave my legs. Wash my hair. Things like that."

"He wanted to be your maid?"

"Something like that. It's just the way he is. But don't get me wrong; he was a good husband. A good father and a good provider. It's only been in the last few months that the whole thing fell apart. No sex for weeks."

Suddenly Laura sought Mrs. Cheney's mouth. Kissed her frantically, lips open, tongue fluttering wildly. Mrs. Cheney held her firmly, put a hand up to stroke her hair. Their mouths slowly drew apart until lips were separated; only tongues touched, darting and sliding.

"Oh," Laura breathed. "Oh, oh, oh."

Mrs. Cheney's skeleton fingers were at the back of her bare neck, stroking, pinching gently. The fingers of the other hand crept craftily inside the loose neckline of Laura's blouse. Long, scarlet fingernails picked persistently at slack nipples. They came erect.

"Have you ever made love with a woman before?" Mrs. Cheney asked.

"Once," Laura told her. "When I went away to school. A slender, small-boned girl. Dark. So lovely. So elegant. We roomed together. I was bigger than she, and stronger. And certainly not as pretty. But she was the one who came crawling into my bed. We did everything. I was so frightened. Scared we'd be caught. But I didn't want it to end. I wanted it to go on forever."

"What happened?"

"I never found out, exactly. She went home for

spring vacation and just never came back. Later I heard her parents had put her in a very strict school in Switzerland. She never wrote."

"But you loved her?"

"I suppose I did. But I used to close my eyes and imagine she was a man making love to me."

"Is that what you do when I make love to you?"

"Oh no!" Laura protested. "No. I'm not sure what I think when you make love to me. First of all, I can't believe that you're actually here. Then I just let myself go. I don't think at all, I guess. It's all feelings."

"Good feeling?"

"Oh God, yes! So good. One orgasm after another. Until it's just one long one, and I get frantic because I can't stop."

"Don't be frightened," Mrs. Cheney murmured. "You know I'll be the lover you've always wanted."

They continued their slow, languorous love-making, hands moving with lazy delight, fingers searching. They kissed, they kissed. Licked. Nipped each other's flesh. Rubbed against each other in lubricious heat. Their whisperings became increasingly wanton. They discussed what they would shortly do. They giggled, laughed. They moved eagerly to the bed, not interrupting their fevered caresses.

"Please!" Laura cried. "Please!"

"Dear girl, sweet girl," Mrs. Cheney said throatily. "Oh, how I love this. How I love being with you. If I could only have you for my very own. To be with you always. Just the two of us. I'd never leave you. Never ..."

Paul Fayette, lying alone on the guest room bed, stared at the black open window with aching eyes. But no matter how strongly he willed it, no matter how many times he muttered his anguished prayers, the white curtain hung damply limp. Mrs. Cheney did not appear.

Finally, admitting to himself that she was not coming this night, he rose and pulled on his robe. He went padding down the hallway, intending to have a brandy or two downstairs. Enough to dull his disappointment.

He stopped suddenly outside the door of the master bedroom. He heard faint cries, giggles, groans of delight, soft hoots of laughter. Twang of bedsprings. Slap of palm on bare flesh. Then more whispered talk. Two people. Two women. It was obvious what they were doing.

Paul listened awhile. Then he went quietly back to his room. He locked the door, removed his robe. He stood naked at the open window, smoking a cigarette. He looked down at himself, surprised to see his own excitement.

It was Margaret in there with Laura, he had no doubt of that. Hadn't the two been close for years and years? Hadn't Margaret slept over several times, in the master bedroom with Laura? Wasn't Margaret now manless and lonely? And couldn't the same be said of Laura?

Their relationship didn't shock or dismay him. He had told Laura the truth; he just didn't care about his family anymore. But this lesbian union might prove valuable during the divorce proceeding. A wife's infidelity, with a lover of either sex, would certainly count against her in any court, before any judge.

He finished his cigarette and went back to bed. He strained to hear, and thought he caught faintly the cries and moans of their lewd coupling. But he might have been imagining; there were two locked doors and a long corridor between them. He fell asleep finally, his mind whirling with steamy fantasies.

"—what I'm going to do," Margaret Stahl concluded despairingly, lank hands twisting in her lap.

"Yes, dear lady," Colonel Benjamin G. Coulter murmured, nodding, serious, "we do have a problem, don't we?"

She was vaguely conscious of his use of the plural, and was comforted by it. But her attention was riveted on his fingers. For while Margaret had poured out her

tale of ruinous misfortunes, Colonel Coulter, listening
intently, had performed sleight of hand. A half-dollar
flipped across his knuckles, disappeared under his
palm, reappeared to dance again. Coins were plucked
from under cushions, from Margaret's ears, from the
air itself.

Then the Colonel produced a deck of cards and
shuffled them in a miraculous manner. The pack was
stretched apart like an accordion, then pressed together again. Cards slipped down in a waterfall, but
neatly, in place. In a one-hand shuffle, the deck folded
over on itself again and again.

They were seated in deep armchairs in Colonel
Coulter's hotel apartment-office. Drapes and curtains
had been pulled aside to allow late morning sunlight
to stream in, revealing the room in all its squalor. In
the cold fireplace, a basket of flowers, daisies and
peonies, at least a week old, drooped limply, scattering petals on dusty tiles.

Coulter had insisted on ordering up tea and croissants for them both. The service set on the long refectory table. The tea grew cold, croissants stale, butter
melted as the new widow recounted her story. She
wore a severe suit of black silk, jacket double-
breasted, skirt straight. A voluminous white scarf concealed her cleavage. Her makeup was minimal and
chaste. Her only jewelry was a plain gold wedding
band.

"I was hoping," she faltered, "that you . . . I talked
to Diane before she, uh, before it happened, and she
said she would speak to you, and perhaps you
might . . ."

"Pick a card," Colonel Coulter said abruptly, fan-
ning the deck before her. "Any card."

Obediently Margaret selected a card.

"Look at it, remember it, slide it back in the deck,"
the Colonel instructed.

Margaret did as she was told. Coulter closed his
fan of cards, shuffled them briskly, cut the deck two
or three times, shuffled them again.

"Would you care to shuffle?" he inquired politely. "Or is that enough?"

"Enough," Margaret said.

"Tap the deck three times."

She tapped the deck three times with the tip of her thin forefinger.

"Presto!" he shouted.

He jerked to his feet, whirled, threw the pack of cards at the blank wall behind him. The deck flew apart, scattering every which way, a snowfall of cards. But stuck to the wall, face out, was the four of clubs.

The Colonel turned to look at Margaret Stahl.

"Well?" he demanded.

Her face was slack.

"Yes," she said, nodding, nodding. "Yes, that's it. The four of clubs. How in the world . . .?"

"Magic, dear lady," Coulter said, chuckling softly. "Pure magic."

He regained his seat, crossed his knees carefully, adjusting the crease in his tan doeskin trousers.

"Aw, yes," he said. "Magic, magic, magic. You do believe in magic, don't you?"

"Well, I—"

"Do you mind if I smoke a cigar?" Coulter asked solicitously. "It won't offend you, will it?"

"Of course not," Margaret said. "Go right ahead."

It took at least a minute or two for the ceremony to take place. Pigskin case withdrawn from the Colonel's inside jacket pocket. Plump cigar selected from the three within. Case capped and returned to inside jacket pocket. Cigar held near the Colonel's ear and rolled gently between thumb and first two fingers. Gold clipper removed from Colonel's waistcoat pocket. End of cigar neatly clipped. Stub discarded on floor. Box of wooden matches produced from Colonel's side jacket pocket. Match struck, allowed to burn a few seconds. Flame applied to cigar end, a half-inch away. Cigar turned slowly to ignite evenly. The Colonel took a deep draft. He blew the smoke out slowly in a long bluish plume.

"Elixir," he breathed dreamily.

He leaned forward suddenly, proffered the cigar to Margaret Stahl.

"Take a puff," he commanded.

"Oh," she said, "I couldn't. . . ."

"Take a puff," he repeated.

She took the cigar, holding it gingerly. She put it to her lips.

"Don't inhale," he said hurriedly. "Not necessary."

She kept the smoke in her mouth a few seconds, then let it leak out slowly. Her eyes were half-closed.

"I like it," she said, smiling, blinking brightly.

"Of course you do, dear lady," he said, snatching the cigar from her fingers. "Delicious stuff. Made up specially for me. Yes, she did mention it, Diane did. About a job of work for you. Best thing in the world—what? I mean, keep you busy, mind off your trouble, money in the bank. All that."

"Diane told me how many people you have working for you. How busy you are. All over the world. A big business."

"Aw, yes," he said. "True, but not *my* business, you know. Oh no! Far from it. Just a tiller in the field, that's yours truly. A very small cog in a very big wheel, dear lady. I have to answer to my superiors, too. I do indeed, Let's say I'm just a soldier, an old soldier. Receive orders and obey. A soldier's life. Oh yes. I mean, I don't *own* the business, I don't *run* it."

"But you do employ—"

"Of course I do," he said cheerily. "I'm a colonel after all—am I not? And so I command a battalion, a regiment, a brigade. Whatever. But," he added slyly, "there are generals, you know. There surely are."

He held out the cigar. This time she took it willingly. His saliva glistened on the tip, but she had no hesitation in poking the cigar between her lips and puffing importantly. Then she handed the cigar back to him.

"Does that mean," she said slowly, somewhat dazed,

"does that mean you must consult your, uh, superiors before you hire someone?"

"Oh no, no, no," he said hastily. "A colonel does have some power—what? It's more or less left to me. Results are what count. Oh yes, deliver results, and the sky's the limit. Like any big company, you know. The bottom line. Tolerate anything but failure. And all that."

"I should tell you, Colonel Coulter," Margaret said, taking the cigar from his fingers, "I should tell you, in all honesty, that I cannot type or take shorthand or things like that. I'm not very well qualified, I'm afraid. That is, not trained or experienced in business. But I do learn quickly, and I would be loyal, and I'd work hard, and I'll do anything."

"Anything," he repeated. "Splendid. That's good to know. Travel, would you?"

"I'd love to travel."

"What about your children?" he asked sharply. "If you travel?"

"Well, they're old enough to take care of themselves. And I suppose I could have a housekeeper in if I was away a long time. I think it could be arranged."

"Mmm," he said, taking the cigar gently from her fingers, "I'm sure it could." He took a single puff, then gave the cigar back to her.

The coins appeared again in his fingers, flipping, leaping, disappearing. He drew a long vermillion scarf from his mouth and discarded it onto the rug. He pulled a yellow scarf from his left ear, a blue scarf from under Margaret's skirt, and a white scarf from nowhere. They all fluttered down.

"Wonderful," she said muzzily. "Just wonderful."

"Isn't it?" he said happily.

"How long did it take you to learn those tricks?"

"All my life," he said genially. He settled back, and she thought how like a cherub he looked. An aged cherub. White hair and military mustache. Pinkish complexion. Plumpish body, faintly bulging. She thought, suddenly, of what he must look like naked, and she giggled.

"Something funny?" he inquired.

"No," she said, sobering. "Just an odd thought. Well, what do you think, Colonel? Is there any possibility? Of a job for me?"

"Possibility," he said. "Always a possibility. We do get recruits from the most unusual sources. Various backgrounds. A possibility? Mmm . . . well. . . Would you mind standing a moment, dear lady? Let's get a good look at you."

She put the cigar butt carefully aside in an ashtray on the table. She stood unsteadily, tugged down her jacket, smoothed the skirt over her hips.

"My," he said, "you *are* a long one. Over six feet?"

"Yes," she said. "Over."

"Wear wigs, do you?"

"Usually," she said. "Not today."

"Lovely suit you're wearing," he said. "Have a fairly extensive wardrobe, do you?"

"Well, yes. I mean, I have clothes I could wear for various things. Office, parties, dinners. And so forth."

He stood up, came close to her, smiling. She towered almost a head over him. Her chin could rest on his forehead.

He drew a blood-red silk scarf from her right nostril.

"But that's incredible!" she cried.

"Yes," he said, moving around behind her. "Now let me show you some *real* magic."

There was enmity in the Fayette home. It was an intermittent hostility, distracted. Laura and Paul each went his own way, silent and intent, morose and withdrawn. They communicated in monosyllables. They shrank, huddling in. They frequently dined separately. They rarely entertained. Their lawyers wrote letters; their lawyers answered letters. Meanwhile they dwelt under the same roof, but passed each other sightless and without notice.

Only Ben seemed at ease in the silent rooms. He

had his milk, his food, a pan of litter in the downstairs lavatory. He went outside infrequently. He
seemed content with the role of house cat, prowling
empty hallways. He curled on couch, chair or bed to
sleep or groom himself with long, pleasurable licks. He
sat for patient hours staring out windows. Or he
padded silently after the human guests, rubbing
against ankles or reaching a clawed paw for a stroke
or scratch.

The house flooded with silence. Dust gathered, and
dishes went unwashed. Roaches were seen in kitchen
and bathrooms, and behind the walls there was heard
a dry scamper. Lamps were rarely lighted downstairs;
Laura waited in the master bedroom, Paul in the guest
room. Nothing seemed alive in the shadowed house; it
might have been a condemned building inhabited by
derelicts. The phone rang, and went unanswered.
The doorbell rang, and no one went to see.

"Brian's letter is on the dining room table."

"What does he say?"

"I didn't open it."

They were already divorced. Not from each other,
but from the life they had known before. Each was
besexed, awaiting the appearance of the woman who
was dead. Neither questioned her corporeality. Their
senses conquered their sense, and they found reality
in a scent, a tone, a touch, a kiss. The vision of Mrs.
Cheney dominated their waking hours and ruled their
dreams. She was their reality, and their lives without
her became chimera and dross. She was true, and the
summer sun a token in an empty sky.

Paul went to work late and hurried home early.
Laura never left the house. Each fearful that Mrs.
Cheney might appear unexpectedly and find them
gone. They could not persuade her. Strain of will did
not help, nor prayer, nor tears. She came to them as
she whimmed. Always at night, for hours. But during
the day, briefly, no more than a touch, a whisper, a
quick caress. Curtain moving. Mirror image fading
the moment it was glimpsed. A scent on the air. A

breeze. A laugh from nowhere. But they knew: she was there.

Each pleaded with her to stay. Each made wild promises and frantic threats. But she disappeared from them as quickly as she had seemed. A tapping of skeleton fingers on the cheek. A sad, wolfish smile. And then the insubstantiality beginning. Softness of outline. Wavering. A thinning of her substance until she was transparent, glassing, they could see her and the wall beyond. Then she was gone, utterly, and the blank wall loomed.

So when their quarrel started up again, it was not so much directed at each other but at their own disappointment and defeat. It was dispassionate, since each had become object to the other. But both were so riled by frustration and regret that they sought release in rancor. It was a venting of passions so deep they could not put a name to them.

"Did you pay the light bill?" he demanded.

"No. Did you?"

"You always paid that bill."

"My lawyer told me not to sign any more checks."

"Screw your lawyer," he said furiously. "We'll be sitting in the dark."

"I don't care," she said.

It could have ended there, but neither wanted it to.

"This place is a pigsty," he fumed.

"Yes. Fit for a pig."

"Is it too much to ask you to keep the place reasonably clean?"

"Yes," she said, "it's too much to ask."

"Then hire someone."

"I don't want anyone in here."

"Then clean it yourself," he said desperately. "What do you do all day, for God's sake?"

"No concern of yours."

He looked at her.

"Oh yes," he said. Derisive leer. "I know what you do all day."

"Do you?"

"Margaret comes over, doesn't she?"

"Who?"

"Margaret Stahl. She's over here every day."

"You're insane," she said.

"Am I? Don't think I don't know. Fun and games."

"Gibberish," she said, shaking her head. "You're talking absolute bullshit."

"Oh-ho," he said. "Beautiful language. Lady talk. Sorry, dear, your secret is out. I heard."

"What secret?" she said, her lips white. "What did you hear?"

He tried to be sophisticated. Nonchalant.

"I heard. You and Margaret. In your bed. The springs creaking. Sounded great. Have a good time?"

They stared at each other.

"I haven't seen Margaret Stahl in more than a week."

"You say. I know different. I heard her in there."

"When?"

"Three nights ago. Wednesday, I think it was. Maybe Tuesday."

"Maybe noday. You're demented."

"I heard it, I tell you. I was going down for a drink. I heard you."

"Lurking outside my door, were you? Put your ear to the wood? Or maybe you used an empty glass, like a private detective? That's a sweet vision. You listening at my door. Prying."

"I heard plenty."

"You heard nothing," she told him. "I was alone."

"No way," he said. "You and Margaret. I heard it all."

"Are you serious?" she demanded. "Do you really think I had someone in my bed?"

"Someone?" he said. "Oh yes. But not a man. I never knew you swung that way. How long has this been going on? For years?"

"You're a liar," she said.

"And you're a cheat," he said. "A lesbian cheat. I can laugh at it because it doesn't mean a goddamn thing to me. The divorce judge might feel differently."

"Prove it," she said.

"Easy. We'll subpoena Margaret."

"Be my guest."

Her indifference infuriated him.

"You think she'll perjure herself for you? No way! She'll admit it. She's probably proud of it."

"You bore me," she said.

"Lesbian!" he screamed at her. "You lousy, depraved slut!"

She jerked the middle finger of her right hand into the air, the other fingers clenched. The gesture so inflamed him that he stepped close to her and struck her across the face with his open palm. The blow smacked her head around. Tears came to her eyes, more anger than pain.

"More," she said. "Keep it up. How about a black eye? A cut lip. How about a broken rib or two? Go ahead. My lawyer will be delighted."

His obscene curses followed her up the stairs. He shrieked, ranted. She turned once to spit down at him. Even after she had disappeared, he continued to rail, emptying himself of venom and despair.

Ben came out of the darkness to rub against his ankles, tail twitching.

8

"My father was a marine engineer," Paul Fayette said. "Home for a month and gone for three. I want you to understand."

"Of course," Mrs. Cheney murmured.

"And my aunt lived with us. My mother's sister. Her husband had left her—but I didn't find that out till later. So there I was in that dark house with two silent women."

"An only child?"

"Oh yes. The strange thing is that when my father *did* come home, things didn't change all that much. I mean, suddenly everything wasn't laughter and brightness. Just as gloomy as ever. Then he'd go away again, and I'd be left with my mother and aunt. Oh, don't get the wrong idea. The didn't dress me up in girls' clothes or baby me or anything like that. As a matter of fact, they were always after me to go outside and play with other boys. You know—sports. I was lousy at sports. I wasn't a sissy, I don't think, but I stayed inside and read a lot. I was very good in school. Still, it did something to me."

"Growing up with two women?" she asked. "Without a father there?"

"Partly that," he said, perplexed, "but also the atmosphere, the shadows, quiet. And they were so straitlaced. My father, too. About sex, I mean. My God, I was a virgin when I was married. That's pretty rare, isn't it?"

"Oh," Mrs. Cheney smiled, "not as rare as you think."

"But now everything has changed," he said happily. "It's like I was rehearsed for a role. Programmed. It wasn't me—you understand? I was playing a part I had been taught. All my life. I mean about sex. When you said it was physical imagination. Creation. A unique form of communication. I didn't believe you."

"I know you didn't," she said, drawing skeleton fingers down his cheek. "You do now?"

"Do I ever! Knowing you has been like peeling off an old skin. Dry and crackling. And underneath I'm new. I mean, everything that I pushed to the back of my mind. Wild fantasy. That was the real me all the time. Sex, of course, but more than that. Personality and character. A man I've always wanted to be, dreamt of being, but never was. Am I talking absolute nonsense?"

"Not so much," she laughed softly. "I understand."

"Do you?" he said earnestly. "I hope to God you do, because it's important to me. Now I'm finished with acting and can be what I am. You know, that first time in the closet, I've relived that so many times. It was really an eathquake for me. It felt like the floor was shaking. And I just cracked wide open."

"You felt it, too?" she said, holding his face between cool palms. "That's the way I felt. I never felt that with another man before. Never."

"Oh God, that's wonderful," he sighed. "That you felt it, too. Both of us, together."

"We've got to get rid of Laura," she said.

"Oh yes," he said instantly. "No doubt about that. There's just no room in my life for her anymore. I don't even *know* her. Is sex a clue to character? Do you think? I mean, if you know how a man or woman makes love, the things they do, then do you know more about them than from what they say, how they dress, what their job is, their philosophy, and so forth? Is sex the main clue?"

"It's the only clue," she said. "To everything. The first to live, the last to die."

"You really believe that?" he said. "Yes, I think you're right."

"How will you get rid of Laura?" she persisted.

"Well, divorce, of course. It's been started."

"It takes so long," she said, pouting. "It could go on for years."

"Oh no," he said. "Not years. As soon as possible."

"You don't love me," she said, lying back, turning her head aside. "You say you do, but you don't."

A turgid night, the air swollen and viscous. He had spread a sheet on the guest room floor, and they lay on that, with pillows from the bed. A large electric fan stirred a trembling current, but did nothing to cool.

He wore khaki jeans and a white T-shirt. His feet were bare. She had taken off her white camisole top. She wore a lace-trimmed bra, a long, unpressed shirt of Indian crinkle-cotton. She had kicked off her strap sandals.

"I do love you," he pleaded. "You must know that. I'm divorcing Laura for you. What more can I do?"

She rolled toward him, up onto one hip. She looked at him thoughtfully. Reached out, put a hand behind his head, pulled him closer.

"When I disappeared," she said in a low, secret voice, "in the coffin . . . Remember?"

"Yes."

"Do you think I really did disappear? Or was it a trick?"

He groaned. "No, no. I believe now, Diane. I really do. You *did* disappear."

"I did," she nodded. "Would you like Laura to disappear as I did? I could make it happen, Paul."

He stared at her, blew out a long exhalation of held breath.

"Laura? Disappear? You could do that?"

"Oh yes."

"Would she—could she come back?"

She released him, rolled away, turned her shoulder to him.

"Would you want her back?" she said dully.

He closed his eyes. His head fell forward until his chin rested on his chest. When he opened his eyes, slowly, with an effort, all he could see was her sinuous back. It was roped with soft muscle, spine cunningly channeled, the line swooping from rib cage to nipped waist, soaring to flare of hip.

He reached out timorously to feel. Above and below the bra strap the flesh bulged tightly. It was fire to his fingers and held the imprint of his touch like a bruise. He sat up, legs crossed, and bent to her. His knowing fingers unfastened the strap's hook.

"Make her disappear," he said thickly.

The strap ends dangled. He leaned forward to rub his lips over the red weals.

"Oh lover," she moaned.

He slid the bra away from her shoulders and arms, and tossed it somewhere. He pushed her gently, and she went down prone, face dug into the pillow. He gripped the elastic top of the skirt and peeled it down, threw it free. She was naked then, arms raised above her head, crucified.

"Don't," she recited. "Please don't."

He combed her hair coarsely with his fingers so it splayed across her bare back. He buried his face in its fragrance. He parted it to run his tongue down the sly channel of her spine, the strong ridges on either side pressing his face.

As always, her helpless complaisance inflamed him. When he pulled her legs roughly apart, she resisted, but briefly. He manipulated her, straightened her arms, turned her feet outward, separated her long hair into two thick plaits lying over her shoulders. He looked down at the quivering star, almost fainting with want.

It seemed to him that her skin was stretched shiny with the force within. No wrinkles, no folds, but all lean, hard, bursting and juiced. Her skin was a pulled envelope, a line that contained her completely. He held a palm close to her thigh and felt the searing heat. She radiated, all of her burning.

His skimming touch on ribs, back, the tender insides of her thighs, set her squirming. He played with her, watching with fascination and a rising lust as her extended limbs flexed, wavered, throbbed. He had never before felt such a sense of mastery and possession. There was nothing he could not make her do.

"Say this . . ." he said, to test her.

And she said it.

"Say . . ." he instructed.

She said it.

"Louder."

She said it louder.

"Now say this . . ."

The words coming sobbed from her lips excited him more; he tore his clothes away.

"Say . . ." he commanded.

She repeated after him and then he said the words, then she, then both together until it was a groaned and feverish litany, and he was atop her, sweated and tearing, and they were rutting beasts, crying out their catechism together, slick flesh sliding, both of them wet with their craze, bruising on the hard floor, intent, intent, howling and grinding, everything lost but the pierce and fire . . .

Laura, at the other end of the hall, woke from a clotted sleep. She lay a moment, blinking at the darkness, thinking the sounds had belonged to a forgotten dream. But still she heard: animal noises, a kind of fight, wild and uncontrolled. She moved from her lonely bed, unlocked her door, went silently down the hall. The sounds grew louder.

She stopped outside the closed door of the guest room. There was no mistaking those wails. Not words now, nothing she could recognize, but frantic gasps, brief shouts, cries of triumph and defeat.

Laura sank slowly to the floor, legs crossed, hands folded in her nightgowned lap. Head tilted to one side, leaning forward, she listened to the guttural mouthings. Her eyes slowly closed. She swayed gently. Hearing slap of flesh and grind of skin. Dreaming, and smiling, nodding . . .

Margaret Stahl came sailing in, caroling in italics . . .

"Where have you two *been?* I've been trying and *trying* to call you. And don't you answer your doorbell *ever?* You're *never* at the club. Hermits. I mean, you've just become *hermits.*"

Laura and Paul Fayette stared in astonishment, remembering her last visit. Now she was pure brio, with giant gestures, flaunting of an auburn fall. She was all gush and teeth. She had never seemed more towering, but that might have been a new posture, almost a military carriage. Proud. There was a feverish glow to her. Her eyes snapped brightly. The Fayettes wondered if she was on something.

She wore a man-tailored jacket of nubby black silk, with a beige scarf knotted loosely about her throat. Her pleated silk skirt was sand-colored, and the shoes on her bare feet no more than thin ribbons of leather.

Paul brought them all drinks. They sat in the family room, and Margaret burbled on . . .

"I'll stay for just this one little drink, and then off I go. So much to do! The most wonderful thing happened; I must tell you. Remember the last time I was here and singing the blues? Said I was going through Clint's papers and records, hoping to find some secret treasure. You know—an insurance policy or something he hadn't told me about. Well, I found it! Can you imagine? A savings account I never knew existed. Left in trust for me. Just lying there and collecting all that lovely interest like mad. The dear, dear man. I suppose he intended it as a reserve for a rainy day, or something to tide me over if anything happened to him. More than ten thousand! Isn't that marvy?"

"Oh Margaret," Laura said, "that's grand. I'm so happy for you."

"Good for Clint," Paul said. "That should take care

of your immediate needs. Any problems with the probate?"

"Oh no," Margaret said blithely. Then she added, "Everyone's been so cooperative. People I never even *heard* of before have been so kind, it makes me want to weep."

They were silent. Margaret looked back and forth, one to the other.

"Something wrong?" she asked. "I'm getting bad vibes. Have I interrupted your plans, or are the loving Fayettes in the middle of a fight?"

"The loving Fayettes are getting a divorce," Paul said harshly.

"As soon as possible," Laura said, face set.

"Shit," Margaret said. "That's a bummer. No chance of calling it off?"

"No," Laura said.

"No," Paul said.

"Have you told the children yet?"

They looked at each other.

"I'll tell them," they said simultaneously.

"It's my responsibility," Paul said stiffly.

"Since when?" Laura said. "I can do it better."

"Take it easy," Margaret Stahl said hastily. "Laura, you tell Christine. Paul, you tell Brian. How's that?"

They looked at each other again, then nodded.

"Well, then," Margaret said, with satisfaction, "that takes care of that. What brought it on—if you don't mind my asking? You know, I was ready to dump Clint, but never had the guts to make the move. Any special reason—or just middle-aged dissatisfaction? Want to do your own thing—is that it?"

"Something like that," Paul said shortly. "Sure you won't have another drink?"

"All right," she said promptly. "To drown my sorrow."

"I'll have another, too," Laura said. "To celebrate."

When he came back from the kitchen with the fresh drinks, Margaret was sitting close to Laura on the couch. He felt a sudden, irrational thrust of jealousy.

He gave Margaret her drink in a hand that trembled slightly.

"Got the shakes, Paul?" she asked lightly.

"Of course not," he said. "I've been working too many long hours. At the office. And the divorce, and all."

"Sure," she said.

"Many long, long hours," Laura said. "Sometimes to three and four in the morning. Hard work. In the guest room."

"What the hell is that supposed to mean?" he demanded.

She turned to Margaret.

"Want a laugh?" she asked. "A really good laugh?"

"I can always use a laugh," the other woman said cautiously. "But maybe I'd better go. I think I'd better go."

"No, no," Laura said. "You've got to hear this. This giant brain thinks we've been getting it off together. You and me."

"What?" Margaret said, setting down her glass. "Let's have that again."

"You and me. Sleeping together for fun and games. He's convinced of it."

"Jesus Christ," Margaret said.

"Don't take the name of thy Lord in vain," Paul said. "I *know*."

"You know shit," Laura said. "Tell him, Margaret."

"Paul, this is insane. I swear I—"

"Swear away," he said, shrugging. "I heard what I heard."

"And shall I tell you what *I* heard?" Laura asked. "Would you both like to listen to *my* story? About what's going on in the guest room? 'Guest room.' That's beautiful."

Margaret drained her drink and stood abruptly.

"That's it," she said flatly. "I'm getting out of this nuthouse. I think you've both gone over the edge. I don't want to listen to any more."

She adjusted the scarf at her throat, smoothed her

jacket, freed the auburn fall so it cascaded over her shoulders.

Laura and Paul Fayette looked at her, seeing her for the first time, suddenly realizing what an attractive woman she was. Not pretty or handsome. But with a unique allure. In her new mood, flushed with energy, there was a peculiar sexiness about her, a looseness, something erotic and frightening. She moved with a wanton profligacy, spread her knees wide when she sat. She seemed naked beneath silk jacket and skirt. They could almost see her body squirm under the stuff, and fancied they heard the whisper of cloth on skin.

"Why are you staring at me so?" she asked. Ironic smile.

Neither answered. She gathered up her purse and hat. It was a man's wide-brimmed fedora with a band of pheasant feathers. The Fayettes did not rise to show her out.

"Did you contact Colonel Coulter?" Paul called after her.

She turned away to adjust the brim of her hat in the hallway mirror.

"No," she said. "I tried his hotel, but he wasn't there. They don't know where he is."

"I could have told you that," he said.

She turned back, stood in the doorway.

"I'm only going to say this once," she said. "And then I'm never going to mention it again. I'm not screwing either of you. Got that?" She gave them a sly grin.

They didn't believe her. They couldn't believe her.

The room was tunnel-black and whispery as a cave. The surrus of their quiet voices brought Ben awake; the sleek beast raised its head in the darkness. They could see green almond eyes glinting with cold fire.

"Of course it wasn't me, dear girl." Mrs. Cheney said, stroking Laura's hair. "How could you think such a thing? Don't you trust me?"

"Margaret said it wasn't her," Laura said miserably.

"Was, wasn't . . . What difference does it make who he was with? We have our own life to live. As soon as we get rid of him."

"Oh yes," Laura said eagerly. "Our own life to live. Together."

"Have faith in me," Mrs. Cheney murmured. She leaned forward to press strong lips against the other woman's neck.

Laura was wearing babydoll pajamas: a short, cap-sleeved jacket of white nylon printed with tiny rose-buds, ribbons and ruffles at neck and hem. Beneath was a brief white bikini. Her breasts were unbound; hard nipples poked sheer cloth, beige coronas showed through.

Mrs. Cheney touched her breasts lightly through the thin stuff. Laura shivered with delight.

"I feel so—so womanly when I'm with you," she whispered. "I want to have long, long hair and wear flowery perfume. I want us to have a romance, a real romance."

Mrs. Cheney glanced toward the observant Ben and smiled in the darkness.

"A real romance? That's exactly what we do have, you lovely girl. Oh, the sex is wonderful and impor-tant . . . You feel that, don't you?"

"I do, Diane, I do!"

"But our romance is more important. Our love. It's what you've wanted all your life, isn't it?"

"Yes," Laura said wonderingly. "What I've been hoping for all my life. Diane, you do exist, don't you?"

Mrs. Cheney pressed cool lips against Laura's tem-ple, cheeks, lips.

"Were those kisses real? Of course I'm real."

"It's just that—I think of you so much. I fantasize about you all the time. About the things we do to-gether. And I wonder if this, now, this moment, is just a very strong fantasy. Hallucination."

Mrs. Cheney was silent a moment.

"Darling," she said finally, "when sexual attraction

becomes as intense as it is between you and me, it has the power to make immaterial things real. It was your love for me, and my love for you, that brought me back to you. Can you understand that? Think of sex as a foreign language that only you and I can speak. A very special, private method of communication. We are imagining, not only with our minds but with skin, blood, flesh, bone, gristle . . . with our very hearts. And with all our senses. That is what makes me real to you. Our love creates me."

"And you can't appear to anyone else?"

"Only you," Mrs. Cheney vowed. "Who else wants me as much as you?"

Laura reached out soft arms, pulled her close.

"No one," she said throatily. "No one loves you as much as I. You'll never leave me, will you? Say you won't leave me."

Mrs. Cheney didn't answer. Her slender, articulated hands slid up beneath the nylon jacket. Fingernails scraped gently at Laura's bare back, armpits, ribs.

"I know what you want, dear girl," she said. "I want it, too."

The ritual seduction, so precious to Laura Fayette, began slowly, lazily: an indolent lovemaking full of play and ingenious exploration. Ticklings. Pinchings. Nipping of teeth and soft pluckings.

Laura went with it, surrendering her will. She felt tissue swell hotly, moisture within and slicking her skin. It was a feverous faintness in which she could dimly hear her own groaned, "Don't, oh please don't." There were strong, masculine hands at her, and she was vaguely conscious of being undressed, pushed back, spread wide.

Then the nimble wand of Mrs. Cheney's naked body was lying atop her, between her opened thighs. Her knees were raised, her arms tight about her lover's muscled back. A dozen tongues lashed mouth, neck, breasts. Hard fingers bruised her. All the openings of her body were stuffed and stretched. She was ravished, torn open and scorched.

It was a flood of flame that engulfed her. She could see the flicker behind closed lids. The calm body of Mrs. Cheney became a blaze that seared. She breathed smoke, smelled ash, and as she was consumed, shouted out her love and anguish, feeling crisp to the touch and charred by lust.

Paul Fayette, deliberately awake, heard the animal wails and tried to resist. But they drew him, in passion and fury, naked down the long hall. He stood shivering with excitement outside the closed door, imagining he heard, behind the frantic cries, the snapping and crackling of a great conflagration burning out of control.

Now he recognized the two voices, and wondered if Clint Stahl, too, had listened, heard, and gone howling to his immolation.

He put his shoulder to the door. Once, twice, three times. Not feeling the pain. The lock wrenched free. The door sprang open, hit the wall, bounced back. But then Paul was in the blackness, fingers fumbling for the wall switch.

Glare filled the room. Pitiless white light. He saw first the frozen figure of Ben, back arched and ruffled. The cat, wide-eyed, was hissing faintly.

And on the bed, in the bed, the naked, gleaming body of his wife, writhing in a spasm she could not end. Harsh, inchoate sounds came from her: moans, gasps, cries, whimpers. While her flushed hips pumped upward into vacant air, a travesty of copulation. Her dimpled thighs strained wide, vulva gaping, as she bucked, heaved, her mouth working wetly, tongue flailing, her curved arms grasping nothing. The thick grunts went on and on, her body bouncing crazily.

Paul looked about wildly. He darted into dressing room and bathroom. He flung open closet doors and bent to search under the bed. He saw nothing but the white curtain at the open window billowing gently outward.

He slapped her face with his open hand. Palm, back, palm, back. Her rantings ceased. Her eyelids slowly rose. There was an opaque film that gradually cleared. She stared at him.

"Where is she?" he screamed at her. "Where is she?"

"What?" she said dully, looking about. "What?"

"Diane," he howled furiously. "Where *is* she?"

When she didn't answer, he began to hit her again. Now with clenched fists. Not punched, but hammered blows on her face, neck, head. She covered up, crossing protective arms. He slammed his clenched knuckles down upon her slackening breasts, open belly, thatched groin, raw thighs.

"Where is she?" he kept shrieking. "Where *is* she?"

Laura curled away from him, bringing up her knees, huddling. When his hysterical assault continued, she rolled off the bed, landing on hands and knees. He rushed around and began kicking her ineffectually with his bare feet, stubbing toes on ribs, haunches, knees.

She grasped the bed's headboard, pulled herself up. She turned suddenly and pushed him with surprising strength, the heels of her hands thudding into his shoulders. He staggered back. Before he could recover, she was darting from the room. Ben went squealing after her.

Paul rushed for the hallway. He caught her at the top of the stairs. Gripped a slick arm. Whirled her around.

"You fuck!" she yelled through bloodied lips. "She's mine!"

He struck her with his fist. He watched with satisfaction as she tumbled down the stairway, over and over, arms flying, wet thighs exposed, head thumping on every stair.

He stood still, thinking her dead, hoping her dead. But she dragged stumbling to her feet, went staggering away. He went leaping down after her, sobbing with the need to end her, it, everything.

When he came bursting into the darkened living room, she slammed a heavy crystal ashtray against his head. He dropped onto his knees, sick and dazed. She started to run by. He reached out a hand, grabbed an ankle, brought her low.

He tried to roll atop her, pin her down. But she hammered at his head, clawed for his eyes. They rolled, and tables, chairs, lamps went crashing down. She grasped for his testicles, and he squirmed away. She made it to the family room, scuttling on hands and knees.

When he caught up with her, she was brandishing a brass table lamp, shade hanging loose.

"She's mine!" he sobbed.

"Mine!" she cried.

The base of the lamp numbed his shoulder. But he flung it from her grip. For a moment they stood clinging, sweated; naked bodies straining and swaying. Her knee pounded for his groin. He turned to take the kicks on his thigh, and she slipped slickly away, leaving him clutching stained air.

The cat was underfoot now, darting, spitting, pawing at flashing ankles. He tripped them, scratched them, leaped to rake bare thighs and calves with unsheathed claws. They both kicked him away, but he came on, fur bristling, teeth shining, eyes wide and burning.

In the darkened kitchen, stumbling, arms outstretched and hands flexing, he found the wall switch and showed the room. She was at the back door, fumbling frantically with the lock. He charged her, and closed until they were grappling once again, striving against each other, skin sliding, flesh rasping in a tangle of sweated limbs.

"Mine!"

"Mine!"

Until she struck him in the throat with her elbow. The pain broke his face apart, and he went falling back, trying to breathe.

What followed reminded him, idly, of the last still scenes on movie and TV screens. Actions caught and held. A quick succession of frozen images . . .

He coming forward. Arm extended. Hand reaching. Face wrenched.

She moving back. Looking down. Knees sagging. Mouth open to gasp.

He caught in midair step. Torso twisted. Hands clenched to fists. Arms swinging.

She at open drawer. Eyes lifting to his. Body suddenly straightened and tense. Muscles taut.

He close to her. Fist aloft. Triumph in his eyes. Penis swung to one side.

She with chef's knife gleaming in her hand. Lurching forward. Her weight behind the point.

He tried to stop his forward lunge. To draw back, stomach sucked in, to avoid that cold flash. But it was too late, too late. They fell together. She thrust the blade forward.

He felt it go in.

Every burning inch of it.

She was muddily aware of a painted concrete floor, cement walls, recessed overhead light covered with wire mesh, iron cot with a bare mattress, a seatless toilet in the corner. And a door of bars.

People came continually to the bars, all during the early morning hours. Some just stood, stared at her, then turned away. Some spoke to her, kindly, and asked if she was hungry, or thirsty, or wanted cigarettes.

She didn't answer any of them. She crouched in a corner of the cell; sitting on the damp concrete, clutching her knees. She was wearing the soiled raincoat they had put about her before they brought her to the station. She sat there a long time, cheek resting on her knees, thinking about nothing. She was empty.

Finally, toward noon, two matrons came into the cell carrying clothing. Her own things. They lifted her up and dressed her, as a doll might be dressed: arms poked through sleeves, head eased through neckline. They put on her shoes. Then they set her down gently on the bare mattress. They moved her back until she was leaning against the wall. Then they left. The barred door clanged shut behind them.

A short time later, a young man with a blond beard appeared outside the bars.

"Mrs. Fayette," he said, "my name is Stephen Willsdon. I'm an assistant district attorney. Do you have a personal attorney, Mrs. Fayette? Or do you wish a court-appointed attorney to represent you?"

"Mrs. Fayette," he said, "my name is Stephen Willsdon. People call me Steve. I understand your name is Laura. Do you understand what I'm saying?"

"Laura," he said, "this is Steve. I want to help you. Can you hear me?"

After a while, the young, bearded man went away. Then a little, tubby man, bald, was admitted. He was carrying a black bag. He talked soothingly to Mrs. Fayette, and didn't seem to care that she never answered. He took her pulse, blood pressure, peered into her eyes, tested her reflexes, felt her arms and legs, and moved all her joints about slowly. She let him do what he wanted. Finally he patched up the cuts and contusions on her face and head. Then he, too, departed.

One of the matrons returned, bearing a paper cup of coffee and two doughnuts on a plastic tray.

"Eat something, honey," she urged. She left the tray, and banged the cell door behind her.

Then Laura Fayette was alone.

"Diane?" she said softly. "Where are you, Diane?"

She remembered what Mrs. Cheney had said, about the intensity of their sexual attraction, their private language, and how it was this passion that made the dead Mrs. Cheney real, that created her.

So Laura concentrated her will on calling up the shade of Mrs. Cheney. She did this by remembering sensuous details of their relationship . . .

Cool fingers drifting over her engorged breast.

Hands cinching on the limpid insides of her thighs.

Tongue darting through her mouth to fence with her own responsive tongue.

Lips flurrying over her closed eyelids.

A long, sapling body pulsing between her burning thighs.

All these things she recalled, and many more. They were real to her. They existed. So strongly, so intensely that she thought any one would materialize the spirit of Mrs. Cheney.

But she caught only glimpses, fragments torn and fluttering. It was like seeing a woman moving away from her through a thick and swirling fog. She passed occasionally under street lamps and Laura saw long hair, or gliding walk, a turn of a white cheek, neck, a hand. Then she was gone. Completely.

"Diane?" she called anxiously. "Diane?"

No one answered. No curtain at the barred door to billow inward, signaling her coming. No scent of sweated flesh. No soft murmurs of, "Dear girl, sweet girl."

"All my pretty things," Laura Fayette mourned aloud, and then, "Diane? Diane?"

She tried again, thinking only of their ritual, their ceremony. She focussed only on that, brow furrowed, eyes squinched. She went step by step . . .

She lying quiet in something frail.

The white curtain puffing in.

The bold figure in sharply creased pantsuit.

The bed creaking.

The greeting kiss and low hoots of laughter.

The necking, petting, stroking.

And then . . . And then . . .

She went through it all, certain that the force of her memory would bring Mrs. Cheney flying back. And on this rough cotton tick, on this hard iron cot, why they might : . .

But Mrs. Cheney did not appear, would not appear. Naughty, willful Mrs. Cheney! But still, she said she would not come to anyone else, since no one loved her as Laura did.

Then why did Paul do those things to her?

Because . . .

She thought a long while.

Because Paul was jealous of her happiness, didn't know it, couldn't share it. Because Paul had only Margaret Stahl or some other chippie he smuggled in late at night. Poor substitute for Laura's romantic love. So Paul, maddened by jealousy, had broken down her door, and Diane had fled in terror, and Paul had beaten her brutally in rage and frustration, and she had to do what she had done to protect herself. She wasn't guilty of anything but self-defense. They would all say that: self-defense.

But also, slyly, she remembered Diane . . .

"We've got to get rid of him. A life together. Just the two of us. No room in our lives for Paul. Our love. Alone together. Rid of him, rid of him, rid of him . . ."

But they would know nothing of that. And perhaps, when she was freed, home in her own bed in the master bedroom, alone, then Mrs. Cheney might come to her again, whole and unafraid.

The curtain would billow in, and there she'd be. Wearing the pantsuit Laura loved, smiling her cool, ironic smile, saying, "Dear girl, sweet girl." And Ben would be lazily licking himself on the rug, and the bed would be spread with fresh starched sheets, and slowly, thoughtfully, Mrs. Cheney would seduce her again, and she could hear herself crying out with fright, but with anticipation, "Don't, oh please don't."

And, in fact, Laura Fayette was crying aloud, "Don't, oh please don't," when the young man with the blond beard appeared again outside her cell door. And with him was the tubby, little man, still carrying his black bag, and one of the matrons, and a man in uniform who walked with a hand resting on the butt of a revolver strapped low on his hip.

"Mrs. Fayette," the young man said gently, "we're going now. We're taking you away from here. We're taking you to a hospital where you'll get a good rest, and your children and friends can come visit you. Won't that be nice? Come along, Mrs. Fayette."

She went willingly, offering no resistance. They crowded her close, smiling determinedly. They came outside into a steady rain. They stood at the top of the courthouse steps. They looked up at the shattered sky. Then hurried down to the waiting car.

It seemed to Laura Fayette that there were many people there to watch her leaving. All bent beneath black umbrellas. She recognized many of them, her friends in Penlow Park. Some of them called out to her, but she could not understand what they said. Some of the women were weeping, and turned away, black umbrellas bobbing. Some waved. Some just stood and stared, eyes blank and helpless.

Just before she got into the car, she turned to look at her friends again. There, in back of the crowd, standing apart, she saw the courtly figure of Colonel Benjamin G. Coulter.

The Colonel caught her eye. He bowed, and tipped his brown bowler gravely.

A thousand miles away, in a motel room smelling of plastic newness, the Reverend Timothy T. Aiken stood preening before the dresser mirror. He wore a jacket of hellish plaid, a knitted sports shirt open at the neck to reveal chest hair as wiry as Brillo, maroon slacks, white socks, and strap sandals with enormous brass buckles.

Most surprising, the reverend's mass of snow-white hair had been dyed a glossy black and plastered close to his scalp. But it curled up in back and over his ears. He smoothed it down with his palms, turning this way and that, admiring his reflection and wondering if a dapper mustache, dyed black of course, would enhance his youthfulness.

Pleased with his jaunty appearance, he turned to the bed and opened the lid of an attaché case. He had packed the bills neatly, each bundle secured with a rubber band. One hundred thousand dollars. Almost. The remaining bills were in Reverend Aiken's wallet. Sighing with pleasure, he drifted his fingertips lightly over the stacked currency before he snapped shut the attaché case, locked it carefully, and slid it into the bottom dresser drawer, under his new silk pajamas and next to the Gideon Bible.

Then Aiken lowered himself into the largest and softest armchair in the room. He examined the backs of his hands critically, and tried to recall where he had read of an ointment guaranteed to remove liver spots. He might also have a face-lift; more and more men were having it done these days. Get rid of pouches and wattles. Then, too, there were vitamins and hormones; they were bound to help.

His dream of the man he would become was interrupted when the bathroom door opened, and a woman stepped shyly into the room. She wore a long wig of honey-colored hair, fine as corn silk. It was parted in the middle and flowed down her back, over her shoulders, across her bosom.

She wore an organdy pinafore over a short cotton dress with little ducks printed on it. Sheer white stockings ended just below her bare knees. On her feet were black Mary Janes with buttoned straps. As she posed in the bathroom doorway, she put on a pair of big horn-rimmed spectacles set with ordinary glass.

"Do I look all right, daddy?" she faltered.

"All right?" the Reverend Aiken said, chuckling. "You look yummy, sweetums. Good enough to eat. Come sit on daddy's lap, and daddy will tell his little girl a story."

Obediently she slid onto the old man's lap, squirming about to make herself comfortable.

"Am I too heavy, daddy?" she asked anxiously.

"Oh no, no," he groaned. "Just right. Just exactly right."

He reached up to stroke the fine hair hanging loosely down her front. His fingertips passed lightly over her breasts. Then he pressed his fingers into her waist.

"Ticklish?" he said. "Is my little girl ticklish?"

"Ooh yes, daddy," she giggled. "It feels so funny and nice."

She rocked back and forth on his lap in mirth. She put an arm about his neck. She pressed her fresh, smooth cheek to his.

"Sweetums," he said thickly. "My own dear sweetums."

She snuggled down in his arms, making "Mmmmmm" sounds. He held her close, sniffing at her scented wig, her neck, shoulder.

"Now tell me the story," she said, her eyes closing.

"Later," he said hoarsely, and thrust a trembling hand beneath her short skirt.

"Ooh, daddy," moaned Margaret Stahl.

From the bestselling author of DEATH WISH comes . . .

HOPSCOTCH
BRIAN
GARFIELD

Before his enforced retirement from the CIA, Miles Kendig
thrilled to the cut-throat strategy of pursuit, the
red-blooded rapture of out-witting his opponents, the
subtlety of human conflict. Now, with the demands of
everyday life so easily accomplished, he felt empty, lifeless
and unwanted.

'You belong in the rubber room' they told him. But Miles
knew he was the best. He would show them. Both East and
West were terrified by his crazy plan. And this was going to
be Miles Kendig's last chance blaze of glory . . . if they
didn't nail him first!

'Brian Garfield is a natural storyteller'
NEW YORK TIMES

Also by Brian Garfield in Sphere Books:
NECESSITY
DEATH WISH

0 7221 3820 2   ADVENTURE THRILLER   £2.99

A selection of bestsellers from Sphere

FICTION

WHEN DREAMS COME TRUE	Emma Blair	£3.50 ☐
THE LEGACY OF HEOROT	Niven/Pournelle/Barnes	£3.50 ☐
THE PHYSICIAN	Noah Gordon	£3.99 ☐
INFIDELITIES	Freda Bright	£3.99 ☐
THE GREAT ALONE	Janet Dailey	£3.99 ☐

FILM AND TV TIE-IN

BLACK FOREST CLINIC	Peter Heim	£2.99 ☐
INTIMATE CONTACT	Jacqueline Osborne	£2.50 ☐
BEST OF BRITISH	Maurice Sellar	£8.95 ☐
SEX WITH PAULA YATES	Paula Yates	£2.95 ☐
RAW DEAL	Walter Wager	£2.50 ☐

NON-FICTION

HOWARD & MASCHLER ON FOOD	Elizabeth Jane Howard & Fay Maschler	£3.99 ☐
FISH	Robyn Wilson	£2.50 ☐
THE SACRED VIRGIN AND THE HOLY WHORE	Anthony Harris	£3.50 ☐
THE DARKNESS IS LIGHT ENOUGH	Chris Ferris	£4.50 ☐
TREVOR HOWARD: A GENTLEMAN AND A PLAYER	Vivienne Knight	£3.50 ☐

All Sphere books are available at your local bookshop or newsagent, or can be ordered direct from the publisher. Just tick the titles you want and fill in the form below.

Name_____

Address_____

_____

Write to Sphere Books, Cash Sales Department, P.O. Box 11, Falmouth, Cornwall TR10 9EN

Please enclose a cheque or postal order to the value of the cover price plus:

UK: 60p for the first book, 25p for the second book and 15p for each additional book ordered to a maximum charge of £1.90.

OVERSEAS & EIRE: £1.25 for the first book, 75p for the second book and 28p for each subsequent title ordered.

BFPO: 60p for the first book, 25p for the second book plus 15p per copy for the next 7 books, thereafter 9p per book.

Sphere Books reserve the right to show new retail prices on covers which may differ from those previously advertised in the text elsewhere, and to increase postal rates in accordance with the P.O.